# This Earth You'll Come Back To

# This Earth You'll Come Back To

*a novel by*

# BARBARA
# ROETHER

MCPHERSON & COMPANY
*Kingston, New York*
*2015*

Published by McPherson & Company,
Post Office Box 1126, Kingston, New York 12402
www.mcphersonco.com

1 3 5 7 9 10 8 6 4 2   2015  2016  2017 2018
DESIGNED BY BRUCE R. McPHERSON
MANUFACTURED IN THE U.S.A.

LIBRARY OF CONGRESS CATALOGING-IN-PUBLICATION DATA

Roether, Barbara.
This earth you'll come back to : a novel / by Barbara Roether.
pages cm
ISBN 978-1-62054-015-2 (alk. paper)
I. Title.
PS3618.O386T48 2015
813'.6--dc23

2015027005

# CONTENTS

# This Earth
# You'll Come
# Back To

# I

## ARRIVAL

2008
*Blanchardville, Ohio*

COURSE you couldn't find it right away. It's not so easy,
what with all the names and pathways, if you're not familiar with the layout to begin with. Not in the heat of July.
Still, there was no need for you to carry on like that, walking around half crying and stumbling sorry for yourself 'cause
you couldn't see it right away. You should have used the sense
God gave you and asked your brother, could have drove you
right in to the place. I don't know why you had him drop you
off downtown, walking all the way out here by yourself in the
blazing crown of the day. You must have come out by West
Main Cross and there's not a bit of shade there now they took
the maple trees out to build the parking lot for the church,
took down Grandma's old house too. That about broke my
heart. Must be more than two miles. Don't you have a hat?
Why you always insist on making things hard for yourself I'll
never know; but it's just like you to take a simple errand and
turn it into a full-blown crusader pilgrimage.

Well there's not another soul around today just the old
maples with their green overall, the grass and the flowerpots,
next to the American flags. And you my daughter walking in
a circle trying to find a landmark you recognize. Reading all
the names; names of the people you went to school with, their
grandparents, parents, uncles. Names you haven't thought of
for thirty-odd years since you left here. All those names you
used to hear in the daylight of desk rows deep in the rapture

of childhood; Weisling, Frankhauser, Riley, Lynch, Slawinski. Each name ringing out with a voice around it, ringing up days in which the names were spoken, and all those days stretching back until you feel the beginning of your life and the end too. It comes over you all the sudden. That your leaving here and living in California all these years, the stories you wrote or didn't write will never matter at all, because you know you can't get away from this, this earth you'll come back to right here. You feel its pull. It's not a bad feeling. Oh the earth is the same earth anywhere it lies, and that is a comfort to you I know. Everything we ever tried or said or dreamed, every finger, backbone, jaw, falling down here like leaves. As if the ground itself were made of our passing lives, compacting into the dark soil of time.

I know you feel the earth, child. You feel its spreading kindness. I remember you wanted me to buy you a copy of *Leaves of Grass,* "every atom belonging to me as good belongs to you." I liked Walt Whitman too, except my favorites were his poems about Lincoln, "Oh Captain my Captain our fearful trip is done." I never did buy it for you on account of he was homosexual. But that's way off our subject. Where were we?

Well at least by now you know you're in with the Catholics, you know you're close. You found the big old Healy stone that's Aunt Marybell's, you know my grandmother's sister. She was so vain she wanted to have a bigger stone than her own sister if you can imagine.

Now there's no need for you to carry on like that. Bleating around like a little lost lamb, making a fool of yourself, hiding behind the oak tree when old Mr. Heinke's wife pulls up the gravel drive in her red Buick. She's out of the car with the pot of petunias, those tacky purple petunias, leaves them and back in the air conditioning in three minutes, and has done with it, like you could have; instead of acting like a child and mooning around with some fool notion. Feeling sorry for yourself, and getting all upset because you can't find your own mother's grave. Well, you can't find anything with your eyes blurred by tears. I'm right behind you but you keep going the wrong way round.

Oh I know when you came today you'd been thinking how you missed being with your mother your whole life and now it's too late. Seems like you've already decided that's the tragedy you're working up to tell. How we lived and died so far from each other. But I was there all along.

What are you around forty-seven now? All swept up in grief and regret about what you haven't managed to write or do. And now you've decided our distance was the reason. Maybe you could explain why you weren't here until the end of the funeral, not to keep harping on that. There's two sides to every story. Now I hear even your own son calls you Miss. I. Regret. Speaking of your son why didn't you bring him along last time you came to see me when I was alive? I asked you to bring him, but you acted like it didn't matter. Deaf ears. I wanted to see him. Every child begins the world all over again. That's why we have them you know.

∼

Well what's any mother to any child? Sounds abstract but you have to shake it out to the doing and dealing with every day. Life is what you do every day, what your hands touch and feel. Remember in *The Odyssey*, when Odysseus goes into the underworld, meets up with poor Achilles, and Achilles tells him that any paltry shred of human living is more precious than eternal glory. I didn't even like that story when Sister made me read it in eighth grade, but now a' course I see his point.

∼

So, how do you measure love? What evidence can be offered of its existence? Is it what is remembered or what is forgotten between those who love each other? Is its measure what is swallowed back, or what is spoken?

∼

Now that you've found my marker you can't see how you'd missed it in the first place. It isn't even a shock, just like death really isn't such a shock. Gave you a moment of comfort, finding my name carved out clear in the standing stone of daylight. There is proof of her being, you thought, for all the world to see. You let your breath out relieved but no more than one breath when oh, so crestfallen an expression I never did see as you looked down. I guess it took you by surprise there not being any grass grown over the plot yet. The earth here brown and bare; green to each side but the square right over me just brown and plain.

But how could that be you're thinking, after six months, after the snow of that frigid day in January, by now by July there should be some grass.

Oh at first you're angry enough to raise the dead or those of them that haven't yet been raised. Why can't your mother have some grass, some deep rich green grass to cover the place like everyone else, why should her place lie brown and uncovered? Scarred with the brown of poverty. Can this woman never have anything abundant? Is grass extra in the price of dying? Why did she have to live and die now too in the ever glowing glare of not enough. Even that isn't the whole story is it? You see your own shame in that brown square, see what you were too careless to attend to. You wonder how the earth could know of your omission. Withholding its blessing because you had been so late for your own mother's funeral? Too far away to make it back until the last minute.

Course in the larger scheme of things a lack of grass here isn't much to speak of. The plot just hasn't fully settled in yet. And oh they're cheap out here. You have to ask them special to put new sod on and it costs. George came by once on the tractor with grass seed but then the floods came right after him, washed it away. On the other hand now, notice your father's place next to mine, all nice green and perfectly mowed. Some things never change.

∼

I can tell this story if you want me to, dear daughter, but maybe not all in a row. That never was how my mind worked, but inasmuch as one thing leads to another, well, it should suffice. You'll have to listen and let me tell it in my own way, which means not just after you were born or not just about you, though you have been the easiest to love, most of the time. I think we had similar temperaments, so we understood each other, though not all mothers and children do. It's not a given, though you'd think so wouldn't you? Some children take after their fathers, as several of mine certainly did and I don't have to belabor that point.

People always asked me why did you have ten children, and did your husband drink because of that, or did I have them in spite of that, well who's to say? Their number and his drinking relate as much as one thing to anything else if you want it to.

∼

This is the first chance I've had to even think about it so much. Someone was always getting born or getting sick, I don't mean just my own children and my grandchildren, but theirs too and uncles, aunts, my brother with that brain tumor. Of course those fools out at Valley Hospital, I call it Death Valley, couldn't diagnose it for two years, you'd think they would know more than they do, well he suffered so, and for what?

But now we're free to talk. Are you still nursing the notion that a lot of what goes wrong for you comes down to the fact of you growing up so poor? Those are your words now, I never thought like that, poor or not poor. Call it what you like, I did the best I could. That wasn't enough for some of my children and it's awful when your own turn on you. Grow up to be whoever they are and then get mad because you didn't do things the way they would have. I don't mean you, you're not so spiteful by nature. But I know your sister Kate is out there bad-mouthing me from her spotless house that I wasn't organized enough. I should have done more. It's not logical. Course logic never stopped anybody in this family. Sometimes I want to say to hell with the lot of 'em. We can always think of a reason this or that happened but just because we think it don't make it so.

You want me to tell you how I raised ten children without any money, but didn't give in to despair. Why I didn't give in? Well, what's there to give in to when you think about it, where you gonna go on God's earth? I guess you can tell me that, since going seemed to be your approach. You want me to tell how my husband never did drink himself to death but not for lack of trying? He died in the middle of the living room sure, but that's no great accomplishment, everybody dies.

Then of course if ten children is too many which one wouldn't I have had? As you're the ninth I'd watch yourself there. I know you've had abortions; don't think that never occurred to me. I asked you several times why you only had one child, and you didn't answer. You don't want me to talk about that but I certainly will. The church tells us it's a sin, but now you see it's a sin against the body, you felt the pain of that sin. And you grieved for those who never came, those you talked yourself out of saying you didn't have enough of something, didn't have enough time or space or help. Took the idea of there not being enough into your own body, didn't you. Still, you ought to forgive yourself. Life does come and go, women know that.

～

Look at the starlings today how they flock and turn, fold together, shake out. European starlings they are, not native either you know, some fool man interested in Shakespeare thought they ought to bring over all the birds he mentioned in his plays, took a terrible toll on the farms around here, I don't know why people can't leave well enough alone. Still they're pretty to watch.

I lay there trying but I couldn't move them, had no sensation whatsoever. Well, I thought, Rose, you have really done it now, this ninth child was just one too many and now your legs are paralyzed. Said you would help that baby but you won't be able to now, not her or any of the others, who's gonna chase after them? I about lost my nerve for the whole shebang right then. Started to shake with the fear of it, or with the blood I'd lost, either way exhaustion took over.

I slept, and when I woke up I felt something in my toes. I kicked off the blankets just to see if my legs worked and they were fine. I was laughing with relief really when the nurse came by and scolded me but I didn't care. Course it seems funny now. It was just the stirrups or something had given me a pinched nerve. I was fine by the afternoon.

~

They brought you in. I recall each child clearly, it's not a memory that dims.

Even from here, I can remember looking into your milky blue eyes for the first time. The hospital walls fade away and there's just a clearing. Pang of shyness I felt (came with each child) noticing you were a stranger I had never met before. At the same instant some voice in the distance that's familiar, a conversation we've had before, like you knew me somehow, some previous agreement you've come to collect on. Your look is troubled, because you know getting born is a bad gamble, it might not work at all, but you have no recourse now, no way to return to where you came from. You're caught in a tiny net of bones all smeared with oil and blood, a body that is of no use to you, there's no strength in it. You have no resources whatsoever. I see the humiliation you feel, can feel you saying "Look at me, look at what has happened to me, I who am a human being, to be reduced to this, alone here, a stranger, helpless, exhausted." There's a sidelong glancing question in your look, you're not sure I'll keep my part of it but I feel a power I don't want to offend, so I say yes.

Yes I will. Tie your life to mine.

Was something familiar I saw in your eyes, looking down that deep distance, like something in back of a dream. Part of me is still there looking. Part of a mother remembers and never forgets that. Because in that first gaze I saw you. Saw who you were in a way I have been losing track of ever since. Just those few seconds are all the time I had to see who you were in the essential before you became my child. All a mother has, three or four seconds to get to look at their child as she came originally from wherever she did. Before I said yes, I would help you. Before who you were was mine, my daughter, to be circumscribed by where or what I am or was, what I could or couldn't do.

1960-63

*Blanchardville*

*Warming up outside finally, hope it holds. You just can't tell. Plenty of times we've shivered outside in a new Easter dress. But it's early spring and no reason to be unhappy today, little Stephanie lying on the couch and the hyacinths poking out of the ground by the porch steps.*

"Why don't you take a nap sweetheart? Listen I'll tell you some rhymes. *I've never seen a purple cow I never hope to see one, but I can tell you anyhow I'd rather see than be one.*"

"Is it bad to be a purple cow?"

"Well a course. It's strange, it's not right for a cow to be purple."

"But what if it is, will somebody kill it?"

"You go to sleep. It's just a little rhyme. Here's a different one. *With rings on your fingers and bells on your toes and elephants to ride on wherever she goes.*"

"Is that about me. Am I the 'she'?"

"Why sure, it could be."

"I'll ride an elephant?"

"You never know."

"How can you put bells on your toes. How do they stay?"

"I don't think it means on the toes, I think gypsies used to have some chains and jewelry they decorated their feet with, and there might be some bells attached. It's just a story for fun. Take a nap now."

*She's asleep. Good.*

*It isn't raining rain you know its raining violets... Wish I didn't have to use this downstairs room as our bedroom; on display for all to see. The front door, opens right off the living room, no door to close, no privacy. But what are you gonna do? It's a roof over our heads. Keep this bed made and the clothes picked up. Floral bedspread maybe isn't the best choice here if I had a solid color that might seem less bedroomish. I dislike these modern polyester fabrics on everything anyway. Mother used to have such beautiful linen bedspreads for summer, embroidered them with daisies, used to stand and iron the linens, Uncle Charlie would move the beds out to the long summer porch, could hear the crickets all night, birds singing in the morning. Oughta get a basket for her to put those blocks in before I step on them again. Damn edges are sharp.*

*It isn't raining rain you know it's raining violets.... Oh she's waking up.*

Out of the darkness of the inner bedroom, and into the living room I'm walking toward you as you wake from sleeping on the couch little one, there you looked startled.

"Hey babe, waking up?"

"Uh huh."

I'm walking out of the shadows; you watch me moving toward you into the light.

"Momma?"

"Dear heart."

"What was my name?"

I stop. You watch my brows knit together, grimace. Maybe fever I think. Waking up with it. "What do you mean, your name? You know your name is Stephanie."

"I know, I know that," you say, frustration in your voice.

"I don't mean now, I mean my real name, before. Before I was here."

Oh I felt a terrible chill like someone sneaking up behind me. I looked around the room, I didn't know what. I stopped, had to think. I could feel you touching another place but it was not a place I knew. I was spooked, tried to answer.

"Your name is Stephanie, I named you when you were born out of my stomach. God created you and you've been with us these three years. You came from heaven."

"I know I mean before…I."

"Feel sick?"

"No."

"Let's have some lunch, how bout some chicken noodle soup."

I came into the living room. I flattened my palm against your forehead to check for a fever, but it was cool.

"But what was my name…" you sit up, searching my face where you see the worry then lie back down and turn your face away toward the back of the couch. The paisley fabric there and the start of something uncertain. My displeasure was new to you, and you were frustrated too, thinking I should know. How could your mother not know such a simple thing as what your name had been originally?

You felt the edges of the world fold up around you, like a wild pony corralled for the first time. Well, you can't be in two worlds at once, or at least that's what I thought at the time. Felt like I needed to hold you here, keep the borders intact, like a rancher mends a fence to keep in his stock, to say here now stay. You only have the name I gave you. Cows are not purple.

First question you had ever asked me that I couldn't answer. Still can't. Eight children before you and not a one of them ever asked me that. Three years old you were and already thinking about someplace else. Was that the first time we parted? You felt alone with your question even then, didn't you. I know that disappointed you.

Though I know more now. How the borders around us are arranged like rippling water.

∼

You were always coming from somewhere else. Used to write your address in my book with a pencil it changed so often. You told me a story once, I wonder if you recall it. You were with the Buddhists, in your Buddhist period I say, like Picasso's Blue Period. Ha. You were staying in a little wooden house on a hillside in Darjeeling, India. For a week, every day was just draped in fog and mist, socked in tight. In the floaty gray dawn you would climb the slick switchback curves up the path, following the sound of the chanting monks in the monastery up above. One day, sitting in that monastery your eyes had been closed ten or fifteen minutes, when something changed in the room and you opened them. The fog had lifted, and there, through the windows in front of you were the snowy diamond peaks of the high Himalayas, stretched out blazing like cut glass crystal against the deep blue sky. Gave you vertigo to look it, was just so beautiful and "to think" you said, "that all that beauty had been there all along and you just couldn't see it." I think of that now because I can see so much more from here too, as if the fog of life has lifted and I can see to some other horizon, but as far as I can tell I think it's life too. Just more life. Far as the eye can see.

∼

Like I started to say earlier you can trace a lot back to geography. In 1886 there were 6,000 people here in Blanchardville, by 1887, 30,000. All on account of the earth you see. Limestone, Trenton limestone, any geologist will tell you runs in a belt through here north to southwest, it's about a hundred feet deep and the gas flows through it in underground rivers. Wells were all over this side of town. You could hear the gas gushing out, some said it sounded like Niagara Falls, all that gas blowing like a huge breath out of the mouth of the earth. Could see it too. Even when you cap a well there's exhaust and they would put a flame to it. Grandpa told me there wasn't a dark night in this town for ten years when the Cargill Well was blowing. You could see it from miles around, the tower and its constant red flame against the sky. This part of town people walked around all night like it was daylight. Grandma hung the laundry out at midnight, while the boys played football in the streets. Was like God had lit a special lantern just especially for the people of this town, that they should always have light. And they did. Fiat Lux.

Advertisements in 1890 said "Whoever missed the chance of enriching themselves by investing in the great cities of Chicago, and St. Paul has another chance with Blanchardville," which was sure to become "the greatest manufacturing center of a mighty republic." Course our hopes were a little higher than turned out to be the case, family and town either one. I always hoped you'd write a book before I died, as you were always threatening, but you never did. Well if wishes were horses beggars would ride. But why don't you, plenty of people do.

～

Still only about 30,000 people here give or take; and damned Republicans most of 'em, but the residents here do feel they're special. If you drive in from Columbus-way onto South Main looks like you really are somewhere, with all those grand old Victorian mansions lining the streets; towers and turrets carved out of the gas boom riches. Some of those mansions still have the old window glass, with the ripples you know, that your great grandfather blew. Of course there was oil ran under the gas and when one ran out they took the oil is why Hercules Oil made its headquarters here. Still our largest employer and the biggest building on Main Street, what is it five stories high? A pile of yellow brick. Doesn't look big to you I know, world traveler.

You must have walked right past my grandpa's old brick building downtown today, you know where it is there at West Main Cross.

Well they sandblasted the old stone façade last year and now you can read the Healy name again, but you have to cross the street and stand in front of the courthouse to see it, way at the top. I thought that last flood was gonna take out the whole block.

Some of those last little downtown businesses just north of the bridge were wiped out, including you'll remember Fowler's Diner that Scott Fowler ran, third generation of Fowlers to have that restaurant. Served the best fresh bass from Lake Erie. Well during that flood your crazy sister Becky in Oregon heard the news, oh it was in the *New York Times* and everything, so she called up your sister Linda here in town.

Becky said, "Linda I heard about the flood and I'm worried about Mom."

"Well what about her Becky?"

"Is she gonna be OK?"

"Well she's gonna be as OK as she's ever gonna be," Linda says.

Becky I guess was worried the flood was going to sweep away the graves.

She always was a little hysterical, remember I had to lock her in the cellar sometimes I don't like to admit it but I did. And truth to tell it didn't hurt her a bit. Well, so I wasn't swept away, and so what if I had been. Not like I was gonna drown. At any rate there was nothing Linda could have done, was there?

They say the river here runs east and west, but I say it doesn't really run at all, it just sort of sits there, looking for trouble. It's too flat around here to have a good river. I haven't been out North Main to Pine Street where you all grew up in a long time. Seems like everything's over here now. Closer to church.

Anyway I'm glad you got away. Seventeen when you left for San Francisco, 1977. Saved your money from waitressing at that Mexican restaurant on Main. After all that had happened I went along with it. Seemed a better idea than you putting yourself in so much danger again, I thought, since your older sister was there. Wasn't like I had that much choice in the matter but I wasn't happy is why I didn't go with you and Dad up to Toledo that morning. You wore that big denim cowboy hat your friend Stacy had given you. I said "I don't know why you want to draw attention to yourself like that," because I had to say something to cover the bitter loss I felt.

Remember just a few summers ago you were visiting and we were doing the dishes together by the kitchen window that looks out onto the neighbor's blacktop driveway, when I dried that plate and put it in the cupboard overhead as Mrs. Walsh pulled her car in from work, and I meant the whole of life here when I said "I'm glad you got away." But maybe now you're not.

1965
*Pine Street. Blanchardville*

You've seen they tore down the old grey-shingled house on Pine where you all grew up. Tore it down some years ago, to make a parking lot for the school. It was an ugly house to begin with, and a course we didn't live there anymore.

The big maple out front is still there if you want to go look at it, its trunk dividing into those two outstretched arms. The tree has survived as living things often do, longer than the works of man. Tree standing there rooted to where it always was.

Along with the house they tore down the peony bushes that used to bend over in the rain, so heavy were the white petals on those blossoms, I can smell them yet, a wet white perfume; and on the other side of the garage also torn down was the spindly ash tree where you had a tree house, over a forsythia bush with its early yellow fingers of flowers and other things that grew there as my children did.

No one now seems to remember how much of the town was full of overgrown gardens with currant bushes and barefoot kids out running around playing baseball and jump-rope and basketball and bicycles, and creating carnivals in the backyard out of piano boxes and cardboard, without all the adult interference that they get now. Now none of the kids even walk out the door. No one walks anywhere, all we have are ugly black-top parking lots and fat kids, I don't call that progress.

I think of that maple tree now and those games of hide and seek that would begin and end at that tree. Summer evenings, you'd start after dinner and go to nine ten o'clock, the whole neighborhood would get involved, some of us parents would sit next door on Cramer's red brick porch with the roof over it, a Midwestern porch, nice and cool in the summer. Be the two Cramer boys and the Weaver girls from across the street and of course the trashy Stone kids from down the street, Decklers from behind us if their crazy Portuguese mother wasn't screaming at them, you younger ones, at least a dozen kids give or take.

"You playing or not."

"I'll play but I'm not counting, I did it last time."

"Did not, Kevin counted last night."

"Across the street is out of bonds."

"Joseph if you're gonna go inside in the middle of the game then don't start playing."

"Oh he's little leave him alone."

"He's a spoiled brat."

"Look I got firefly rings on every finger."

"That's gross, you're gonna kill them all."

"I like to pull their guts out, see how they keep glowing, and sticky too. Here eat one."

"Get away from me."

"Come on let's play."

"Carrie you have to count, and your head has to be touching the tree, and eyes closed."

"Five ten fifteen twenty twenty-five thirty thirty-five forty forty-five fifty fifty-five sixty sixty-five seventy seventy-five eighty eighty-five ninety ninety-five a'hundred, apples-peaches-pumpkin-pie who's not ready holler I."

Course one of the younger children would always holler I.

"Hurry up then, five ten fifteen twenty that's all you get."

And off you'd all go into the spaces behind and between the houses, behind the juniper hedges, or into a car parked at the curb or behind the barrel where we burned the trash, behind the tool shed door, between the houses and the pine trees, and under the grape arbor in old man Turner's yard. The game, you know, is to come out as the seeker is off looking for someone else and run to the tree before they see you. But you never seemed to understand that, and you stayed hidden, listening from under the tendrils in the grape arbor to the crickets thrumming, to your own heart pounding, watching fireflies and the stars overhead, breathing in the smell of rotten fruit, listening to the voices of your friends and their running footsteps in the dark, waiting there in the hidden place wanting to be found or wanting to never be found but to live there by yourself in some other life than the one you had.

"You didn't find Stephanie?"

"Don't even look for her, she always hides somewhere you'll never find her."

"Ollie, Ollie in free, Ollie Ollie in free," one of the kids would shout and you'd have to come out. But otherwise no one ever found you. Not the places you hid.

～

You've been in Ohio longer this summer than you have been since you were seventeen. Wouldn't you know it, now that I'm gone you have cause to come. It was ever thus. I'm glad you're getting another degree, somewhere up there by Cleveland where we used to live.

You didn't expect that being on your home soil, breathing in the humid Ohio air would make you feel better but it has hasn't it? Just the feel of the air has been healing to you, not that dry or harsh salt-sea air you have on the coast; we have softer air here, and it's the air you're made of. That moist smell of the earth coming out of the cattails along the road, the powdery smell of red sumac, deep set white wooden houses. Houses that seem to sag under the weight of green shadows, and of course the storm's thunder and lightning, you been watching the storms out your window at night, but don't go out in that, I don't know if you remember what lightning can do. Just the sound of a lawnmower in the late afternoon, perfume of the cut green grass mixed with a little gasoline it's all a comfort. Even the feel of your feet walking on the worn blocks of a limestone sidewalk, the texture of the Ohio earth. Those sidewalks you used to walk on to school and everywhere.

∼

Must have been your twelfth birthday, you were walking. You'd be surprised how easy it is to get from one place to another now in memory. I no more start thinking of it than it all appears. Maybe memory lives inside our lives like water lives in a stream, as if water could weave together every scene. Now I'm not making any poetic claims, but maybe memory lives its own life. One day I was home and you were at school.

January 1972
*Blanchardville*

*What time is it anyway? Better get up. Where did I put those slippers, damn, I wish I could find them. This linoleum floor is cold, how cold is it out there I wonder. I'll turn the TV on. get the weather report while the water boils. Oh doesn't look like it snowed more, some sun coming out now. 30° not so bad. Stephanie's birthday. Oh it was bitter cold the morning I had her. Wasn't such a good year, but things got a little better after she came. Rusty started working again. Count your blessings. Oh hell I'm almost out of instant coffee. Guess I better try to get over to Food Town. Can't remember what Stephanie did say, had Girl Scouts or Campfire, whatever it is she's in. I think she's coming home late after some thing at school. Well I'll make supper early, so we can eat before I have to go to work. Noodles sound good, she likes those. I'll see what meat is on sale. Oh there's the 12 o'clock news. So Tricky Dick is going to China. That'll do us all a lot of good. Damn heathens all of 'em. Poor Oolan, Mother said. I heard Pearl Buck once at a Chautauqua up on the lake there near Erie. Oh that was a sad story poor Oolan, her husband stealing the pearls from off her neck. Terrible. Dear Sister Ursula. Always had us sending pennies to China. Better carry that laundry to the basement. Then I'll clean up, take a mop to that dining room floor like I've been saying I would, not that any of 'em would ever turn a hand to help. I bet I can find an angel food cake over there. Stephanie likes that. I better get a move on.*

You were walking along thinking.

No one's going to remember my birthday, not that it matters now it's already 4:30 they didn't even know it was my birthday in the Girl Scout meeting, the center is just behind downtown at least it's a little closer to home, I can go straight down West Cory, I want to get a camping badge it will be getting dark soon have to walk fast to get home before dark. It's hard to walk over the black patches of ice on the sidewalk, can't go around it cause the snow is piled up so high on the sides, but not here on the green arching metal bridge the frozen river below looks solid but you can't walk on it or you might fall through like the relative in Michigan did in a lake behind his house he was only seven, only a little boy that never even got to be twelve. On the other side of the bridge solid land, the machine shop door is open the men still welding how the sparks run out in front of them like a fountain of fire what do they make in there. Don't even think about your birthday, there won't be anything at home so just get used to that. Even if anybody remembers, they don't have any money to buy presents or cake or anything, you're not a baby, you've had a lot of birthdays it's not like you're a little kid. Earlier just after school, the sun was out, the icicles hanging over the front porches were dripping and water ran across the street, but now the melting has stopped it's getting colder. So quiet now except when a car comes by a peeling sound, no one else is out all the other kids walked home an hour ago, only these same old everyday houses on both sides of the street with their rectangle window eyes shut and dark their pointed heads settling into stillness, snow shovels leaning next to the door and the frozen tricycles on the grey porches.

What story is this like maybe the Dickens story *Little Dorit*. I'm very tragic, a poor little waif, threadbare like my coat; or I could be in a Fitzgerald story a careless adventurer, a very sophisticated traveling woman, a woman who is walking to a hotel in Moscow. Dickens seems more realistic. Still hurry up home because maybe someone remembered. Make your feet go slower because they haven't. The sky is pink and purple in the west you can feel darkness coming. It doesn't matter whether there is anything or not. Why do tears keep getting in your eyes then? If anyone sees me I'll say it was the cold. Maybe if I were a better person. This morning mother wasn't awake when I left for school, since she works at the newspaper she gets off at two in the morning so she tries to sleep. The oven in the stove doesn't even work so even if she had remembered she couldn't bake a cake. Sister Linda or Annie might remember and bake a chocolate cake and come over. Maybe they would try to surprise me. I can picture them. But probably not. Besides it doesn't matter. It's just sinful and selfish to just think about your own birthday. Why did you have to have a birthday and get your hopes all up anyway, that's the worst part. It's stupid that there are tears in your eyes again if they came all the way down would they freeze.

A lot of people are in Vietnam dying and you're just worried about your stupid little birthday. Of course it's irrelevant, birthdays are stupid anyway you've had already twelve of them; you're not a baby. Would it be chocolate? If there were a present what would it be? Mother has enough to do just to get dinner cooked before she leaves for work at six anyway, sometimes she can't even finish it, so how could she do more. Here's the corner of Defiance already and the stop light at Main Street. It's only two more blocks, one down one over to Pine then you'll know. Legs are frozen cold on the thigh where my coat doesn't cover, these books are heavy. I don't really want to get home, it doesn't matter what happens, my birthday is almost over anyway.

You opened the door and the warmth took you in, the living room had been cleaned and vacuumed. You could smell chicken cooking and hear me singing in the kitchen.

I heard you come in, "Hi, Honey, I'm in the kitchen"

I was just finishing up the dishes. You didn't answer, so I came down the hallway my hands still wet with dishwater, I wiped them on my apron, before I reached out for you.

"Hi Sweetheart, Happy Birthday, baby girl" and I wrapped you in my arms and, kissed your cold stiff cheek, but noticed a salty trace there. Your face turned slightly away.

"Now what's wrong?" I asked.

"Nothing."

But I heard the lump in your throat. Girls at that age are emotional I thought. Nothing wrong with that. Let 'em be.

Well you saw the cake on the table; an angel food cake from the store, whipped cream and pineapple to go along with it. There was a card, candy. You didn't say anything. Maybe couldn't I see now.

"Well sweetheart I didn't have a chance to get a present, maybe later this week. I'm making chicken and noodles; I know that's your favorite."

~

That was a day you have always remembered, when you dared to be tender which is not often; that day you realized that what you or anybody wanted when they were out walking in the cold alone was just for someone to be waiting.

Someone holding you in mind, though you couldn't see them; holding you in the net of their mind and pulling you nearer. Wasn't gifts or cake or any of that mattered, except your mother's arms coming out of the steamy kitchen and wrapping around you where you wouldn't have to be single or apart or anyone else.

All along I've been waiting for you to come home.

# II

## DEPARTURES

I WANT to talk about my own mother now as talking brings her close to me. Edna Catherine Tindal Healy, born in 1897, died in 1976. She was born on Center Street here in town. Did you know that wasn't her given name. She had been named Adrianna originally, for her paternal Grandfather Adrienne Tindal but when she was young no one wanted to be a foreigner and she called her self Edna. No one knows why she picked Edna but she did. Oh Steph, you never saw her when she was young but she had the most beautiful fine brown hair, that had a light blond streak in back; one eyebrow and eyelash was blond, while the other was dark brown.

When my mother and father were first married they lived over on Washington Street, and after some time then his family thought that he should try his hand at the farm. My dad's mother had bought it at a sheriff's sale along with several other properties and businesses. No one ever could figure out where she got her money, they say Grandpa made it running his card games on the Interurban, but he died just before this time.

Well this farm had absolutely no modern facilities. There was a privy, a well, no tractors, team of horses called Captain and Chester, big custard-colored Belgians. This farm was five miles out on Dixie Highway. My sister Jeanne and I were both born at Grandma Tindal's in Blanchardville at 403 Griffin Avenue. Mother came into town to have us, but Bess was born at the farm.

So, no amenities whatsoever there, a pump, a woodstove. Neither Mom nor Dad had any experience with farming but they liked the idea of having the farmhouse, all the space; there were lovely old black walnut trees in the yard. When you went off to Oregon and you wanted to live like that with your woodstove and lanterns, I thought now haven't we all been through this before? What's this family got against progress anyway? Although through the first war and up to about 1922 you could make some money from farming in Ohio, as Europe was all torn up and most of its food supply was coming from here. Farming was a going concern. I remember the horses, how big around their feet were, their sharp warm smell. How mother loved the horse called Captain, and would feed him apples from her hand.

We lived on the farm for about five years, and it was when Bess was a baby that the gypsies came.

Women cooked everything from scratch in those days of course, on the woodstove, so if you wanted to make a soup or stew, well it would take some time, and it was hot in the kitchen in the summer so you would put something on and leave it to go do some other chores.

1924
*Blanchard County, Ohio*

It was a day like that, late summer when Mother had put a nice beef stew to cook on the stove and took the children out to the yard with her. Dad had driven into town that morning. She was hanging out the laundry by the side of the house admiring how nicely her flower border had come along on the side border this year, bachelor buttons, the blue was so noticeable, and phlox, the phlox just gave and gave its bloom, since June it had, but the red zinnias clashed with the pinks and blues. Now the lilies you could smell even over here, so tall this year, and secretly, for she thought it sacrilegious, she held the inside of the lily flower as good proof for the glory of God as anything, the delicate pink stalks topped with the dangling umbrellas of pollen, there like a Chinese festival of abundance and rain. She noticed then how her white sheets seemed to be dancing in the wind as the children began pointing at the road. She heard the sound of a waltz come spinning across the grass with a carnival sound she knew was an accordion, met a few minutes later by the jingle of the bells on the wagon horses coming along the road. She could see them from the slight rise of the lawn to the side of the farmhouse, the back of the wagons covered over with green canvas and the bottom wood painted red like a circus. On the first wagon a young man was sitting up front next to the driver, swaying and singing as his hands played over the accordion keys, his words were in a strange language but it was a catching tune. The children clapped and ran to look closer, but Mother called them back, "No, now you stay. Right here." There were three or four covered wagons. Some boys along the side led a string of horses. They often traded horses. Dad said you could always tell the stolen horses because those were the ones they were most eager to sell before the rightful owners a few counties back might catch up. They used to stop at the small pond down the road and camp there for a few nights. Some were metal smiths, tinkers you know, they would mend a broken pot handle or a harness, they weren't all bad.

Well mother stopped her laundry to look and called her collie dog that was barking at them terrible, back into the yard and held my hand while Aunt Jeanne hid behind her. One of the gypsy women saw her, and got off the wagon and came over pulling a flowered shawl around her shoulders. She said to Mother "I will sell you some pins for sewing."

"I don't need any pins," Mom said, "no thank you."

Well the woman kept patting Jeanne's hair as she was very blonde, saying, "So yellow, so fat."

Then the woman called back to the wagon, and two skinny

little barefoot girls came running over to her and she pushed them in front of Mother and said in decent English, "See how small, my children. So hungry." She put her hand to her mouth gesturing, "Sooo hungry." Well they did look awful skinny.

Mom couldn't bear the thought of anyone going hungry, but she didn't have much on hand. She had some summer squash in the vegetable garden, and motioned to the woman to follow. She opened the wooden gate and put the children in front of her still wary, she picked an apron full of squash with the yellow blossoms still hanging on the tips all big and bright to give her. The gypsy woman took them in a flour sack she seemed to have been carrying along but she didn't look very happy about it.

"Hard to cook," she said, and looked so upset.

Then Mother said, "Well, if you bring your children back later I may have some stew for them."

That seemed to cheer them all up, and she thanked Mother and walked back toward the wagons, which were a little further down the road now.

Mother finished hanging the laundry. She had Bess in her pram and me and Jeanne whose job it was to hand up the clothespins. She was careful to keep us all with her cause there were stories of gypsies stealing children though she didn't really believe that as they seemed to have plenty of their own. Jeanne went into the house and brought out the book of fairy tales and Mother sat on the grass and read us Thumbelina. When we were finished we gathered up the basket and walked out to the chicken coop behind the house, where I was allowed to fill the water tank in the coop from a bucket by the pump; then she scattered some corn from the bottom of her apron pocket, stopped to tie Jeanne's shoes and to pick a good handful of fresh parsley from the herb patch out the back door, then lifted Bess from her baby carriage and put her on her hip. As she started up the back porch steps she heard the front screen door slam and wondered what that was. Well she walked into her kitchen just in time to see the back side of that Gypsy woman hurrying down the front walk with her stew pot still steaming in her hands. Mom hurried out the front door after her but there was a wagon waiting right on the road out front, and a man helped the woman with the pot into the wagon and off they went at a good trot.

Mother was livid, and walked after them yelling, "That's not right, my husband will be after you."

She was carrying Bess in one hand and the parsley in the other, and in the midst of her anger she thought to herself 'damn it now that stew's not gonna taste right without the parsley,' but that thought made her all the madder and she threw the parsley into the road and stamped it into the dust. They weren't just taking her stew, you see but taking her chance to give it to them, was like they stole it twice, took her good pot and her good intentions too. She stood there in the middle of the road looking back at the house where Jeanne and I stood peering off the porch, and back down the road where the wagon was rolling, looking back and forth, stomping her feet and we didn't know which way she was gonna go.

Stay or leave us we didn't know. And when you disappeared that time, it was like that. I didn't know. You took something too. Well this is all related if you'll just be patient. So many things are vivid now.

July 2, 1976
*Blanchardville Hospital*

*Was good of Jeanne to drive up from Columbus well of course she would be here right away. Saint Jeanne, my sister who never said an unkind word about anyone, and I don't have to talk while we sit here. Is Mother dying, I think it may be. I didn't expect it not this month of July, just had her 82nd birthday but at least I can imagine she will go to heaven because her devotion to Mary was absolute and Early Mass at 7 a.m. every Wednesday as well as Sunday, but my Stephanie, I don't know where she is or will go. My baby girl. Where is it she has gone, not where the old go when the heart stops beating or starts again God's will be done. Something else controlling where she is and I don't know what it is. My mother's body here, her hand bruised from the IV, her bony hand purple, but warm. She responds to my touch she squeezes my hand, her face is calm, almost smiling I think. But my daughter's body, where is she, what if someone I have never seen would take her put their grubby hands on her. I can't lose both. What then, more than a soul can bear. They say fluid is filling her lungs now, cardiac failure, heart disease, heart's dis-ease. Would to God this had not. I sit when I can. Jeanne is here, thank God Jeanne is here. We're just sitting with her, not much more that we can do.*

～

"Rose, have you heard anything today" Jeanne asks. Her voice is so gentle its gentleness catches in my throat, I clench my teeth to keep from crying, I do not want to sob by my Mother's bedside.

The pump of the respirator.

"We think she went off with the older Taylor girl from across the street, she was in town with a boyfriend and they were on their way somewhere, left about the same time she did."

"Uh huh, I bet you'll hear something soon."

The pump of the respirator, in and out as if wind is blowing my body away.

"She doesn't know Grandma's here in the hospital does she?"

"Well the day before she left Grandma was first admitted here, said she didn't have anything to do and I said you can go visit your grandmother in the hospital…" but I couldn't explain to Jeanne even.

"The police said they're looking of course."

"Chris said he would bring Bess out during his lunch hour."

"That's good. Is Chris still working for Sunny Delight?"

"I think so. So funny I never could stand the taste of that stuff. But I would never say that to him."

"No."

"She's resting, should we go for a smoke in the cafeteria."

"You go Rose, but you should consider giving it up after this."

"I know Jeanne but not now."

"I know. Go ahead I'll wait for you here."

～

*I'm walking down the hall of the hospital and it's not a good place to be, smells of antiseptic. I can only think if my daughter is dying also, if death has come where I can not see it. At least here in these awful yellow brick hallways of Blanchard Valley Hospital I can see what is happening, where I gave birth to her, yes it's true. Same place. I hear moaning from one room, look at that old man twisted in his sheets. In the elevator now, that mother has a baby has an infection in its eye, so swollen and pink. "The fever has gone up" the father says, then the baby cries, now thank God it's the first floor.*

*Cafeteria that way, sign says. Sit back here at the empty table, there's an ash tray. Up to now I've survived by doing whatever it was we had to do taking care of the babies and feeding them, pouring milk in the bowl, frying a dozen eggs on Sunday, making do with what you had tried to read to them send them to church what have you, none of it enough, we had to keep them fed but that is not enough not nearly, I wonder what it was.*

*She doesn't have it so bad must be those drugs that make her crazy or depressed, it's sad she said the other day "I want to kill myself." A beautiful young girl like her what a sin to say such a thing to your mother, they must have destroyed her mind.*

"Are you alright Ma'am?"

"Oh yes."

"You had your head down on the table there I didn't know if you passed out."

"No, I'm just tired, could I get a coffee?"
"Why sure."

~

*Waitress in a pink polyester dress, do you know where my daughter is, could I get an answer waitress. This death I don't know how to make do, with this not at all, if it comes I cannot say I will pay later or borrow from my sister I cannot last longer by adding powdered milk to the milk that I have or put on an extra sweater to save the heating it's too near Labor Day it's hot. Rose your mind's going, that terrible fear comes over me, here in the cafeteria. I need to walk outside.*

*That's better here on the bench by the zinnias. Mother always knew the names of all the flowers. Forget me not. Who are those men all dressed in black going into the hospital, everyone looks like death, I worry that he may come in a way I can't recognize.*

*I have too much for death to take. That's the problem. Oh death would make a fortune if he came to see me, death would call me a Golden Calf. I have so much life to keep from him, so many lives, some others have only one but just think how much could he get from me, what a temptation I am for death don't think I don't feel it. Could come from anywhere, it's just this hospital puts me so on edge. As if the dying might linger around and take more, once it has started.*

*It's just like after you have a baby the womb is open you know, susceptible to infection and you shouldn't take a bath, or sit in water anywhere, don't dare go in a pool or river, the womb is still open you have to be very careful. Eight weeks at the minimum, a break from your husband and you're glad of it because being close to the baby is all the closeness you can feel at once. I don't know why I'm thinking about babies now. After birth the womb is open. Death is the same I think but I do not know what is open. I need to know what part to keep from being entered. Is it time?*

*This old wooden bench is what holds me sitting up here,*

*I could not even sit except that the bench sits and I am in it, haven't slept much in days. Oh mister please turn off the truck motor if you're waiting there to deliver, the diesel exhaust is nauseating. Every piece of clothing sticks to you in this heat, I'm perspiring like a pig. She could have waited and run away some other time, she knew Grandma was sick. What do you protect to keep death away? Protect your nerves is what you should do so you can pray. When death is near when you smell the antiseptic or see the purple line above the lip then light a candle get out your rosary. I think it's in the bottom of my purse here somewhere I think it is, oh all tangled up terrible in with the house keys. I can't even untangle it, can't even get my rosary out to pray. Goddamn it all to hell.*

*When death comes near when death comes you must protect your face, protect your faith is what I mean. Don't lose your faith then, don't ask questions whether it is true or not that heaven waits. Let it alone, let it lie unbroken there in your mind. You must now. What is opened in death is not the gate to the body the round red gate to the inside of the body where the beating of the heart echoes in a warm current of blood, what is opened in death is the gate to the mystery of Jesus Christ and the resurrection of the flesh. What is opened are doubts are opened that lead only to a dark threshold in a sleepless night so you mustn't let it. You must protect your faith when death comes that's what you must protect. Let us proclaim the mystery of flesh, no I mean let us proclaim the mystery of faith. Christ has died, Christ has risen Christ will come again. But will my daughter?*

∼

It had been three days now you'd been missing. Bess called, and said Mother had a bad morning they weren't sure what would happen now. So I came to sit after I finished at the paper at 2:00. I just came direct to the hospital from work. Already missed three days of work, won't be able to eat if I don't go. I was awful tired but I thought I could doze off there easy as anywhere I suppose. They wouldn't allow us there if they didn't think it was near.

Don't know how anyone rests with all the lights and machinery going up here in ICU. It's Jenny on duty, she's Carolyn Lynch's daughter that used to live next to us on Lima Avenue. Whole family over 6'2", and flaming red hair. I wouldn't want to wake up to Jenny personally, but she's good-hearted. Speak of the devil and he always shows.

"Hello Jenny"

"Good morning Rose, come to sit with your mom?"

"Yes I did."

"Well your brother just left. You can take over the recliner."

"I will, has she been awake?"

"Her lungs were clearer so we were able to take the tube out and let her breathe on her own. I think she was talking to Jim maybe, the doctor has her on a lot of sedatives because he doesn't want her blood pressure to go up. Now you call us if you need anything, I'm on rounds."

"I know, Jenny I will."

"Hello, Mother it's Rose here. I see you're breathing on your own again."

She's reaching for my hand, my mother is reaching for my hand as if to comfort me, does she know of my other worry?

⁓

*Yes, daughter give me your hand, so I can feel what a living person feels like I can feel the good warmth of living flesh not this machine incessantly beeping that sound will be what kills me if nothing else does first. Passing through little towns with the changing traffic lights, lights turning green, no hills in the entire county as far as your eye can see over the clothesline. Out hanging up clothes on the farm when you were a little one sitting by the wicker basket handing the clothespins up to me, and I clip them into the shoulder of a white shirt wondering how a shirt even without a man in it reminded you of a man, just the shape left but nothing inside, or a short white smock with a little girl's shadow in it. I sewed the satin rosebud on the collar of that one on your first birthday there, see how the clothes-line sets right on the horizon and the horizon is straight except for the heat waves. Now you've dropped your doll, go looking for it between the ends of the white sheets, billowing white sheets where did you go? Now what is that sound, not the wind but like a wind, it's knocking oh it's the police come for the whiskey upstairs. Need to warn them to hide it. I don't think I can climb up the stairs now. Rose can.*

"Rose, go tell your father they're here, run child and hurry," she said, clear as a bell.

Gave me a terrible start, her talking all the sudden right out of the blue from her hospital bed. Said it clear as day, and I panicked for a second thinking where is Dad, except he's been dead these twenty five years. Well she'd been dreaming of course.

"It's alright Mother, everything is alright." I said. I worried she was raving but she looked right at me with her blue eye and her violet eye and you won't believe it but they were twinkling with merriment.

"I know it is," she said. "Gypsies took the soup but they didn't take the children." She paused and smiled. "I guess I will go on then."

Then she pulled my hand to her chest. That was the last thing she said.

But she was still dreaming and tending to her things inside that dream. I don't know what you would call it in that place being or not, so near one to the other. When you're there, it doesn't much matter what you call it so much as paying attention to the way. Call this a dream but soon every dream and every day mend together along the seams of memory. Just sit still for a minute and listen.

～

1976
## *In my mother's dream. Blanchardville*

Something she had forgotten woke her. She rose up from her bed and stood listening to the rhythmic breathing of the summer night on the farm. Her husband's chest rose and fell, the curtains on the open window blew inward then back against the soft screens. He has been sleeping for such a long time she thought, still she stepped quietly, leaving. She paused at the doorways of the children's rooms, felt their breathing spreading through the dark hallway as ripples through water, stood in the intervals of their breath, breathed with them, smiled that their father was there to watch over them. At the front door she bent to put her shoes on then stepped out onto the wooden porch. The moon was almost full. The dog stirred from his place under the porch, but she said, "No, you stay." And he did.

It was easy to walk on the road all white with moonlight. Poplar trees shook their silvery leaves, it was refreshing and cool where the trees held, warmer now the corn fields began on either side of the road. How obediently the corn stood in its rows like an army of thin men, stretching as far as the eye could see. Just stay there she said to the corn, if I need you I will call. She walked down the road toward the pond where the gypsies were camped.

She could see faintly now the golden shadow of a fire up ahead, a spark bursting and falling; hear the buried swell of an accordion coming and going. When she neared the widening in the road where a path led down a slight embankment toward the pond she paused. She smelled the pungent musk of the horses, heard their coughing, stomping, then made out their shapes tethered in a line. A grey horse looked up as she approached and met her eyes, nodding as she passed. Orion the Hunter visible overhead, three stars in the belt, sparks rose from the fire as she approached it.

The gypsies sat around on stools and rugs, a dense dark ring around the red center. Mother recognized the back of the woman who had been to her house earlier by her paisley shawl, an old man on the other side of the fire saw her approaching and stood up alarmed.

Hey who is it? and they turned to look. The wind changed just then blowing smoke low into the faces of the seated gypsies, who coughed and turned.

Who are you what do you want here?

I've come to take my cooking pot back, Mother said.

And why do you think we have your pot, the old gypsy man asked.

Because it's right there, Mother said pointing. Her rare and valuable French copper pot hung on a spit over the fire.

That's my pot. It has the mark of Thomas' forge on the bottom, I can show you. This woman stole it from me and I've come to take it back.

Mother pointed to the woman. Earlier today you were at my house.

I've never seen this woman before, answered the gypsy woman to her neighbors. Never.

You've seen me before and begged food for your children.

There it proves it, said the Gypsy woman, I don't even have any children. And all the gypsies laughed.

I offered to give her soup, but she took my cooking pot instead. It's not right.

Ha, it's not right, the old man said to another, mimicking her voice. It's not right, this queen of the night has come to tell us what is wrong and right. As if we are children.

She was confused for a moment, not knowing what else she should say when the warm breath of the grey horse, sudden on her shoulder, startled her.

The grey horse walked forward.

Give her the cooking pot, the horse said.

The old man raised his arm above his face as if bracing for

a blow, but nodded then pushed at the curly headed boy next to him. The boy searched among the edge of the fire for a stick; he stood up and with his stick, slid the pot to the side of the spit, lifted it, to the ground.

He dumped a dark liquid into the grass.

It was only holding water, he said. It will need a minute to cool.

She stood, waiting in the glare of the fire and the other language. The half-light illuminated the fronts of their faces while the rest of their bodies were submerged in the darkness. They spoke softly now to themselves, as if they were frightened.

She took a clean cotton hanky from her pocket to pick up the handle of her pot. It was warm and clean, shining in the moonlight. She carried it toward the road, afraid to look behind her. The accordion player started up in the invisible distance.`

After climbing up the slight embankment to the smoother road she paused, took a deep breath of the night air, warm and green smelling. She lingered to hear the crickets, a dove cooing somewhere, the crackle of the fire, the crackle of the stars, the corn standing at attention in its vast formation. She looked down the road she had just come, the road to home, but turned the other way. She began walking.

It was only then, once she had started away, that she knew she wouldn't be going home after all. She thought of her children asleep in the house, wishing she could stay with them, but knowing that was impossible now. They had their own children to tend to, in other houses in other nights than this. And truth to tell, she was curious to see what was down the road. She walked on, her cooking pot dangling from her hand. Now that she had her pot back there was no end to what she could cook, anyone could take the food who was hungry, she would just make more.

For some miles she kept walking though she could not tell

how many. Walking toward a faint grayness at the horizon, must be the coming morning she thought, if I walk quickly it will arrive sooner. She tried to hurry but her feet seemed to move so slowly, and her left hip ached where it always had. I am tired, tired feet, tired knees, tired hips. Can't fight nature she thought and slowed her steps. Suddenly she heard the pounding of hoof beats behind her, turned with a last pang of fear, then sighed. The grey horse slowed to a walk as he neared her, then knelt in the center of the road, panting softly, or was that her. A sound like a greeting came from her mouth though she couldn't recognize the word. She climbed onto his back, wrapped her hands deeply into his wiry mane. They rose.

July 7, 1976

*Pine Street, Blanchardville*

My mother, your grandmother, died that evening. I kept thinking of the happiness in her eyes or had I mistaken it? Next day I couldn't think to do more than fry an egg.

People need to eat. I have no appetite but need to keep going. Frying eggs like every Sunday. Ringing, I hear a ringing someone get the phone. Can't be that Mother's gone because that call came last night. Maybe it wasn't true maybe she didn't die, hospitals calling to say it wasn't true. Calling to tell me.

"Luke do I hear the phone?"

"No Mom I don't hear it, it isn't ringing."

*I thought I heard it. Ask not for whom the bell tolls it tolls for thee. Tolls for me apparently no one else can hear it. Maybe the oil sizzling there in the skillet. Or my ears ringing. Been a while now since I slept, couldn't sleep last night after I heard. Stayed with her long as I could she wasn't conscious at the end and Jim wanted to sit with her I left at 5 p.m. they called at 9 p.m. How can Earl sit there and read the sports page?*

*"You want your eggs over easy Earl?"*

*"Over easy, but don't overcook them."*

*Don't overcook them have half a mind to throw the whole skillet on his head. No consideration from him don't know why I'd hope for it. Day after my mother died he might be kind but why hope that. Cauldren-Crates they said, the funeral home we always use, tomorrow at noon and five, don't know what I have to wear that's black maybe that navy skirt, but it's wool, be awful hot in this weather.*

*It is ringing now I hear it, again.*

"Luke the phone is ringing, isn't it. Get the phone."

### July 1976
### *Near Oxford, Mississippi*

Their voices had come through the unpainted wood slat wall like splinters, waking you from sleep. "No, please don't," that was your friend Katie's voice, then her boyfriend Dale's slowly, "I'm gonna use this gun see, I have these guns for a reason."

You tried to pretend that you couldn't hear, turned your back to the bare wall in that old Southern cabin, pulled the covers over your head, afraid to listen. Afraid not to listen. They stopped for some time. Maybe it was just a dream.

Then it started again, their voices growing into a solid something, wrong. All the doubts you had about Dale in the past few days, the drugs, his paranoia about strangers, talk about the end of the world, why he wanted to come here to his grandmother's old homestead in rural Mississippi, Katie's submission, you understood.

A light shown under the door that led from your room to theirs, you knew the door was locked from the other side, he always locked it. You thought maybe if you listened hard enough you could be in the room there with them, you could stop them by your hoping, Katie would know you were hearing wouldn't she? You tried to picture what he was doing, in the light, holding her, or hurting her, then his shouting.

"What I wanna know about this arrangement is what am I getting outta this deal, what do you do for me? What do you give me?"

"I give you my love." Katie answers, but her voice is too meek and hopeless, you know she's doomed now. You want to tell Katie, don't answer like that, don't act as if your love is nothing. Then his reply.

"I don't know what I can do with that."

Their voices pausing, then going on. More threats, pleading.

It went on until you could hear something else, the shape of a story unfolding, and a role in the story that was yours. It had to do with going, with rising up and going away into the darkness of the night. You saw that leaving home had started this going but it was not the end, and you saw all the going you would do, all the leaving you were assigned to in that night, felt it come for you clearer than any dream. Still, you lay there a minute longer as if to tell the going that you were still acting on your own time.

The darkest hours had passed, there was a pale lightening somewhere distant that gave you the courage to go. You realized you had been waiting for a little glimmer of light. Trying to be as quiet as possible, before he heard you, before that other door opened, you rose from the bed. There was no time to find your shoes, the room too dark for that. You put on your overalls, found your shoulder bag, your wallet with a few dollars.

Passed their locked door trembling, held your hands out in front of you to find the doorway into the front room then to the front door, the knob turning. Outside there was a just enough light to show you the three stairs leading down from the porch, a mist cowering against the ground. You didn't know where you were going, or what you were looking for, but there was story you felt yourself inside of, it said go get help now, save yourself, save your friend.

The hard packed clay of the road was cool on your bare feet. In half shadows, skinny pine trees rose up on either side, their shape engulfed by a smothering tangle of kudzu vines, a rampant grasping growing whose power you felt as it threatened to cover you too. You walked slowly because you didn't know where you were going. What was in the shadows, you're worried, wondering in your worry, what might be happening to Katie. But you did not fear for your own life, you felt your own life in this story unfolding even as you walked.

You walked until real morning came, and watched the mothering light of the rising sun embrace the trees, the pastures fence posts, the green grass by the road, yourself. A lightening of all darknesses ever descended, ascended. You felt that morning had come as a gift to you alone in the whole world and you wept to see it. Stood there in the middle of the road, your face raised up weeping and smiling overjoyed in the profound blessing of plain daylight.

You slipped out of the haze made of fear and there you stood, in front of the driveway of a farmhouse with a gate. It seemed like you had been there by that gate for a long time, like you had always known it.

Then you saw the sign on the fence that said Beware of the Dog, and you laughed at the sign, couldn't help but laugh because you knew the universe was telling you that Dale and every evil thing like him was the dog you would have to beware of, oh the world was talking to you that morning. The other sign said No Trespassing and that threw you off, that didn't make you laugh, maybe they would want to shoot you too. People around here were like that.

You stood there looking down the driveway toward a house you could just make out, hoping to hear or see someone. You didn't hear anyone, you lost your nerve, walked away. Turned around, walked back. Thought well you weren't trespassing, there's no crime in asking to use a phone is there. They can't shoot you for asking to use a phone. Just go ask. You were still walking back and forth by that gate when a real dog began to bark. The woman that lived there pulled up in a station wagon back from sunrise service with the Baptists and rolled down her window.

"I had some trouble, and maybe I could use your phone." That was how you put it, "I had some trouble." She was a nice woman, said I thought we heard some noise from over there, like they'd heard trouble from there before.

"You might as well get in or the dog'll chase you." You told her you had run away from home but had changed your mind now.

She took you into her kitchen that smelled of sausage and coffee, her mother and husband and two grown sons were eating breakfast, and looked up awful surprised as you came in.

"You want a cup of coffee?" she asked. "She needs to use the phone to call her family, telephone's over there."

July 7, 1976<br>
Pine Street. Blanchardville

"Yeah it's ringing now. I got it." I hear my son Luke answer. "Hello? Stephanie! (Mom it's Stephanie.) Yeah where are you? She's coming."

*Turn off the stove don't burn the house down on top of everything else, I'm coming, I'm coming down the hallway give me the sound of her voice living, here please give me her voice in my ear.*

"Hello, yes, where are you?"

You may remember this. You said I'm in Mississippi, I want to come home, things haven't gone so well, you said things haven't gone so well, understatement of the year. Are you alright, I said and you said yes. You sounded nervous but not hurt. Oh I could hear it all in a minute, hear it all in your voice. You still trying to sound nonchalant but I could hear what had happened. The people at the farmhouse agreed to take you to the closest town, which was Oxford Mississippi, they had to go that way anyway, when they were finished eating.

Would you like another cup of coffee they asked and you said yes. They were having Sunday breakfast, eggs, sausage with grits, gravy and biscuits, they offered and you accepted. You sat there in your hippie overalls and braids, no shoes on your feet. What they must have thought. But they were quiet people, didn't say too much among themselves, Praise the Lord and nobody ask any questions. You felt awkward alright. Sitting there thinking how you really did understand Faulkner and Flannery O'Conner in a whole new way now, and you wondered had these people read Faulkner too?

Well you were thinking of Faulkner of course because he lived in Oxford, you knew that. You had agreed to wait there at the police station. The policeman there was kind to you, even though you asked him right off if he was a redneck, oh you had no fear that's for sure. Your father had called and left word he was on his way, so the policeman arranged for you to stay with a woman in town for the night, because it would take that long to get down there. She picked you up at the police station and took you to her Victorian house, she had six children herself and a drunken husband though they were all very religious. She wore a nylon dress, printed with red and blue Liberty Bells for the Bicentennial and that stuck in your mind a long time her dress covered with Liberty Bells. You've remembered that dress a long time, and that night because of how near to an end it was but you never felt that end, you felt that you would rise up in the night and dawn would come and you would get help and you did and saved Kate Taylor's life on top of it.

Might as well tell. You were still asleep in that woman's house around 11:00 a.m. when your father got there. The two of them were out front talking when you were woken up and you walked out. "How much do I owe you?" your father was asking her? He was always so polite.

"Oh ten dollars is fine."

No kidding he paid ten dollars for you.

As you got in the car he told you. "Your grandmother died, night before last."

Then he drove you back to Dale's house because you still needed to get Kate.

That was when Dale came out onto the porch with his shotgun.

"What do you want here?" he yelled. Then he just stood by the door and started shooting.

"Get down behind the car," your dad shouted and pushed you down by the shoulder but he didn't seem to be afraid at all did he?

Dale kept shooting into the air over your heads into the trees, how long would he go on. "This is my house" he yelled. "I'm defending my property, you get off my property." Then he shot into the air some more.

"We're gonna do that sir, we're gonna go as soon as we pick up our friend here." Your dad yelled. Then Kate came out and she too was brave all the sudden.

"Dale stop shooting, please." And he looked at her as if he had never seen her before and put his gun down a minute.

She went inside to get her things.

Then he started shooting into the air again, looking up, just shooting at the sky. Without rhyme or reason.

It took a few minutes for Kate to pull her suitcases onto the porch and your dad helped her load up her stuff, and then you were all gone from there.

～

It was the strangest thing. Once your father called to let me know you were on your way back, I could feel Mother leaving me then. I could feel her body start to recede into the distance like she was walking away, each step wrenching my bones with the force of her pulling away. Oh I knew it's all attached somehow my mother leaves my daughter returns.

There is a thread that runs between them needs be, tug of war across the river Styx.

∼

I thought so many things at once, I was glad you'd be back in time for the funeral, so I wouldn't have to explain losing my daughter to everyone trying to console me for losing my mother, why that would have been just vulgar, to lose that much in one week. Ask not for whom the lord giveth and the bell tolls. Oh what's the verse. "Job arose, and rent his mantle, fell down upon the ground. Naked came I out of my mother's womb, and naked shall I return, the Lord giveth and the Lord hath taken away; blessed be the name of the Lord." Or the telephone.

Whatever else you might want to say about your father remember that he didn't hesitate on that occasion to drive a day and a half to come after you and get himself shot at into the bargain. You make your own peace on that.

Your father dropped you in the front yard so he could go round back to park.

"Your Mother's waiting for you."

You walked up the three steps. You opened the screen door and came in.

I was standing in the room alone, facing the door, waiting.

"I'm glad you're back," I said. We embraced briefly, but you turned your face away.

You didn't know what to say, because you were trying to decide just who I was. I looked like a stranger to you I know, my face all ravaged by grief and worry. Dark shadows around my eyes the kind of shadows that looking at death leave, my skin dry and cracked over my bones like the parched earth of a long drought. A drought you sensed was of your making. I was so much thinner. Smaller.

You saw the fragile girl inside of me inside of every woman, a small wounded creature in place of your mother who had always before in all difficulties stood solid and fierce. But then I was a child who had lost her mother, but I was also a mother who had believed her child lost. I was a grotesque, a crossroad curiosity, that's what you saw. Standing right there in the living room. All the sudden I remembered that quote from Dante: "The long theme drives me hard and everywhere the wondrous truth outstrips my staggering pen."

"I'm sorry I worried you," you said. "I didn't mean to worry you."

"Are you okay."

"I'm okay."

"Please tell me you won't do that again, I couldn't bear that again."

"I won't I'm sorry."

"We can work out whatever it is, I don't want you to be so unhappy."

"It's not your fault." You said not knowing what else to say.

～

You didn't know enough to say the truth. I didn't either at the time. You didn't know to say I had to go mother I was trying to find my life, trying to find where life was. You shouldn't have worried see. Here I am in my overalls, my bag, here on my shoulder, my body, my long hair hanging down. I knew I would not die, you didn't know but I knew.

You stood there at sixteen and saw for the first time that some damage cannot be taken back or fixed; and the realization of that came over you like a chill. You put your head down and cried. That was worse than any punishment I could give. You knew a bond had been broken, and you broke it. Snapping it underfoot as you left. Didn't even stop to look, so eager were you to get away. Hoping to break the bonds of this town but you broke our bond. Or at least bent it to where the mark would show through.

～

Well seems like you've stood there for thirty years now, looking into my ravaged face wondering what part of that pain was you.

Is that what you left here to get away from? The closeness of death in my face, and something else small in the corner, you could see it too, the mark of your own death. Erased for this time but still showing through. I think that's what it was. You were young to have seen that. But there it was.

And now look at yourself, raving through the graveyard. A full-grown woman with a husband and a child. Never chose to live close by when I was alive and now all the sudden desperate to find me, to find that heartbroken woman. Is this what you came to tell me? To stand there again. And still the answer not clear?

You did ruin forever my hope that some love could run a smooth course, that's true. But in time I did forgive you, a mother's love is deeper than forgiveness. Problem was you didn't forgive yourself. And you stayed away from here because of that. Maybe.

I think in that headlong rush of yours to find who or what you were you left the only person who knew.

But you couldn't see that then. You didn't know it was me you were trying to talk to, it was your mother you were trying to ask. Who am I. See me. Tell me.

So you're asking me now. I can only say what I know.

~

Do you remember the story *As I Lay Dying.* Comes to mind by coincidence, but of course the Oxford connection reminds me and I know you loved Faulkner. Do you remember the story. The family is trying to bury their mother, but the husband is so shiftless and stupid that he ruins everything he touches. Trouble is piled on trouble until you have vertigo from all the bad one fool man can do. By the time they finally get the mother buried one son is crippled, the daughter has been raped, the other son in the insane asylum and the husband gets a new wife. It all begins again.

But I think now, we can step outside if we like. Was it Herodotus who said "the same river twice?" How did that go?

A river is the same then as now, or there is only one. It goes backward to lead us to the future as the Blanchard flows into the Maumee flows into the Ohio flows into the Mississippi on currents that move like the summer into autumn which is a shift isn't it of light more than anything, a milder light, clear and blue. What if we are the stream that stays time together, a cord in the center of the rope wound round and round. Still I think the world, in its hands, its light, bones, water, trees, has memories of its own. Sometimes I can hear my great-great-grandfather, his voice like the sound of rushing water.

# III

## ORIGINS

### 1856
### *Charles Healy: New Orleans to Cairo, Illinois*

*I*T SEEMS *that I have been held and burdened down for
so long but now I am lighter moving ever deeper into the
stream until I am held up floating easily, in the moss skin scent
of fresh water I am in this river that is in the heart of this country and I dive under. I feel in each hip joint a looseness while
the water holds me. I swim while the water brushes along my
ribs, my chest. I breathe and dive, in rhythmic stroking. When
I turn on my back to float the voices of Malachi and Christo-
pher cheer me as when we were boys. "Alligator's coming," he
shouts but I know there are no dangers here. I come up, up
through the golden water, it tastes of earth. I can hear the river,
hear the roaring of its passing, hear the gravel scrape against
the bottom. I am in this river that is in the heart of this country
and I dive under. I swim back against its pushing, swim against
the current refreshed in the water I feel free to move, stretch
my arms far in front of my face, something new awakes in me
a salmon that has lingered in my blood, and I am strengthened
to swim upstream. I dive deeper under the surface swimming
under water against the current. I move into it and it sweeps
me, southward, a few yards. Many trees are buried in the water
their branches just breaking the surface, one must steer clear
of those or be scraped from underneath. Everywhere there are
things buried that I cannot know. Caressing my shoulders as
I move, sliding along my ribs as I stroke, slipping and sliding
along my side and along my legs as I move. I walked until*

*the water came to my waist and I swam forward. I peeled off my damp clothing with pleasure, and waded in slowly at first finding the water cool but not cold to the touch feeling with my feet the mysterious bottom of this river, to find my footing on this ground that is always unknown to me, I found that it was sandy and sunken under my weight. Malichi and myself disembarked and following the suggestion of the young first mate walked a slanted sandy path through a bramble of willow and cattail to a gravel point that juts forward into the water convenient. Since landing at the wharf we have been searching out among the shore a place where we could go bathing in relative modesty in consideration of the local women, though I do not see any houses here. Though they may be near just the same, I never know it seems how things are arranged here. So I am told. It has been hellish hot as we go, even on the river the temperature they say is over 100. The water, though murky to appearance has a fresh odor that brings over us a longing to dive in, but swimming near the churning wheel of a steamship is the most dangerous and accidents of a grisly kind are common among children and boys who venture into the river along this way. So we move slowly on the deck of the boat that also seems to move slowly. The heat here is a presence unto God, a stupefying heat, as wet as hot, and in it we move like lost memories.*

*The boat is never quiet slapping and churning the water behind us. It seems as if the boat continues to move forward but we seem to get nowhere though the river comes and comes and comes long unending, now the light and the day that plays over it has become beautiful to me. A hundred small streams slip their water into this one and the sound of their running is a cooling sound. At two the heat is too intense to stand out in, and we take shade under the canvas.*

*I watch the river. Still at a month feel I cannot see this country cannot see what it is, or what it is saying. At any rate there is no help for it, for where we are going, there is no backing*

*down now. Sneaking into the interior. Floating. Floating is a
strange way to enter a country. A river that flows like a vein I
think in an invisible body or a thief down a dark alley, I still
have no firm idea, but we go and I am in this going. Perhaps
that is all there will be, just this river and the light upon it, the
clouds overhead. I think I'm trying to find what this country
is. I do not know what it is I am trying to find in observing the
light and the scenery as I do, but feel obliged to remark on it.*

    *Daylight changes over the river as we go up.*

    *When rain is in the air the trees turn their green leaves to a
silver side, that is how you know a change is coming, a breathing in the great canopy of branches as a coolness. Then the
dripping from the silver leaves. Oh there are great trees here,
larger than any I ever saw. At noon on a clear day the glare
from the river is molten bronze, and brash and the voices of
the deck men too, full of profanity at noon, but later there will
be sun on hillsides behind the shady shore trees, and the dark
green of the tree's lattice work reflected in the surface like a
mirror and there will be twilight where the light slips from the
land yet finds a loose edge of water here like the Celtic ham-
mered cup the Church had for a chalice, and there to cast in
gold and reflect upon. Once I saw in a streamlet entering the
river two otters on a log practicing diving. Later in the morning
fish flip a spangle at the eye, and the light catches an edge of the
water white and eddying. In early morning when I crawl from
the shelter of our canvas there is often a pale blue light on the
surface that the river finds from the sky, though the eye cannot
yet see it, it is between them only there are low wisps of clouds
and mist rising like laundry drying by the stove. I have found
it thoughtful to watch the daylight as it comes and passes over
the river. This brown river lies always before us narrowing at
the horizon but spreading to each side slow and swollen.*

∼

    *The plantations along this stretch put a flag out at a land-
mark downstream so that the pilot knows they are to stop.*

*There was one this morning we came to with a wooden wharf along the water, black slaves standing by to load barrels of molasses and to carry from the hold of the ship two whole crates of Irish whiskey, which when appeared the Irishman cheered it, as the slaves took it and loaded it onto a wagon driven by a white man. There were two younger boys with the older slaves who ran alongside after we called out shouting.*

*"Take me on, take me on." Until the man in the wagon yelled at them hush and then stopped running and hung their heads.*

*There was a second plantation today, and as we pulled alongside an oak tree at one end startled me with its girth, larger around I think than a crowd of ten men. In the dark shade of its wide branches there are two black men standing without shirts, leaning against a stack of bundles. One is an older man with white hair who raises his hand in greeting but the larger young man beside him says naught but follows the boat with a set jaw and a harsh look that meets my eyes and gives me a strange chill. I wonder what is in the bundles could it be meat of some kind as there are flies hovering about them. The old man gave some instructions I could not hear through the steam whistle of the boat when it stops, then a gangplank is thrown down from the deck to the wharf that clatters and at its noise the boy turns, I was on the edge of the boat watching and I saw this, saw the boy turn his back to the ship and bend to lift the bundles there, and when he turned I saw a shining wet field of red welts, planted in neat lines like corn, raised on the flesh of his back bothered by the flies. My bowels churned at the rawness of it, I turned away as quickly as I could, while a young American man standing on the deck beside me saw what I had seen and said "Aye he was whupped pretty bad, that one, nasty business isn't it." I couldn't speak at the moment for the nausea and surprise, I've never been a strong one for gore, and walked to the other side of the boat.*

*Later this young man who is very fair and full of stories, training he says to be a boat pilot, talked with me a long time. He said slaves are often whipped with a horse whip for all manner of offenses until the blood flows, and while many think it wrong on a Biblical basis, those in favor control the dollarical basis, in which its value cannot be overstated and so persists. His words. Much dislike between the northern and southern people of the country arises over this.*

*I liked this young man as he was a great teller of stories and merry. We talked as the river darkened to a thick tea color in the slanted afternoon, such as how the English let us starve like dogs but did not break open our backs, that being too violent a measure for the proper English gentleman, who prefers that we hunger to the death and freeze in the winter as the corpses that way are lighter and less odorous. He liked that quip, aye, he said, and it's often the English here too, they say and Scots that do the whippin'; though the mean violence of those bleeding welts and the general public acceptance of it have ruined my taste for this country. Thoughts of going home come back to haunt my days, of going backwards down this river and backwards across the ocean.*

*Why do I want to live among men who would lower themselves to mortify the flesh of other men who labor on their behalf, and cannot defend themselves but stay on to serve their children.*

*Malachi says I am all yellow and weak, and best put my mind to tomorrow but I am longing for home and cannot see the good. Many here have come from home; it is heartfull to hear their voices but two have been upriver and back, they left a sister in New Orleans, work now as railroad men in Missouri. They tell us Irish are hated wherever they go, but the railroad takes them until they drop. NINA they write for the boys here who do not cipher, this is what you see in the cities, this stands for No Irish Need Apply. Best to stay clear of the larger cities, they say there are bogs of Irish in them already and much else. But why I ask him, why is the Irishman despised? Because we drink, and fuck he said, better than any of them. All the fellows laughed at this but not I.*

*～*

*Towns here seem to rise and walk along the bank of the river until they kneel down again, appearing as they do all the same to my eye. The trees that grow along the banks of this river are mighty and tall, where there are not levees, that is walls built to keep the river from meandering which block the view of the land from the water. I watch the countryside rise with a red dirt road here and there, with small towns that look built all in a rush of leaning planks newly hewn from the tree and nary a church steeple to be seen. The trees that go to fuel the fire of these boats are greater in number than all the beams from every cottage in our village. I wonder that they use the trees this way but they do not expect a lack as far as I can tell of anything.*

*Each boat I step aboard takes me further to where I do not know. Though I try now to look ahead at the countryside and it is a distraction of wonders. I seem to be at times only a tool of wonderment. Often I think it a terrible sin that we made in coming here, as I don't see how we will survive it, and often it is hard for me to sleep, with worry and not knowing. That feeling is torn in me still by an unwillingness to continue this journey for another moment. The heat, and the smoke, the noise almost overwhelms me, though I too am borne along in this hurry and frenzy to go. Malachi and I were paid a half day's wage to help with loading and that has sustained us for these few days while we have waited by the wharf to find a way north. The docks swarm so with coming and going it is like the ocean's edge, surging and withdrawing and again it is a wonder to see. There is but a grim determination that serves to drive the men here, under the vise of the heat that is only increased as steamboats fire their boilers in preparation for leaving and spew a cloud of dark smoke over the wharf. There was a small blond boy carrying a bundle of shirts almost larger than him-*

*self, then a large Creole rolled a cart across his feet, oh the wrinkled tears on his sweat-stained little face was heartbreaking to see, but the little fellow carried on, as if the weight of his load was the final difficulty of his life. I lost sight of him in the pushing crowd but would have liked to offer a hand or a word of kindness, though such feelings are rare here. The departure of the boats was so busy, so packed round with bodies and goods being pulled or rolled up gangplanks, sweating and shouting from faces of every appearance, Creole and black, boy and man, all groaning under the weight of barrels and bundles until stowed, then the loading planks taken away and the ropes wound back on deck.*

*Two days ago we left by steamboat from New Orleans headed for Cairo, Illinois, and onward to the Ohio River.*

~

The Healys came from a famine you see, but I think they brought a hunger with them. You look like that side.

Like I started to say earlier my mother's life was unusual for the time. Before she was married she worked outside of the home, which was not very common. She started out at the Krintz Brewery. Old man Krintz's sister worked there, she was an older woman, and so Grandpa Tindal allowed my mother to go, thinking she would be supervised. He was terribly strict. I can picture her clearly now, that office where she worked. All kinds of things I can see now, or hear so plainly.

1915
*Krintz's Brewery. Blanchardville*

Might have been about three in the afternoon but the winter light fell limp and spent against the broad windows of the Krintz Brewery office. Mahogany desks floated like old boats at harbor in the interior gloom. At the front desk, Mother bent to her work, thinking how the scratching sound of pen on paper was like the tree branches scraping on the eaves.

Wind like this you could hear it all day. The figures she was copying into the large green ledger were getting harder and harder to see. She stood and lit the gas lamps, two on each side of the dingy, cluttered office. Now the gas light caught up the rich color of her fine brown hair as she paused to look in the small mirror on the hat rack by the door; smoothing her stray blond streak into the back. Few people knew that one of her eyebrows and lashes was also blond, she checked to see if it was still covered over carefully with mascara, and it was. She felt that even Thomas would find it too unusual if he knew. Most people noticed her violet-blue eyes. The room felt warmer now as she sat back at her desk.

She noticed how early this winter dusk arrived, almost time for the girls to go home to their supper. She went through her accounts, Let's see yes, I've written up bills for tomorrow's deliveries to McComb, and Arcadia, and put the grain mill bills on Evelyn's desk. There comes Harlan's wagon with the last kegs to fill. I'll give him a wave through the front window here. We're always waving at each other, she thought, ever since he'd moved down the street from the house a few years ago. It was nice to have a neighbor like Harlan, if you didn't want to walk somewhere alone he'd come with you just for the walk. It's nice he still uses horses, I like the sound of them better than the trucks, and they work better for deliveries. She listened to the doors rolling apart in the back of the building as he pulled in, his booming voice rising, and laughing with the girls on the bottling room floor. Where Harlan was loud and certain Thomas was soft spoken and thoughtful, but merry in his own way. Thomas Healy had been in her mind all day, she had compared Thomas Healy's watch with Mr. Krintz's watch, had compared his handwriting to her own. It slanted to the left. It was just a small note she touched in her pocket asking if she might like to see the vaudeville show. The Walter Ambler players were coming to the State Theatre tonight, just a few hours from now, but she wasn't sure she could. My mother'll want me to go to church with her for St. Lucy's day, 7:00 p.m. Mass but I won't do it. Silly girls with candles on their heads. I've gotten paid. Five one dollar bills rolled in my pocket. Must be about time to go. What's that noise, oh now who would that be knocking from the door to the factory. Harlan never comes through the front, and Bill the night man has a key. Strange thumping sound too. Oh it's Ismelda's voice I think and Maria and Wistala. Hello, I'm coming, let me get the key, hold on I'm coming.

She quickly unlocked the back doors and admitted into the office the three Polish girls. Their blond hair was wet against their faces where the wash water had condensed and when they stepped into the warmer office their heads began to steam. I hope they're not planning on walking out like that, Mother thought wondering at their visit. It looked as if they were ready to go but their winter coats were hanging open. Ismelda Apful whom the local children mocked by calling "I smelled an apple" spoke the most English of the three.

"Please Edna if you help us with the buttons" she said, motioning to her coat. "Now our hands from washing all day are swollen and too sore our coats to button."

They stood all three of them together as if to prove the truth of it, held out their six hands to her. Their hands were wrinkled and raw, red from the lye soap and hot water they were submerged in all day scrubbing the beer bottles. In places peeling skin cracked into bleeding sores that must have stung painfully and a pink raised rash spread up their tender inner wrists.

Swollen and empty, those women held their hands with their palms facing upward as if they were asking a question, a question about whether they should have come to this country at all, or what a woman was to do. Why, Mother wondered, was it allowed for them to suffer so?

She pulled the worn black wool coat around Ismelda and buttoned it, and Wistalas too, an even older coat with a long row of hooks and eyes that took some time; and then Maria the youngest with two golden braids so frail around her shoulders that when you pulled her coat closed it seemed there was hardly anything inside it.

Mother thought of fat Krintz the brewer's hands, how plump and smooth they were as they held the pen to sign the checks. Why couldn't they be given gloves. Workmen had gloves. There were rubber gloves. They were costly, but they did exist. They could have had gloves if Krintz would pay for them. She felt ashamed suddenly that she worked for him at all. It was wrong to work for a man like that.

"You poor things," she said, "there must be a way to protect your skin, you should tell Krintz you need gloves."

"No miss we are to ask afraid for other girls will here work and not gloves have."

"We very happy except for coats problem."

She wrapped them all up as if they were her little children, she even patted them on the shoulders without thinking and that made Ismelda started giggling, she said "Thank you Mama." She helped them tie their woolen scarves, careful to wrap their wet hair under the finely crocheted wool.

"Before I came who helped with your buttons?" Mother asked.

They looked at her pulling their coats tight around them and shivering, shaking their heads no. No, they had simply gone cold, walking the mile to the north end where they lived with the other Polish immigrants. They did have knit muffs they put their hands into. Mother put on her own beaver skin coat and they turned off the gas lamps in the wall.

She left with the Polish girls into the gathering dark, snow starting to fall as they walked onto Blanchard Street. They pushed against the wind like a herd of little animals, their shoes leaving dark tracks in the white snow on the sidewalk. Across the street the façade of the new water works was being raised and blocks of stone and brick sat stacked and waiting for the future. To the west the red glow of the Cargill gas well warmed the sky like rouge on a pale woman's cheek. From the tracks down the block a whistle sounded, bringing with it the last Interurban train of the day lit up from within and carrying, she was sure, the father of her Thomas, who she hoped was moving now too, and walking toward her house to call. They stood and waited for the train to pass.

1915

*Blanchardville*

*Standing inside the empty Interurban railway car for the final ride of the day into Blanchardville, James Healy, the ticket manager, watched the winter streets slice by. He held the overhead leather strap as the rocking motion at the crossings lulled his long tired body into a standing doze. At Western Avenue he took off his cap and rubbed his eyes with the heel of his hand and when he opened them saw the Krintz Brewery sign shining up the block. "God damn it!" he said out loud stomping his foot, because he hated beer. More than anything he hated beer, though he believed in whiskey. Not only beer, but he hated the idea that his own son, flesh and blood, would court a woman like the one that worked at Krintz's, even if she were clever with numbers. A bluestocking she was and rarely to Mass. Was that her right there in that group of skirts moving away into the darkness? Move away harlot! He thought to himself, then asked God's forgiveness. The irritation of home is upon me once again.*

∼

*Give a man a bottle of beer and it's drunk in one sitting, he thought. Now give a man a bottle of good Irish whiskey and he can sell it by the glass to the tune of twelve small glasses per bottle, he had counted, and the cost then is wise. Whiskey by the glass, you could make money selling whiskey by the glass, as he well knew, touching the several flasks that he kept neatly stashed in the deep pockets of his blue uniform. Whiskey was a small service he provided for certain regular customers, along with the newspaper and cigarettes, but beer competed because beer was cheap. James was a man who made the things that bothered him serve. He had married Theresa Neimeir, a Protestant German because he blamed the Protestants for everything and thought having a wife of that persuasion could simplify the troublesome situation of marriage by concentrating all his causes for complaint into one location. He had courted her with a troubled heart, struck with lust toward her thick auburn hair and refined manners, while petrified at the sin he made in doing it. He had gone to work for the railroad despite what it had done to his family, or because of it.*

*He thought how unfair it was that nothing was set ahead of time, a gamble it all seemed from start to finish, so one might as well. Gambling's no sin when God does it, so why should I feel any God damn differently. Every man in his family, chasing some rotten bet, because a bet at least left you a whiskey-breath of hope.*

～

Well, after that incident with the Polish girls' hands my mother refused to go to church for a year afterward. She was setting the table for Sunday lunch, tossing the glass plates down a little hard because her father had scolded her again about staying home from mass.

"I'm not setting foot in St. Michael's until the brewery girls are treated better. Their hands are bleeding is why they sit in the back row, it's not that they're shy. A lot of good God does them. They need gloves not God. Aren't the Krintzes Catholic too?" she railed against her father. "What's it mean to be Catholic if they don't have the faintest idea of Christian charity. Fine for them to say the girls will be rewarded in heaven but who is going to button their coats in the meantime? Not to mention that railroad, yesterday, two brake-men killed up in Detroit and the trains kept right on rolling."

～

Over on the west side of town the Healys, especially The-resa Neimier with the passion of the convert, thought Mother a little dangerous and forced Thomas to delay their engage-ment until she would agree to go to church. But she wouldn't be stopped. Even when she was finally asked over for Thom-as' birthday, she went on about it in the parlor over coffee. "Where was the church when your uncles died in the fam-ine?" she asked James. "They care less for your soul than your dollar."

"Oh it was a Protestant famine, and if nothing else brought my father to this better land; so you wouldn't have met Thom-as would you if not for the famine so God has his ways lassie and he's ahead of you bluestockings thinking women ought to vote when they can nary reason out the obvious workings of the world."

James had gone to work for the railroad despite the fact that its coming had torn through his father Thomas' farm and ruined him, or because it had, he couldn't really say. His hap-less father, off the boat from the famine scarce twenty years 'fore they took it, and his voice always whispering under the chug of the wheels. "From Ireland came I to this field to plow it, now another machine will carry it away. Where does all this going lead to, son, where's the end to it?"

Well, where the hell did you think it was going, you poor mouthed dreamer, it's going forward. Cringed when he thought of him. Was heart trouble had been coming on any-way, James told himself whenever he remembered as he did now and crossed himself, then took a shot of whiskey from the flask in his pocket.

How he had stood before his father's chair and said "I'm going to work for the railroad," whereupon the old man had clutched his heart, pitched forward, and died at his feet. No one else was home at the time so no one heard. Died of a heart attack sure as shootin'. Didn't seem any reason to give the job up once the old man was dead. Though there's more to that story.

James was convinced that railroads were the wave of the future, and thought that he should ride them. But in the twenty years since that day, two of the three railroad companies that had criss-crossed the old farm went out of business, their tracks pulled up for scrap iron; while his Protestant wife had gone and converted to Catholicism claiming that her mother had been Catholic all along. Well we didn't know at the time did we. Can't live according to what hasn't happened yet he told himself. So that left only the whiskey. Its effect at least was reliable.

～

But my Grandma Tindal defended Mother whenever the Healys questioned her about her morals, and said they didn't have a leg to stand on in questioning the engagement since that month James' brother, Patrick, had been found floating face up in the Maumee river, just downstream of Toledo, looking from his pained expression to have been murdered. James had never been close to him, he hadn't been spoken of in some time. Word was that Patrick had a drayage business that hauled liquor barrels, but no partners were found.

Just the fact that James didn't pursue the investigation of the case raised suspicions of foul play all around.

"Heartless of James Healy not to follow up for his own brother. I bet he knows something. His own brother, well!" Grandma Tindal said.

Well, it did always seem like there was something low life about that Healy uncle, and I can only say if it appears that something is amiss or that people are doing something illegal, then they most likely are. They probably will keep doing it too, as the men in the Healy family later did prove.

～

1916
## *Riverside Park. Blanchardville*

My mother was still not going to church when summer came and didn't care if Thomas' family was shady or not. She was glad he had contracted tuberculosis as a child so he wouldn't be drafted yet for the War because the politicians and police were as bad as the church.

Was almost like she wanted to prove their wrongness you know. You're a little like her, never cared what anyone else thought as long as she thought so. One day, it was a sweltering July day, she and her sister Nora went out to Riverside Park to the bathing pool there. Well they were on their blanket in their bathing costumes when to Nora's dismay mother took out a cigarette and started smoking. The smoke started wafting across to the neighbors who were turning their heads and muttering, but Mother just kept chatting with Aunt Nora like nothing was amiss, until Nora said she needed desperately to go buy a taffy just then. It was a popular summer, and crowded that day as there was a pair of monkeys that had been brought to the park to live in a cage by the lifeguard cabin, courtesy of the county commissioner. To prevent further mortification the lifeguard in his striped costume was summoned to come and speak with the "Young Lady" who was smoking in front of the children.

"Please Ma'am," he mimicked smoking a cigarette with his first two fingers, "women are not allowed." He meant of course they were not allowed to smoke, but she answered as loudly as she could.

"You mean to tell me that monkeys are allowed here but women aren't?"

Well the young men nearby all laughed, and asked each other who she was, while one man, she thought she recognized Thomas, climbed up the high wooden platform and launched out in an arching swan dive that seemed to capture the challenge of her remark in a rising flight before disappearing with a question mark splash into the golden water.

Under the Blanchard River in Riverside Park Thomas Healy, he wasn't my father yet was he, or is your father always your father? Anyway he smiled at the thought of this woman, and wondered if he was ready for what the future might bring him. His up-stretched arms pushed the water aside propelling him from the depths toward the daylight air. When his head emerged he was still smiling. He was proud of her but he wasn't sure yet what to say, and wondered about it as he turned onto his back and lay floating there.

When the sky failed to answer he got out of the river and went over to where she was sitting. "Where did you come from, Thomas Healy ?"

"The water."

"I see that. I mean when did you get here?"

"About fifteen minutes ago. Just about the time a small crowd gathered in front of what appeared to be a cloud of smoke, I thought maybe there was a cookout?"

"You saw us and didn't bother coming over."

"I honestly didn't know it was you until I was already up the tower. I saw you then and dove in. I was hot. Would you like to take a swim together?" He gave her his arm and they walked across the lawn past the monkeys and into the water.

∼

When Mother cut her hair above the shoulder in September Grandma told her: "You'll never find a husband now as the story is all over town what you did then said in the park. Now add to that looking like a Hottentot, while being Godless, and immodest and just because there is a Revolution in Russia doesn't mean you have to get into the act."

I might have called you Godless too I suppose. I know you're thinking of the time I threw away those Alan Watts books you were reading. Anyway, at that time Mother's sister Nora lived just around the block so she went over one afternoon, and they got to talking and she cut Nora's hair in a bob too, and Nora cried so after it was all done. Mother said, "Now stop Nora I can't put it back on can I?"

But Nora kept looking down at her brown curls mixed among the pattern of the linoleum of the kitchen floor crying.

"Oh what will Norbert say, what will Norbert say?"

Mother said, "Well it wasn't Norbert's hair was it?" Then stood in the back doorway smoking.

There was a knock at the front door.

"Oh no he's home," Nora cried in panic and scrambled out of the chair and on to the floor where she began brushing the curls together, as if she might yet redeem her condition.

"No it's not going to be Norbert, will he knock at his own door."

"No, I guess not."

She went to answer it. It was Thomas Healy.

"Your mother said you were over here."

They were married in October the next year.

1930
*The Zane Lunch. Zanesville, Ohio*

The men shuffled up the four blocks of Main Street on one side of the street and then came back down along the other side.

"The poor men," my mother said, looking up to the light as she wiped a table.

"Where are they going?" I asked.

"They don't have work," she answered.

"If I didn't have work I'd read all the time."

"Seems like you do anyway so count your blessings and get your dirty paws off the clean glass."

"Are they going to find a piece of work just laying there on the sidewalk?"

"Well you never know," Mother said, wiping the table in a broad circle, "where you'll find what."

I can hear her say that plain as day, "you never know." I should have said that to you. You never know where you'll find what, unless you keep looking from where you started. Maybe you could have found what you needed right here .

Well, as I was saying. We never went hungry because we had a restaurant, we were lucky, everyone said so. There were lines at the church where people waited to get bread, a man sold red apples one by one right on the corner.

From the table by the window I watched the men passing; watched their long woolen coats sway, their arms swinging gently. I saw the sides of their faces, saw their ears sticking out as if they were still trying to hear good news, but their eyes were hidden under the brims of hats, pulled down tight to keep them from having to look at people because they couldn't look up and smile very well, because of the Depression, or say good morning because it wasn't really, and everything then felt like a hat pulled down over your eyes.

The name of our restaurant the Zane Lunch was written in gold leaf letters across the window, but backwards, so it was right when you looked at it from the street. I had read that Leonardo Da Vinci wrote backwards and read his work in a mirror but it puzzled me. Why if he were so smart and invented airplanes he would be so difficult and mean. I didn't think you should be mean if you knew better. But Sister Cecilia had visited Italy and saw where he had painted the Last Supper, so people forgave him.

The sky that early morning was deep grey, it had been raining but stopped for a minute with a little blue breaking through, and some white in between the clouds, I could see just a line of it above the red brick building across the street and it looked like a sky Leonardo might paint. I got to thinking about the sky I could see and the sky above what I could see, and it occurred to me that when God looked down on us, down at the window of the Zane Lunch he had the same view as I did except backwards. Through that slit of clouds, he was peeking in just as I was looking out. Did he see everything, the sky and the earth and the town of Zanesville and the rivers and the Y Bridge and the chimneys of Weller's pottery factory and the hill up Main Street where we were, and the words Zane Lunch? When God looked down was it exactly the same as what I saw only from the other direction? The men passed again.

The men were always walking together, groups of three or four, smoking, and the cigarette smoke mixing with their breath when it was cold, and their talking, I guess talking of what they once had, or were, or didn't or weren't. Each time they went by we forgot about them, so that when they came by again it was a surprise, like noticing your own breathing.

Whenever something happened like Uncle Charlie got his car stolen, or Jeanne cut some new paper dolls out of the cardboard of the cereal box, or Tom swallowed a bean and almost choked to death, the men would be walking past the window again. They walked to keep warm in the winter and to keep cool in the summer. Dad said it's easier to walk than to stand still. So every day they started out as if they were going somewhere, but they didn't have anywhere to go and I thought maybe a person found a place to go by going on anyway. Just like I would sometimes get caught up in finding the next piece of the flower or boat side, or water reflection in one of the jigsaw picture puzzles Dad always kept on the back table, and it would be late but I would keep looking for the right piece. Seems like you went on like those men, going from one place to the next like you didn't have any choice in the matter, but of course you did. You had all kinds of choices you never used.

～

Those days we took for granted that men would always be walking by, so that morning Mr. Moscke turned and opened the door and came in sticks out in my mind. Jeanne and I had come downstairs and we were sitting at the counter where we had our breakfast. Well, we had hot coffee with lots of cream and a sweet roll before we went off to school.

"Morning Jeanie, Rosie."

"Morning, Dad."

We would spin on to the chrome stools with the red cushion I remember, and the coolness of the marble countertop.

"Charlie, the potatoes get delivered?"

"I've got them, Tom," my Mother said, "over here, but my hands are full of pancake batter so you come get them."

"You girls are gonna need rain coats today." There were a few figures moving past under black umbrellas.

The banker Mr. Weidemier came in first always, always in a big hurry, we called him Charlie Chaplin 'cause he had a bowler hat and a belly from all the bacon he ate each morning. He swaggered too just like Charlie Chaplin because *The Tramp* was Jeanne's and my favorite movie. After Weidemier left we imitated his walk teetering back and forth in tiny little steps, which we were doing right then when the door opened and one of the walking men came in.

It was Mr. Moschke. I remember he put his old felt hat on the umbrella stand on account of it was so wet the water was trickling off and Jeanne and I smiled at each other.

"Morning," my dad said, "What can I get you?"

"Can I just get a hot water Tim, I got a pill I'm sposed to take."

"Sure thing," Dad said, and went over to the big silver urn where they kept the water, pulled back the little black lever. He set the mug full of hot water on the counter.

Jeanne and I watched Mr. Moschke as Dad went back to the kitchen.

Slowly wrapping both his hands around the cup he hung his head down and sat for a few minutes. He reached out and took the ketchup bottle that was sitting on the counter, and poured a whole lot of ketchup into the cup.

I looked at Jeanne because Dad said not to waste the

ketchup and so I got off my stool and went back by the stove where Mom and Dad were cooking and I whispered Mr. Moschke's drinking the ketchup, but my Dad gave me the worst look put his finger to his lips said "Shshsh, you never mind now, get your breakfast." So I went back out to Jeanne, shrugged my shoulders.

We sat and watched him.

There were saltines on the counter too and he took a pack, just one, like he wasn't being greedy and crumbled those up and put them in the cup. Didn't look up to see us, or to see if my Dad was watching which he wouldn't have because he knew all along what was happening, and was too kind hearted to stop him.

I'll never forget the way Mr. Moschke sat there so intent on that ketchup soup, looking down at it as if it was alive, how his hand shook when he raised it to his lips, and his cracked-up lips around the rim of the thick white cup. He slurped it slowly. The place was quiet except for the sound of his drinking, which was like a restoration of something you could feel it in the room, how hungry he had been and the sighing sound of his breath. How each drink brought something back, when he put down the cup, then raised it up again and sighed again and in that sigh was the sound of sustaining saying this will suffice for now, until what is next, this is enough to get by. He sat like that with his old tweed coat still on, giving off a strong wet wool smell, slowly drinking in what he could to get by, it was like we felt him get bigger and more solid as he sat there.

I realized then that you weren't supposed to say anything if you saw somebody stealing ketchup and crackers to eat because being hungry was beyond saying yes or no to. We felt it too, Jeanne and I wouldn't look at him though we looked at each other, because we didn't know if that would ever happen to us, that we would have to sip from a little cup of ketchup soup to live on until the next little bit came from somewhere. We didn't know if that was so common or not. The way children don't know what in the world is strange, because it's all so unfamiliar.

∼

Now, his sitting there like that comes to mind from time to time when I think of having just enough to kept the body going to get by on. You hardly hear of that anymore, having enough to get by. Will the body have enough to eat? Now there's a question. There was a reason God made his son human, made flesh, so that he would need to sustain himself just as we do, from the fruits of the earth, which is why bread is the whole point of Mass. I know that's not exactly what you wanted me to talk about, or my area of expertise, not that that ever stopped anyone in this family from giving an opinion. But you'll see what I'm trying to get at. And what was lost when they stopped doing the Mass in Latin, I'd like to talk about that too, but later.

Well now I remember that same morning we continued up the hill to cross the Y Bridge to get to St. Nicholas school, which was up on quite a little bluff, and sometimes the bridge would make me afraid, as it seemed high above the river. I would sing hymns as we crossed, "Ave, Ave, Ave Maria." Jeanne had no fear. She was two years ahead but I had skipped first grade since I could already read, so we were just a year apart. From the bridge you could see a lot of the downtown and the factories beyond and their chimneys spewing coal smoke in a slow rising that reminded me of the lines in *Evangeline,* because sister had given me a copy last week for helping at the library.

*"There, in the midst of its farms, reposed the Acadian village. ... Softly the Angelus sounded, and over the roofs of the village. Columns of pale blue smoke, like clouds of incense ascending, Rose from a hundred hearths, the homes of peace and contentment."*

Well the smoke anyway was the same, I thought, and at school you could hear the Angelus ring from the church next door at noon, though we usually went home for lunch, and Dad would have the radio on listening to a horse race, so you couldn't really hear the bells in our home of peace and contentment. It had dawned on me that the world rarely lived up to the images portrayed in literature, and I wasn't sure if that was the fault of the writers for not seeing clearly how things are, or of everyone else for not seeing how they were supposed to be.

It was cold and damp and my socks were falling down, I complained to Jeanne.

"Well if you wouldn't go so slowly it wouldn't seem like such an ordeal probably. And you might consider pulling your stockings up."

"But they always fall down and I can't put my books down or they'll get wet."

Jeanne was always so perfect, her coat was belted and her muffler neatly tucked in, her books in a tight little satchel.

"Your stockings fall down because you're not careful fastening them and no one is forcing you to carry so many books either, you read more than necessary. Give some to me." Saint Jeanne we called her in later years.

Well I did give her some books and I trudged up the hill on the narrow little sidewalk to St. Nicholas where the sisters were pleased that I could read so well. Especially Sister Jeanne D'Arc, or John Dark as we pronounced it, she was over six feet tall and suffered an eye disease that caused her to wear a patch over one eye, which, with her big black habit made her look a lot like a pirate. But I liked her because she had given me the little green bound copy of Longfellow. Each day I watched her in her black woolen habit, wondering did she have any hair under her veil and was there a hole under her eye patch leading into her brain well you don't know; or what else she might have in those big pockets which were very deep too. I had seen many things come out: so far a rosary, a round pitch whistle she would blow to get us on key to sing, blue cambric hankies, a fountain pen, and a picture of a pagan baby.

That day she came in and said, "Look, children!" She pulled her hand from her pocket and opened it and there was a chirping yellow downy baby chick, with tiny jet black eyes, I thought it must have hatched inside her pocket. It was a beautiful little thing just the color of sunshine. I was a little confused and thought maybe being religious gave her a special relationship with eggs because she was married to Jesus and didn't have children of her own, but it turned out she had just put it in her pocket to protect it from the rain as she carried it across the street from the convent where they had a hen. She put it in a box with a light bulb on her desk.

"Now we must take our seats. Good morning, children."

"Good morning, Sister John Dark."

"As it is almost the beginning of Lent we will have a Bible story on each Wednesday. Open to Luke chapter 9, the parable of the loaves and fishes."

I liked the Bible stories though I daren't tell my father because he would laugh and tell a joke about St. Peter and his keys, as if he had already been to heaven and had a drink with everyone.

You know the story of the loaves, at least I hope you know the story, should know something of your faith. Jesus goes into the desert after hearing of the death of John the Baptist and all the people follow him. Night comes and there's no food for the crowd except five loaves and two fish, so Jesus says a prayer and the loaves and fish multiply until there's plenty for all and leftovers too.

And when he had commanded the multitudes to sit down upon the grass, he took the five loaves and the two fishes, and looking up to heaven he blessed and brake and gave loaves to his disciples and the disciples to the multitudes. And they did all eat and were filled. And they took up what remained. Twelve full baskets of fragments.

I sat in the classroom thinking of the loaves and fishes, thinking maybe there is something that sustains us if we ask or if we wait. I got to thinking, well if Christ can turn water into wine, and Mr. Moshcke can turn water into tomato soup, then this must be quite a common occurrence.

Or that an animal can live in a nun's pocket.

Since then I never doubted that you could find a way to eat if you really needed to, or that nuns might lay eggs. Well you know how children think, and it's just the kind of thing a nun would like, an egg, all white and pure on the outside with a golden glowing little creature inside, like Christ.

That was a memorable day when I learned that life can spring out from plain water or a dark woolen pocket. And the very same day my friend Joe Fergusen said he was moving because his Dad was a potter and the factory was closing down, and he wrote in my little green autograph book a jingle that just seemed to sum up the whole day. *I went to the show tomorrow/ And got a front seat in the back/ I fell from the pit to the gallery/ And hurt the front of my back/ Joe Fergusen*

## 1932
### *Zanesville*

I had started walking to the library right after breakfast, before anyone could notice and say I couldn't go. And even that little sin came back to haunt me. Well I must have been twelve or so. Old enough. It was a Saturday and springtime, warm on my bare knees walking across downtown to Fifth Street to our beautiful stone Carnegie library, had a big stairway out front and floor to ceiling windows. Oh I loved that library, went whenever I could. I know it's sacrilegious but I thought the library must be like the inside of God's mind, so cool and deep, and quiet. Had a big Reference Room and that tall wooden rack holding all the colored maps of the whole world. They were on rolls like window blinds, and I would stand there and pull them down, continent by continent.

You loved the library too, I know. I remember you used to ride your old white and pink sting-ray bike to our original library before they tore it down and built that oversized dentist's office they call a library now. Old man Clooney designed it and five buildings around town all look exactly alike. It's an eyesore I think but nobody around here would notice.

Most people in Ohio are practical to a fault. Troubling notions like beauty and memory have no place here. But memories are in a place, they have a door we came out of, and a place we went from there.

That morning the horses came in. Of course I didn't know it yet, about the horses or anything, even the horses didn't know, kicking at the wood in their stalls. Just like you don't know at first that it's your life that's shaping up like it is, until one day you see it, and say that was it, that was the time I lived in and there's what happened. But I was thinking no such thing at the time, I was wandering through looking for something good to read.

Mother didn't think I should read William Faulkner because he was on the church list of books to avoid, so of course when I saw the *Sound and Fury* on the shelf I grabbed it. I had read in the Plain Dealer that it was considered modern and I liked the sound of that; so I took it along with some other books and *Smokey the Cowhorse* for my little brother Jim.

I was worried our librarian old Mrs. Lydek would question me at the checkout, but her grey head stayed bent over the counter, I don't think I ever did see her face, come to think of it just her gnarled hands rustling over the books like mice, taking out the cards, stamping them with the purple date, slipping them back in the pocket, pushing them toward me. I made sure I carried *Smokey the Cowhorse* on top as I walked the springtime mile downtown, into our lunch counter where Mom was working, and put the books on the table.

"Where have you been all morning? Oh, you went to the library. Everyone in this family is into the damn books," Mother scolded, "Reading them or making them."

"I got one for Pat and Jim," but she had already turned away. The phone was ringing and she'd gone in back to answer it. Mother had been short tempered lately, snapping at us ever since the Zane Lunch closed because no one could afford to eat there. Now we had a place down the street, which was just a small lunch counter and across the street the Cigar Store. Dad sold cigars there but also in the room above there was a "game."

A game is all we are supposed to know, not even what the game is, because the men drink up there and run "that damn bookie joint" as Mom calls it. Jeanne and I are not to mention this to anyone even the younger children who might not know enough to lie, but if any men at the lunch counter asks where the Cigar Store is we are to point it out, but only if we've seen them before.

When we closed the restaurant we moved house down the street to a little two-story wooden house with a yard. The horses actually brought in more money than the restaurant ever had, and Mother had wanted to move because she was worried about the noise of the corks popping when we lived above the restaurant. Well it was Prohibition you know, so everybody made homebrew, beer in the bathtub. But Dad could never get his bottling just right and the corks would pop out at night, wake us all up. But that wasn't the worst of it. They would blast off during the day too; customers down in the restaurant would think they were hearing gunshots. One day Miss Peale the schoolteacher was in, having her afternoon tea, when a few corks went off and she spilled scalding hot tea right down her front. "Oh dear me what was that explosion?" she asked, and we all shrugged our shoulders like fools, like we hadn't heard a thing. Next day the new police deputy, Dave, was eating his corned beef when three went off bang, bang, bang like that, well he was up on his feet, pulled his gun out and headed for the door. Mother said it was only a matter of days before even "dumb deputy Dave" would figure out what the source was, so we moved the whole operation.

～

Anyway, soon after I get back to the lunch counter that morning Mayor Weatherall's yellow car pulls up to the curb. The mayor gets out wearing his tweed suit, even though it's hot, and he starts across the street to the Cigar Store. His short wife barely shows above the dash board but she's in there, I can tell by a feather I see fluttering there it must be sticking up from one of her fancy hats, I think she must be looking up in the rearview mirror to get it on just right before she gets out of the car. She's Mother's good friend so she'll be coming in; she'll sit and have pie and coffee—now that's the mayor's excuse see for the car being here. I can smell her before she's even in the door, Lily of the Valley like you wouldn't believe, a cloud of it, and a hat like a stuffed pheasant, always makes me catch my breath.

"Hello Rose is your Mother here?"

"Yes Mrs. Weatherall, she's just taking a phone call. I could get you coffee."

"That's alright honey, I'll wait."

Mom came back, but she looked worried. Even Ms. Weatherall noticed.

"Hello Catherine, you look like you don't feel good."

"Well things are tough all over. Rose you can go on home now, but take this note up to your dad on the way. Get those books off the counter, and take a turn with the little ones when you get home so Jeanne has a break."

"I know, I will."

She had written a letter and put it in an envelope with Dad's name on it. There was no phone in the Cigar Store and I had taken notes up before.

It was a warm afternoon on the Main Street of Zanesville, and the shift at the pottery factory that changed at 2 p.m. had let out. Men were walking home, their clothes all smeared with clay, looking very tired. I had to walk around the long block and go down the alley behind the store because a twelve-year-old girl shouldn't be seen going into a cigar store, and we needed to be extra careful now.

You would never think looking at the nice front of that downtown block, all so neatly painted and the sidewalk swept clean, that the back of it would be as dark as it was. I always noticed that, how the world doesn't even match up right, like the face of a sinner all nice on the outside but around the back all grey, like the back of these buildings. No paint on the windowsills, left over piles of coal and bursting trash cans covered with flies. I clanged up the rusty metal steps that led to the back entrance, knocked at the glossy green door and waited for the peephole to open up above.

"I'm Rose down here," I said, because I wasn't quite tall enough to be seen. The bolt slid back and Dad opened the door wide.

"Come in come in Rosie, Rosie, Rosie." He put his arms around my waist and held me to him, twirling around and around. All the men there were laughing, saying we won we won we won. The air was thick with cigar smoke and his squeezing me so around the ribs took my breath away, my father was usually a quiet man, so I was shocked at this, and dizzy as he set me down finally amidst the smoke and the shouting men.

"Rosie we won big time now. Go tell your mother." Uncle Charlie was pouring drinks from a bottle to all the men standing around, he was pouring so fast, spilling it in-between. They were all talking at once.

"How in the hell did you know it, Charlie; you gave Beltz that horse five to one."

"A Florida horse, I told you, likes the heat."

"Who said anything about the heat?"

"Oh shutup Bill, the mayor'll hear you."

"He was so sure it was winning. Said he talked to a man in Toledo all about the race, who knew. Hell yes he talked to a man in Toledo, that was our brother Lawrence he talked to for Godsakes. I called Larry earlier, I said now when this guy comes in tell him to put his...."

"Oh hell the way Weller came and followed him in with that fifty dollars, like it was nothing. Fifty dollars!"

"We got a hundred-and-fifty apiece, times five almost. Rain of dime notes."

"Poor sucker."

"Horse ran like the wind, what a hummer, I love you Treasure Chest. Here's to you." And he raised his glass.

"Wasn't named Treasure Chest, Charlie, it was Tracer's Best."

"Not to me it wasn't, it was a Goddamn treasure chest."

Fat Mayor Weatherall sat at the table in his suit, smiling too. He was watching Charlie sort dollar bills into a stack and pull a rubber band around them, then slide the stack toward him. Charlie did another stack and the mayor waited for that one to come to him too, then put them both in his chest pocket and sat back looking dignified.

That room had once been the hotel dining room, had green fern-patterned wallpaper and a big table in the middle of the room, which had been put there to be safely away from the two front windows. The table was covered with racetrack tickets, glasses, beer bottles and dollar bills. They slapped the table with their hands until the glasses all shook and they started singing.

"*Camptown racetrack's five miles long doo da, doo da, Camptown racetrack's five miles long oh de doo da day.*" One of Dad's friends was raising his beer bottle. Everyone was laughing, all excited and then Dad was singing *Night and Day,* repeating how the voice within him was repeating you are the one.

"*The voice within me keeps repeating you are the one. Night and day, day and night.*"

I remembered I was supposed to give Dad the letter and I put it on the table in front of him amidst the glasses and race tickets, a white envelope with mother's handwriting. He picked it up and held it as he continued to toast the other men and then they sang *Camptown Races, "Going to run all night, going to run all day."*

I watched him open the letter, saw his brow furrow and his smile disappear so I knew the news wasn't good.

He laid the letter down and put his face into both his hands like he needed to think. He dropped his hands and pushed himself away from the table.

"Goddamn it. Hey Charlie. Mother's sick, we need to go down to Blanchardville. Aunt Henrietta called."

"Is it bad?"

"Says to come right away."

"Well Lady Luck sure drives a hard bargain."

The two of them just stood there looking stricken and scared and that scared me too. Felt like it was my fault. They had been so jolly, but I had brought the note that ruined everything. I wanted the men to keep singing. I thought maybe I'd start it up again, start to sing again, but then the shame hit me of singing when Grandma was ill. I felt the shame and the cigar smoke and the spinning around all the sudden and felt all shaky and sick. I ran to the door, slid the bolt back and ran out.

"Now what's got into her?" I heard my Dad say.

I ran down the stairs and down the alley, though I stopped and walked normally once I hit the street so as not to attract attention. I just wanted to get home, away from the men and the smoke, wanted to talk to my sister Jeanne who would know what to say and hold my baby brother.

What were they talking about anyway? What did it mean when he said Lady Luck drives a hard bargain. Who was she? How was Dad's horse winning connected to his mother getting sick, I tried to see it. He won the horse race and got money, but Grandma had to get sick. Must be related. Maybe. Like the downtown block, every building with that gray worn side in back and the nice one out front. Did he use up all his hoping and his attention making the horse win, but that left his mother weak and sick. Things must be connected somehow we can't see. Well the church was right, maybe I should have never picked it up, that Faulkner book. Maybe it's not Dad's luck at all, it's mine. Now that's silly. Gambling's a sin church says. Supposed to pray to Mary for the healing of the sick. I think he has mistaken Lady Luck for the Virgin Mary. Maybe they are the same person. Is Lady Luck the Virgin Mary. I'm thirsty, and my stomach hurts, I haven't had anything since breakfast.

Well I felt the hand of fate in that springtime afternoon, and it made me feel nauseous. I felt some force that snags at what is too wild, or exuberant in us, some pressing down force that keeps us rooted. It doesn't exactly make sense but since that day I have never found life to be any different than that, one horse coming in first and the other lying down sick. He won all that money, but then my Grandma died a few days later.

~

Just like I got you back the day after my mother died. I'm telling you this because some of your sisters hold anger toward me that I didn't try to do more to change our situation than I did, but I was never so sure that trying to change what was would make it any better. Could have left your father, but what if I couldn't find work or feed all of you, then what would happen. You might have ended up wards of the state. Would that have been better? I tried to bear what the situation was, because I was afraid it could get worse. A bird in the hand you know. Well maybe growing up around all that gambling turned me against taking chances.

~

A few weeks after the horses, I heard the front door open early one morning and voices downstairs. I was still in bed but

I snuck down to see who it was and there's that woman Martha in the kitchen with Uncle Charlie. They're bending over the table toward each other laughing, and drinking coffee. I think well she visits very early in the morning that must be an Italian thing because I know she's Italian. That explains why her hair is so jet black, and her fingernails painted red. Her dress is so tight because Italy is an old country and people's clothes are still small there because they are not as big as America. Probably because they use olive oil in their cooking, which Dad won't allow in his restaurant, says isn't near as good as lard which makes you bigger and tastes good, but they're just Italians so they don't know any better. Uncle Charlie saw me standing in the doorway.

"Well good morning Rosie, aren't you going to come in and say hello?"

I wanted to, but her black terrier dog Fritz started barking at me, and woke up Mother who came downstairs a few minutes later.

When Mother came into the kitchen Martha stopped laughing and stood up.

"Well now I have to go."

Mother didn't say anything to stop her so Uncle Charlie followed her outside and I started to follow.

Mother said "Oh no you don't. You stay right here. You don't need to follow that woman anywhere. She must be twice his age and I'm sure there was a husband along the way somewhere. One of these days he's gonna show up and Charlie will be in real trouble you mark my words."

"I think she's pretty," I said.

"Pretty something, but I don't know what. Get yourself dressed."

I heard Martha say to Charlie, "Ciao Bella," she always said that Ciao Bella, and we heard her car pull away.

～

Well a few minutes later we hear the doorbell ring and

mother says, Oh Charlie must have locked himself out, you go let him in but when I opened the door it isn't Charlie it's two other men in dark suits and one says. Is your mother home?

Mother comes, says "Can I help you?"

The man pulls a star out of his pocket and shows it to her. He says "Is this the residence of Charles Healy?"

I see mother pause, like all the sudden she couldn't remember.

So I think well what's wrong with her and I pipe in, "Yes sir Uncle Charlie lives here."

Mother gave me a terrible look.

And the man says, "Oh does he sweetheart? Is he home?"

She pauses again standing there frozen because she doesn't know if he should or shouldn't be home.

Just then I hear the back door open and Uncle Charlie walks in from the kitchen with the newspaper, and hands it to my mom.

"Hello there."

"Hello, we're looking for Charles Healy."

"That's me," he says.

"Can we ask you a few questions?"

"Yes sir."

Well Jeanne came downstairs, then Dad carrying baby Jim, and they asked if he was the Healy with the Lunch Counter and all. Said they were the Bureau of Liquor and Firearms. Oh Dad went so pale at that, started to drop the baby and Mother had to step over to catch him. One of the policeman asked Charlie.

"Were you in the vicinity of Chillicothe in the last day or so?"

"Why no sir, I've been here at home."

"You were here last night?"

"Yes sir."

"Mrs. Healy can you tell us if he was here."

"Yes sir he was here all night."

"Charles is your car missing, by any chance? "

"Why no sir my car's right out behind the garage here, I'll show you."

So we all walk out, Charlie leading us, across the back lawn and to the back alley where he usually parked, then he stops stock still like he's in shock.

"Well I'll be…car was right here, just last night."

"Well that's what we thought. We have some good news and some bad news. Good news is we've found your car. Bad news is it's wrecked in the middle of a field in Kentucky with a load of liquor in the trunk. Looks like the drivers were badly intoxicated, as one was found passed out in the front seat, he swears that you lent him the car."

"Oh officer I never lend my car."

"Have you ever met these two men?"

They showed Charlie handbills with pictures.

"Why no officer, I never have. Never heard of them or seen them before in my life."

"That's what we thought. They've been stealing cars across the state. Held up a store at gunpoint down in Dayton."

The police asked Mom if she had ever seen these guys and she said No and everyone agreed with Uncle Charlie.

"Well these two swore up and down that Charles Healy had leant them the car, and we thought sure he did, sure he 'lent it to you.' Uh huh. These types of men, they'll say anything. We know they got your name right off the registration papers, which were right on the front seat. Those men are wanted for armed robbery."

Well they kept talking for a while, Dad and Charlie and the policemen, about these two horrible criminals and how they were on a car stealing crime spree across the state. They had Charlie sign some paper, filing charges against them. When the police left everyone looked pale. Mother climbed the stairs and slammed the door to her room. Dad went up. I could hear them arguing.

"Have enough trouble without him bringing a federal marshal to my home, and it will be all over the papers now, is that what you need?"

"Now come on and give the guy a break, he couldn't see this coming," Dad answers. "I talked to him about getting mixed up in the games and he understands. Wasn't any way he could have seen that coming, why would they steal his car like that, could have happened to any one of us and…anything he could do about it."

"Ha, nothing he could do except mind what he was doing to start with. If you think Weatherall is going to help you when the Feds are sniffing around well you have another think coming."

"I don't know maybe they'll think they already checked everything out here good and they won't suspect anything."

"You're taking terrible chances here Tim …"

"We don't have a lot of choice if you want to eat…"

⁓

I go downstairs and Uncle Charlie's in the kitchen with Jeanne, and he could tell by the way I was looking at him that there was trouble. So he put on his white apron, sat Jeanne and me in the kitchen to make us pancakes and told us all about it. How he lent his car to those two men, but then they stole it instead and didn't give it back. As he told it.

"Everyone had thought Fat Lester knew the two guys because he had brought them up to the game. Fat Lester you know used to wait tables for us, your Dad always said he was honest as daylight. So nobody gave it any notice when the three of them came upstairs and joined the game. Said their names were Phil and Bill; and I said well who fills and who bills but they didn't laugh. Looked like they had been wearing the same suit for a long time, but a dirty man can be honest can't he. They bet a lot of money playing 21. I was playing them and won $50 off the two of them, but they wanted to keep playing. Said to give them some credit and they would pay me back once they made a delivery.

"So I just went on playing with them and I kept winning until finally they said. 'We can give you the money tonight but our car's broken down." And Charlie did the voices of the bad men, showing his teeth and growling like the cat does when a dog comes in the yard.

"So, I said you need a ride?" then he flipped a pancake.

"That's right, that's what we need," they said.

"No problem, I told 'em." He picked up the metal pitcher and poured some batter onto the sizzling griddle.

"You girls hungry today? Well we no more than get in the Packard and get on the road than I know there's trouble. You take that one while its hot, Jeanney, here's the syrup."

"Why Uncle Charlie, why is there trouble?"

"Well trouble starts with the beverage delivery as it often does. They needed to pick up some important bottles from a barn near Marion and deliver those to a man in Chillicothe to get the money they owed me. I said they could drop me off at a friend's so I wouldn't be in the way."

"Was it Martha?" Jeanne asked. She lived near Chillicothe.

"Well it looked a lot like her," he said winking, "problem was, they never came back."

"You had to stay all night at Martha's?" Jeanne asked.

"I'm afraid so," Charlie answered.

"Martha brought you home this morning," said Jeanne, "just before the police came."

"Wasn't that a lucky break? You want another pancake? The griddle's good and hot."

"No, but make some for Bess and Pat, they'll be waking up."

There was a big article in the newspaper next day. "Thieves Allegedly Steal Car from Charles Healy, Brother of Proprietor of Zane Lunch Counter."

Dad was mad at Charlie and Mom was mad at Dad for allowing him to act that way.

I loved my Uncle Charlie so much. He was about twenty when he came to live with us; he was the youngest son, and didn't have anywhere to go after Grandma Healy died, so my dad took him in. He was so jolly always; laughing telling jokes. Remember I had a portrait of him hanging in the living room on Pine Street for many years. My dad's little brother. Died of cirrhosis of the liver before he was forty.

～

We didn't always follow all the rules, there's no doubt about that. I grew up thinking laws didn't apply to my family the same as others. Was like God was a close relative and said it was all right for us to gamble and bootleg, long as we went to church. Law's one thing, sin's another. So when you started skipping school, running around and reading crazy books, it worried me, but not for the reasons you might think. Worried me because I knew then that you have to start making all kinds of your own rules, and that's not easy. Start picking and choosing what you'll go along with as the situation dictates and that's a slippery slope. So hard to find the right way. Maybe you should have given up on Robert Frost and taken the road *more* traveled. Just kidding, but you did make it difficult at times.

Not that difficulty is any stranger at my door. Things are tough all over. I remember my mother, whenever one of us was being greedy, would tell us the story of her father's hen to remind us that any thing you tried hard to keep, you'd probably lose.

She told how one year her father, my Grandpa Tindal, the glass blower, had been reading books on poultry, and decided to get a special hen, called a Barnevelder, a breed from Belgium like he had had as a boy. This one came one morning in the post, the mailman came up the walk with a carton that was squawking to kingdom come. He took the carton onto the back porch and took out the hen. There was a lovely iridescent green on its lower body with a scarlet ruff and red top feathers. He held it under his arm as he scooped out a handful of corn from the larder, and held it in his palm while the green chicken ate right out of his hand.

"C'est vraiment un bon coquelet," he murmured in his low bass voice. His chest was huge from blowing glass, but he spoke softly.

"Get that animal out of my kitchen," Grandma scolded, she didn't like him speaking French. Well I laugh now when I think how in later years when I took French my teacher said my Midwest pronunciation was so bad that it was better if I didn't try to speak, and just learned to read.

Occasionally this chicken laid a brownish egg, but he said they were gold and that it was a hen that laid the golden eggs. Every night when he came back from work he took out this hen and stroked it as he sat on the porch.

"Feed it a sunflower seed Adrianna, Tu est bonne poulet, avec les plumes de vert, n'est-ce pas?"

"Yes father its feathers are so silky."

Grandma would come scolding. "Get that animal away from the house."

Well, a few weeks later he had to leave for a job in Toledo. In those days the glass factories had times when they went into production on certain items and called for men. It had been raining for a few days already and folks said the river was rising though no one worried too much. But that day Grandpa, who rarely took off his jacket, stripped to his white shirtsleeves out in the woodshed, rummaging around in the drizzle, to build a special cage with wire and boards on top of the hen house. Moved his hen up there, and left my Grandmother with the three children to get on as well as she could. By then he had caught a cold working out in the rain, but he rubbed his chest with Vicks, and off he went. My mother was about fifteen at the time.

It just kept raining and raining and when the water came seeping into the parlor one morning, they grabbed some crackers and the vinegar jug to take upstairs. Vinegar quenches the thirst in the heat you know. So up they go to the second floor.

There they sat listening to the rain and the river rising, and Grandma sewing. Mother sitting in front of her bedroom window looking down on the wide brown lake that had been the garden just yesterday, when all at once it came into view from the right, the whole hen house floating by, rocking like an old wooden boat as it moved into the current and away.

"Oh Mother" she shouted, "the hen house is going. Hurry we have to go after it, oh Father will be so upset."

But Grandma just kept sewing and muttered under her breath, "Bon Voyage."

"Oh how could you say such a thing, the hen was so beautiful," Mother said, and added her own flood of tears to the general lacrimony.

When the water came down, and when grandfather came back he was sick with pneumonia, well a lot of folks were sick. He recovered but the damage to his lungs, well he could never blow as smoothly as he once had, and Grandma blamed the chicken.

~

As I said before this town is prone to floods on account of it originally being what they called the Great Black Swamp which was created in the last Ice Age. Well one direction the glaciers came up and scooped out Lake Erie, and the other direction you get this swamp.

I never will forget the flood of 1965 it was, that your brother's dog saved us. We had a gas hot water heater in the basement on Pine. The water came up so high that it put the pilot light out but of course the gas kept flowing.

I woke up to that little black dog barking and barking, right at my pillow, then I smelled it. Well the house was just filled up with gas, it was a wonder we weren't all asphyxiated. With the lights out too, and if we had lit a match, it would have blown us all to kingdom come.

~

2007
## Southern Michigan, Northern Ohio

Coming back this summer you flew into Detroit didn't you. Chicago had long delays as thunderstorms grounded all flights coming in or out. How many times have blizzards and storms delayed my children in Chicago from getting to Ohio, but it's hard to find flights that don't stop there.

I have always paid attention to when and where you all were traveling, and in what weather, following your progress when I could. You used to poke fun at me glued to the weather channel, but I liked to know where the storms were in relation to my children. Could always call at least and warn you.

Finally that night flights were cleared to fly to Detroit. It was already 10 p.m. Then the planes waited on the runway another hour to get cleared. Once you were in the air the turbulence got bad didn't it, so no one was certain what would happen, my grandson closed his mouth and looked stoic. The plane dropped and shook and once dropped so far that several women were screaming. It didn't last long. Still when the plane landed the weather seemed fine. Passengers had gotten their bags and gone up one endless escalator, across a glass walkway and down another, now you and your son were standing outside in the diesel fumes and the neon lit darkness waiting for the shuttle to the rental car place. The air was still. Hot and humid. Suddenly a wind came, a warm wind, and the van driver pulled up and opened the door saying:

"Now that is a wind, coming awful fast."

Then an alarm went off in the airport or what sounded like an alarm, the driver called the headquarters on his phone, oh it's just a storm, that's the storm alert. But where could you go. You stood there with your son and you weren't certain what to do about the weather, to seek protection or go on as if everything was fine. You decided to keep coming toward home.

You two pulled your luggage up into the glass-sided bus

and the driver took off headed for the rental lot several miles away. During the ride the bus swayed with the force of the wind, soon hail began to hit against the sides. Were just a few other passengers all of you mumbling, "awful big hail", "will it break the windows?"

"Oh here it comes," said the driver as he spoke again to his boss.

"Drive on through he says." Then he drove through the hail which was only briefly followed by a rain that eased the worry of some passengers as rain is rare in a tornado, maybe after but not before, and so the rain was welcome. Your son cursing you by then, why the hell would you make a reservation to come through here if you know there are tornados. Why the hell would anyone live in this place with tornados, why would we come here? Talking to you terrible. His anger disguising his fear. How stupid is this? But I don't know who taught him to talk like that.

I didn't think you were going to make it into the rental car the way that gale tore at you as you ran into the parking lot. You were soaked through in an instant. You'd left your son inside while you ran out and unlocked the car door, wind ripping at its hinges, and it took all your force to close the door against that roaring onslaught. Dripping from head to toe, and you finally get the boy in the car. You're shivering and shaken, soaked to the bone. Then you're arguing with him.

"I'm freezing can you turn the heat on."

"It's going to be hot in a minute," he says. "As soon as it stops raining."

"I'm shivering can you just work the heater please."

"It's going to be hot, you don't need the heater." He was arguing with you because he was afraid; but why you would sit and argue with a teenager is beyond me, you should have given him a good slap. That storm raged on awful dark. You had to go slowly.

"Do you even know where we're going?" he asks.

"Yes, we need to catch I-75 South."

But there was a detour of course. It's not easy always to simply go home. Weather can get in the way, roads rerouted. The dark and the not knowing the way. Following words on signs that seem to appear at random. Only the headlights to guide the car through the blinding rain, windshield wipers desperately waving. No vision to either side, just black darkness.

The lightning that filled the sky was startling and huge, curtains of light and branching neon lightning both blinking across the sky in front of the car. Driving through the downpour through the dark highways, so ill lit compared to California, so poorly marked. There are no yellow lines or the raised reflectors of the West because of the snow here, remember. I bet he had never witnessed a thunderstorm of that magnitude. You could make it if you went slowly. Inside the car, you felt the dryness, the safety of the thin domelike shelter, its seats soft on the flesh and the dim blue light inside.

"You have to help me read the signs. Says the detour is taking us to the east of Perrysburg, oh and around the outskirts of Toledo. Looks like the rain is letting up."

"No it's not. Maybe that was the calm before the storm."

"Wow it's really pouring now."

"You should pull over, Mom."

"But where? The road is really flooded here. I could really use a cup of coffee if you see a sign or a restaurant let me know."

"Just get off at the next exit."

"But there's nothing down there."

"Just take the exit."

"Says Moline Township Road 460. I'll go." So you turned the car swinging right in a neat arc away from the interstate and onto a two-lane country road. There was even less light there, no car lights passing.

Up ahead was a railroad crossing on a slight rise and just then the black and white arms fell down to block the tracks. A train came slowly, heading south, its headlights illuminating the slanting blades of rain. Sitting inside the car you were relieved to have a reason to stop for a few minutes and turn off the engine.

1885
*Thomas Healy's Farm. Wood County, Ohio*

This land I have bought has a bird singing in it, Thomas Healy thought to himself and smiled with pleasure when first he walked along the swarming April-green hedgerow he had just purchased in Wood County Ohio. 'It has a bird singing in it, but I don't know the name of the bird' and his pleasure passed like a cloud overhead. His throat tightened for a moment with a homesickness that still came on occasion like a dizzy vertigo. A tall man, he had stopped walking to steady himself, to gather his balance against that feeling of falling forever into an endless space, for he would never be held rooted, never he knew be home again.

It will have to be this, he thought to himself, I will have to find it here, on this land. He stomped his boot to hear the solid answer. Still, he doubted that he had actually gotten anywhere in the larger scheme of things, and the new land made his doubt and loneliness worse, for he knew there was no further place now where he might hope to find it.

This land with the woodlots still thick and lush on two sides, with poplar and maple coming into leaf and the green-yellow furze of the new grass tips on the meadowed ten acres already cleared before him.

Rich earth it was too, he stepped into the open from the hedges and took some in his hand, and marveled at its blackness, how it held together in a thick clod that bore the imprint of his fingers. Not the crumbly peat of home, or rocky with sin and need, worn of its vitality from the hungry it fed, no it was so much richer here, but not home. He felt ashamed at himself for thinking this, then rose up carrying some dirt absently in his hand as his thoughts ran ahead into all that there was to do, his feet following steadily. A breeze carrying the stony smell of water from Lake Erie a few miles north dried the sweat on his face, there were pheasant in a bevy racing zig-zag in front of him when from behind suddenly something wrapping around his legs.

His daughter Mary looked up at him, her mouth made large and purplish with blackberry juice, her white pinafore speckled with blue." Help me," she squealed, "the Indian's coming!"

"Who is?" Thomas asked as he wrapped the child in his arms and lifted her to his chest, her head burrowing into his shoulder. With fear pounding in his heart he turned round scanning the woods, an Indian there too now, a new danger he didn't know as he didn't know the names of birds, though there were rumors. Some said they were all gone, others said they hid and waited, who could tell. "Where Mary, where?" he pleaded, as her face contorted in terror and she pointed wiggling screaming from his arms! "There he is!"

His son James, four he was then, came running. Little James.

"Oh Blessed Jesus Mary you set the fright on me, you shan't say things like that..."

The children ran on into the field where their mother had just appeared, and their father followed.

1899

*Healy Farm. Wood County*

James Healy was walking past the open door of the barn where the light fell square on the empty milking stand inside. It struck him how much it looked like some ancient instrument of torture. He hated the very sight of it, with its empty O yoke waiting for a neck to hold still, because he felt it was always his neck that was held there not the flaccid old cow's. He hated the manure reek of the pasture gate beyond the barn where he would have to go find her now wading through the morning's rain water mixed with urine and mud and the flies that hovered there attracted to the stink. He hated the way the flies bothered them both as they sat fastened to their task. So it was with great relief that he heard the sweet sound of Lilian, Frances, and Evelyn, the neighbor girls, walking down the road from Lilian's to Evelyn's and he fell into step with them as they passed.

"Hello James Healy."

"Bet you don't know where the bottomless well is."

"Is that how you say good afternoon?"

"You want to see it?"

The girls looked at each other and decided they did.

"This way," James said, and led them off the gravel road and along the woodlot edge to the limestone embankment where a sway in the earth led out to the flatter land of meadow and field. There was indeed, at the foot of the crumbling green mossy rocks, an opening in the earth, about the size of a rabbit hole by which they could hear water running below, though not quite see it.

"Put your ear right here." He bent over to show them and the girls obliged, not wanting to appear effeminate as they were a whole year older than James to begin with, while the miners lettuce with its tiny dot of white in the green fairy cup and the fresh moss smell of the ground there were pleasant when they bent toward the earth.

"It's true, you can hear it," Evelyn declared, and the other girls agreed, and so they stayed there for some time listening to what ran beneath the earth and noting the three wild iris that grew there; the different sizes of each other's hands, the budding chests, and the light freckles across Lilian's nose as if they had just then discovered all of this. All these wonders had been buried beneath their chores with the rush to spring planting. For a few minutes the new green earth ceased being the field of their work and opened its gates for their pleasure.

Even the dark crows whose jagged calls tore at the pale blue sky seemed beautiful.

Just as suddenly the girls remembered that Evelyn's father was coming to collect her from Lilian's farm with the wagon, or else she would have to walk the two miles alone.

As they started back James heard the poor cow Jesse lowing in the field. As they neared, the cow followed him along the pasture fence.

"Someone loves you I guess," Evelyn teased.

"Someone wants to get their teats squeezed," James answered, watching Evelyn and the girls turn red and cover their mouths.

"Ohhh James Healy, that is so rude, if I told your mother she would wash your mouth out with soap."

"Well who said I was talking about you?"

"Goodbye," Evelyn said.

"We will not see you later," Lilian added, and the three of them turned toward the road, chattering.

James walked toward the house to get the bucket he had left there this morning. There was a strange buggy sitting out front of the house, which explained why the old man wasn't out chasing him yet, he wondered who it was. Quietly, he stepped onto the back porch, took the bucket from the sink and went to his work. Two hours late now and if the old man found him it would be the full dirge of the grieves of old Ireland on him and the poor cow as well. But he was sixteen damn it, far too old to be told always what to do.

An hour earlier his Mother Eliza had been rolling her pie dough out on the polished wooden table when she heard the buggy outside. Now Thomas's hands were moving across the map Herbert Fleischman had brought to roll out on the same table in front of them in defiance of all expectations of their future and his. "You can see it here," Fleischman was saying, as his index finger traced the blue ink line that marked where the Railroad would put its new track, a line running clean through Thomas Healy's farm. "Couldn't they put it here?" Thomas asked, a quarter mile over was all that was needed and this was, after all, just the beginning of his farm but it had supported them most years and if prices rose it could work well. Fleischman said the county had already agreed with the railroad to change the zoning because they stood to make more from the taxes they could levy on the railroad than they could put on farm land, on account of the federal protections for the farm land, and with the tax rate it was now at you could nary afford it, Thomas, so better to agree now.

Thomas saw the straight blue line run across the crisp white paper toward the nexus with Maumee, a corner where three railroad lines came together. He saw the line and saw it cross his creek and felt that the line crossed him like the Ash Wednesday X of the priest, to remember now that you are dust and to dust you shall return. Thomas crossed his arms in front of him where he sat and let his head fall to the table. It wasn't manly in front of Mr. Fleischman, but the weight of his misgivings since leaving Ireland twenty years ago were right and the great store of melancholy he had been cultivating had finally fallen on him like a stone.

Eliza because she was a woman didn't see this as the end of the world, they would have to continue to feed the children and raise them up anyway somehow, put clothes over their naked bodies in the morning. She poured coffee from the pot into the two cups her own and Thomas's and Fleischman's too, though she hesitated to fill his cup; then set them on the table. There would be a price for the land, and there would be a time, after this year's crop, Fleischman said and left saying he had to go. After this years crop that's when they would have to go, there would be other men coming from the railroad, the county too, then there would be rails of steel pulled here on the shoulders of tired horses. Thomas knew then that they had been coming toward him all along, toward his farm and all he had planned. They had started out a long time ago when this strange country was named and wrought from those it rightly belonged to; for a land like a child belongs to those who love it only because it is, and nurture it as it is, who aren't dead set on all it might be or do. But the men with the rails had been coming, moving forward away from where they started, that was all, northward along the river or westward from the coast or Inland from the lake across the mountains, it didn't matter. He knew they moved and had always been moving scattering men and strong women with them who nonetheless stood on desolate doorsteps wondering why here. Why have we come to this place, this desolate plain, at a run; what is it we are hurrying to get to all this running moving, we have tried to stop but now they say run, and run again, and no one ever coming home in America no one ever coming home.

"Don't be crying, Thomas, when your son comes in," Eliza said, but didn't touch his shoulder as she thought to, for fear the warmth of him would move her to pity or panic, either one.

She spread the apples out like a hand of cards inside the piecrust, then put it in the oven.

## 2007
## *Wood County*

You were still sitting in the car waiting for that storm to end and the train to pass. Thinking of the days you would walk to the end of Pine Street to watch the trains just so you could wave at the conductor on the caboose.

The two eyes of the red signal lights alternated their garish blinking red, red, red, red, and the slow freight went north angling back toward Lake Erie. Norfolk & Western it said. The conductors were almost always there, almost always waved back. But you didn't say this to your son. He doesn't care about what you did as a child in your little town in Ohio. Born in San Francisco like he was.

The train slowed to a crawl, almost stopping.

"Let's turn around again this is crazy," he said.

"We need to cross this to loop back up to the freeway."

"No we can follow the road up where we turned at the exit."

You tried that road but saw it wasn't going back to the freeway at all but toward the railroad again and so you pulled up into an old gravel driveway to turn around. In the headlights where the rain had let up, in the dark green night grass in front of the car you saw three stone steps leading to nowhere. You've seen the like before, out in the countryside; you'll come across a part of a foundation, or a cellar step. But those steps right in the headlights so unexpected that you wondered where the house had gone, wondered how those stones always lasted so long after, as if the coming and going were the last things in a house to get cleared away. Maybe those steps were waiting for you to see into the darkness beyond them.

～

I'm fairly certain that was the place your great-grandfather homesteaded. Maybe we are always in the same place, and the world moves around us. Copernicus might have been wrong. Maybe you're drawn to home without even knowing it. It may seem like just a convenient plot twist that you would be turned around in a storm and not knowing it, arrive at the threshold of your great-grandfathers' homestead, but as I always said "Truth is stranger than fiction."

When you finally pull into Blanchardville a few hours later your son looks at the cars parked in the motel parking lots out by the mall.

"Why are there even cars at these motels. Why would anyone come here, to the middle of nowhere?"

"Plenty happens in the middle of nowhere," you answer.

～

This is a big country and there is distance in it. I think one thing that made a distance between us was just the distance. Oh I'm teasing you but you get my drift.

There were so many places you lived that were just too different for us to talk about, there was no common place to begin. Although it's not like you knocked yourself out trying to fill me in. Don't take offense now but you're not the best storyteller in the world, not for just a good description of how a place and its people are. Or maybe you move too fast to ever see it. I always looked forward to you visiting and telling me about India or some exotic locale but you never were forthcoming. To think you lived so many years in places that I never even laid eyes on. Like that college you went to in upstate New York. I'm sorry we never did come to your graduation there at that Barnes College. I never knew quite where it was; always meant to look it up. Degree in poetry was it? I don't know that you find poetry by study. Poetry you left home with was fine if you had let it be. You were ahead of styles by your very nature. Going to San Francisco didn't add anything to that. Slowed it down if anything. But you know I wanted you to go to college, wanted all of my children to.

# IV

## MARRIAGE


### 1940
### *Blanchardville*

*I*THINK *next fall I can go to Antioch to study, Dad says he will help me. With what I'm saving up from the switchboard now, and they say older students are welcome there because of the Depression and all. A lot of folks have to work at the same time so I wouldn't stand out. Wouldn't it be fun to read all day long? No one saying STOP READING! Grandma Healy even likes the idea because they let women go there so early on. Some of the professors there are women too. Their motto is so beautiful. "Be ashamed to die until you have won some victory for humanity." I talked to Mary Pernunzio after church, she went there, now she's going to teach at Kenyon. She speaks Italian, she said because her father read her Dante's Inferno on Sundays, so now she learned to read the original. I think that would be so interesting. Or maybe learn Russian and read Brothers Karamazov since we read it in 10th grade but skipped the whole middle section on account of Sister said it was not an orthodox Christian view. I could be a teacher I think and teach history maybe, or theology but Mother says women shouldn't mess with God, since that is a man's idea to begin with. I meant to ask her what was the woman's idea to begin with; I think she'll say everything else. Maybe I could teach history, I like history, so many good stories. The story of Joan of Arc, or Saint Theresa of Avila, though the Franciscans frown on her sort of extremism. Our neighbor Dennis Deidelbach went to Antioch he said he wanted to work for the*

*National Geographic as an ornithologist but he spent most of the year working for the county game warden making sure no one shot too many pheasant. We could afford it working part of the year. I could do stenography or shorthand and typing since I did have that business class Dad made us take just out of high school, my but that was boring. I was pretty good at Latin in High School maybe I could study more Latin or Greek I could read Homer, but not Chapman's Homer, the original Greek one. Sing to me of the Muse! Or sing to me of the Man which was it? If it's sing to me of the man I'm not sure that's anything to sing about. Of course it would depend on who the man is.*

*Now Bess she'll sing about any man. Here she comes. I can tell it's her feet on the stairs. She'll push open my door without knocking.*

"Bess, what a surprise."

"Can you believe it?"

"Well I'm sure I can, if you tell me what it is."

"After I went and spent money on the dress just for that."

"For what?"

"Oh Rose don't you ever look up? Louis Armstrong's coming to Detroit but Carl has to work at the elevator all night because it's harvest time, so now he can't take me."

"That's a tragedy Bess. Tell him if he really cared about you, well they would just let that wheat crop rot in the fields."

"Oh go back to your book why don't you."

"I'm trying."

1941
## *West Main Cross Street. Blanchardville*

Was a sticky summer afternoon. My sister Jeanne and I were rocking on the front porch swing, trying to find a breeze, swinging always seemed to cool things off. Jeanne was just pregnant with her first child, she had recently married Jack Jones, so must have been visiting from Columbus where they lived.

She was talking about the ice business his family ran.

"Day like this wish I had my own ice factory."

"We could move in for the summer."

"Now Mike and his dad are starting a delivery business, delivering ice to stores all over, he's gone a lot. But they're saying they're going to install ice machines in all the big stores. Don't rock so hard makes me nauseous. He says ice machines are the next big thing."

I was thinking it was sad to be married to the iceman of course because well it just seemed cold, and years later after Eugene O'Neil's play, and after Jack got rich off the ice machine business we all kidded him, "the Iceman Cometh" we'd say. Course that's a sad play all about drunks and nightmares, don't go see it. That day on the porch, at the time you think you're gonna have a hundred days like it but maybe you just have that one. Oh poor Jeanne! The way she went so suddenly, without any warning.

One day she was in her kitchen making a ham casserole, only her backward daughter Francie there, who never left home. Did you know the FBI caught her running naked on the White House lawn once? No one ever knew what was wrong with Frances well she was an RH baby had to have a blood transfusion when she was an infant and I always thought that had something to do with it. Well poor thing she was sitting there looking on when Jeanne just dropped her Pyrex dish and fell over dead of a heart attack in the middle of her kitchen. Had she been feeling bad? We don't know because she would never have said anything if she had, so selfless always and she'd already been nursing Bill for some years. Though she had said she didn't want to be buried next to him, so she bought the plot next to mine said she wanted to be buried up here in Blanchardville near her own family on account of Jack was not faithful to her. Had a girlfriend they said. I always wondered why her five boys, all so handsome, but seemed so angry, seemed like. Once he was gone they came right out and said he was a horror. Oh it hurt me when she died, so sudden too, I missed her a lot.

I missed her when she was alive because we never lived in the same town. She lived down in Columbus and we lived in Cleveland or here in Blanchardville. Oh I suppose I got off the point there. But I remember that day I was with Jeanne thinking about what it must be like to be married.

Swinging on the porch swing, the spring creaking and our feet tapping, when out of the blue we hear a strange sound clumpity clump, clump, sounds like horses galloping. Well this was already 1941, everybody had a car by now, so it was quite unusual to see horses in town.

"What on earth?' Jeanne says and we stand up to look. Then round the church corner they come, these two young men cantering down the middle of West Main Cross street on the prettiest Palomino horses you ever saw. They were going fast, racing I think. Jeanne and I are standing on the edge of the porch watching so of course they see us.

"Whoa," they say and pull the horses right up to stop, making a big to do.

"Hello ladies," they say and tip their hats. Both of them wearing cowboy hats, that was also unusual, like a Tom Mix movie. We were a little hesitant, didn't know 'em from Adam.

"Nice day for a ride isn't it?" one of them says and we grin and shrug our shoulders. Then my little brother Tom comes out, and says, "Hi Rusty, hey Bud." Tom was about fourteen but he washed dishes at the bar and knew everybody in town.

"Hey it's Tom Healy," Rusty said then they rode the horses right onto the sidewalk in front of our house till you could smell the horses and the leather boots they wore, all glistening in the sun.

"How ya doing Tom, I didn't know you lived here. You didn't tell us you had sisters."

"Oh I have four of them. This is Rose and Jeanne."

"That's right he's our little brother Tom," Jeanne said, protectively.

"Nice to meet you ladies," Rusty said, and I never will forget, he made his horse bow his head.

Was a beautiful Palomino horse with a creamy white mane and a body the color of caramel sauce. I guess I liked his horse.

"We know young Tom from Healy's Bar, that your family's place?"

"Yes it is." Jeanne was doing all the talking.

"I occasionally do some business there."

"Is that right?" Jeanne says.

*I occasionally do some business there.* First two minutes I knew him he told me the truth. I should have marked those words. Don't you know it. All the clues in life are always there early on but you don't know what you're looking for to explain what's going to happen, because you don't know what's going to happen in order to look for the clues.

"Yes ma'am. We were just as a matter of fact thinking of a cool drink. Though I'm feeling refreshed already." Said that looking right at me and smiling.

Later I asked Tom about him, said Rusty and his brother were sort of notorious in town for riding their horses around. Bud, and Rusty, short for Lester and Earl. Bud the dark haired one is older and some say crazy. Rusty he's the younger one I think he just rides along. It's all kind of silly I think but the girls fuss over them. Their father raises horses right on the edge of town there, Palominos. Dad says he's seen them at the bar, and they tie the horses up to the light post, while they drink. While the men drink, not the horses.

A few weeks later, I was walking down Main Street on my way to lunch. As I passed Beltz's the men's clothing store, there was a man leaning against the window smoking a cigarette.

He stood up and tipped his hat to me. Said "Hello Rose, how's your family?"

I said hello just to be polite but for the life of me I couldn't place him. He looked so different without the hat and boots. Well he must have noticed I looked confused and said:

"Oh I'm sorry, you probably don't recognize me without my horse, I'm a little shorter. Rusty Koehner."

"You're right," I said, "Different hat too." We laughed.

"What brings you to the commercial hub of the great metropolis?"

Oh, he was witty in his day. Said "I saw your Tom the other day, he said you work downtown at the phone company."

"That's right."

"Well I guess then you must get a lot of fellas calling you." He made me laugh and before I knew what had happened it turned out I was going to the dance in Toledo with him because Benny Goodman was playing so if I didn't have any other plans.

"Suppose I give you a call at home," he asked.

"That's fine," I said, "but will we be traveling on horseback?"

He thought that was funny. "I got a jalopy, don't worry. A'course my horse is a little faster."

I don't know what it was I liked about him at first. It's hard to remember so many years back. You've been in love. There's a reason they call it falling, isn't there. Because whatever you were thinking or doing beforehand rushes by and disappears. Who can explain it. The course of love never did run smooth. He was going to Blanchard College which was ambitious at the time. Always had tickets to the dance, had a job too, and some wit. He dressed well too, not that I cared so much about that. His hair was even more red then than you probably remember it, and he was rail thin, like your own son.

That day he wore high-waisted pants and a light tan suit, with a watch on a chain that attached to a belt loop that hung down and draped into his right hand pocket, a little outrageous. Had matching tie clip and cufflinks, that kind of thing. Everybody in town liked him; he had been the high school quarterback. Natty Bumppo from *the Last of the Mohicans.* Well he picked me up in an old Model T, and we went to Toledo, he was quite the dancer. I wasn't so swift and deft as he, he loved to dance, was so athletic you know.

I was dancing with Danny Lynch for one dance, cause I knew Dan and we had been friends. Dan worked as a photographer at his family's studio in town, well Rusty was dancing with as many girls as he could, took his jacket off.

I was sitting and talking to Dan, having a beer when he finished and came over to the table.

"Thanks for entertaining my date Dan, now get the hell outa here! Oh I'm just kiddin ya, how ya been?"

"Well good, but I didn't know she was your date on account of all those other women you had your arms around."

"Well Danny boy you gotta hold 'em up once they get going or they get all floppy and fall off their heels. I was just trying to be helpful, give 'em something to lean against."

"Otherwise they'd be falling all over you," Dan nodded.

"No, now my Rose needed to rest her little hooves, I've been trottin her around the ring a few times."

"Oh I'm not gonna talk to either one of you now," I said, "you're both all wet."

"Come outside, for a breath of air," he said. I think that was the first time I kissed him.

I'm telling you what I can remember that he was then, having lived since with all that he wasn't, though the seeds of one must have been in the other. He was very attentive, and he was intelligent. I never denied that. Not a literary person not bookish, but he was intelligent, good at math. More alert than a lot of the boys I met. Always moving, playing something, tennis, swimming. We used to go for picnics out at the limestone quarry where everybody swam, well I didn't. I watched him mostly. Watched him dive off the rock ledge in his perfect swan dive into that clear green water. He was a polite man deep down, that sounds strange but there was something about that, even in the worst of his drinking see he was never coarse or violent, he was always trying to make it all right. Opposites attract they say but that's not it exactly. He wasn't ever patient, of course when you're a young woman you don't want someone who is patient you want someone who is a little ambitious and he was. That was part of the difficulty.

~

Was just the winter following the summer we met, 1941. It was a cold Sunday in December, and I was sitting in front of the switchboard thinking of doing some Christmas shopping. Telephone Company was usually quiet on weekends, not that many calls to put through.

I had gotten this job at Ohio Bell and had been promoted to long distance switchboard supervisor; headquarters up on Main Street. Those days you sat in front of a big board full of circuits, had a row of little sockets with lights above them to show what circuits were free, you took a line from one side then put it on the open socket to connect the call; but like I said there were very few calls that day.

I was sitting there looking out the window watching a fireman on a ladder hanging up the Christmas wreaths over the street. Then all the sudden the whole board just started buzzing and lighting up like fireworks on the Fourth of July, every circuit blinking, and buzzing. I didn't know what had happened, I tried to put a call through but all the lines were busy. Wasn't anything I could do. Betty Riley was there, it was just she and I up front.

"What in the world? What do you think it is Rose?"

"Well the equipment must have gone haywire."

"I don't know what to do, Rose."

She got all upset, waving her hands around all flustered, and pulling back from the board like it was gonna come after her. "I don't know what to do."

"Now just sit down Betty," I said.

"It's not gonna all blow up is it Rose?"

"No it's not. Maybe Roosevelt died, he's been sick."

"Oh no."

We went through each wire we could, "All circuits are busy please try your call again."

Mrs. Wilson the manager came in from the back about five minutes later, we knew it was serious when she came in because she was a fat lady who never got out of her chair.

"Oh girls" she said, "say your prayers the Japanese have attacked us."

We couldn't believe it. In Hawaii, she said. Well that was cold comfort, we knew it was far away but Betty burst into tears and said, "I want to go home to Mama."

Mrs. Wilson said, "You will Betty, right after your shift is finished," and she sat her right back down. Well we were busy all night see. At that time we didn't know, nobody knew if they were going to attack somewhere else, or what. We stuck it out for hours.

Next morning of course all the papers had the story and that evening was busy at dad's bar, Healy's Bar it was called then, on Main Street. Well it was just the thing to do in an emergency was go get a drink, we all went, all the regulars there, and everyone had their opinion.

"We ought to go in there, have the whole thing over within a month or two. Mop up the whole shebang." Stranahan, the mailman, he was a loudmouth, started pontificating.

"Suppose your neighbor sneaks in your back door and takes your wife and kids."

"He can take mine," Bill Walsh says.

"Now Walsh I'm on the level here, it's a dirty underhanded thing to do."

"Oh hell," Howard the clerk at the hotel next door said, "What's the use of worrying about what's gonna happen, I had a good sleep last night, and a good meal this morning and I'll enlist this afternoon if anybody asks me to."

I remember Howard saying that, because later when he died in the war it seemed like he knew somehow.

My dad was a pacifist see, no one thought there should be another war, said we should stick to diplomatic methods. No one was looking for a fight, people were worn down, seemed like we had all been fighting enough just to get through the Depression, no one wanted to go to war. But the bombing changed public sentiment and a few days later Roosevelt made his declaration. We all listened to it on the radio at Grandma's house, supposed it would only take a few months. We were sure it wouldn't last.

Course that wasn't the case. But it was Bess's idea to join. What year was that it was the springtime after, so 1942. Would have been the next summer.

Mom was cooking a roast for Sunday. There was a breeze coming in through the back porch and we could hear Mr. Weiserman mowing his lawn with the push mower which he did on Sunday being Jewish, and it used to make Father Drake so mad on account of the back of the rectory and Weiserman's yards backed up against each other, as luck would have it. Dad called that yard "Where the Old Testament Meets the New."

It smelled good in the kitchen, like pork roast and I was sitting reading the paper, when Bess comes downstairs.

"Mom have you seen those posters downtown for girls in the military. Margaret Swanson is going to be a WAC. I saw her today at Wilson's. She said they have a woman in the office right next to the enlistment guy, just for the women to go to, right there in the office next to the bakery. I saw Kathy Reninger go in there and she can't even be out of high school. Margaret said you might get to go to New York City, I'd like to live in New York City."

Mom was checking the roast and put it back in the oven for a few more minutes and closed the oven door with her knee as she always used to; and wiped her hands on her apron.

"Theresa if you think your father is going to let you run off like that you got another think coming. It's fine if you don't have anything else; Reninger closed his store a long time ago. I don't think those girls have much to look forward to, but you have a good job. You could go to college if you save your money like I've been telling you instead of buying clothes you don't need. "

"Mom, we need clothes. And besides I'm not the one who wants to go to college, Rose wants to go to college. I don't want to sit around all day in some stuffy room, I want to see the world. Look Rose, I went in and got the brochure."

She sat down at the table and spread it out. We poured over it.

"Here are the requirements, we could do this." She read it all out.

"WAVE Enlisted Candidates: Applicants of Enlistment must have general and physical qualifications described above. Age bracket is from twenty to thirty-six years. Educational qualifications must include a certificate of graduation from high school or business school or evidence of completion of courses at business school and subsequent business experience sufficient to be considered the equivalent of a high-school education."

"You're just twenty last year."

"Well twenty is twenty. We have all that. Plus we know the switchboard. That's maybe worth something. "

"Is that on the list?"

Says, "Applicants may fill the following positions. Storekeeper. Ship's cook. Baker. Radioman. Specialist. Chauffeur. Mail-room clerk. Messenger. Librarian. Information Bureau line Assistant. Escort. Waitress. Mess cook. Mimeograph operator. Yeoman. Pharmacist's mate. Aviation machinist's mate. Aviation metalsmith. Photographer's mate. Aerographer's mate. Parachute rigger."

Mom was looking over our shoulder. "Rose maybe you could be a librarian."

"Yeah. cause you already act like one," Bess added.

"Whadaya suppose an aerographer's mate does?"

"Graph means to write so they must write in the air?"

"Oh stop being silly Bess," Mom talked stern but never raised her voice.

"Who looks after those girls so far from their families? All those soldiers around God knows who, anyone can join up who wants to, you don't have to take a character test. You don't know how men are. Why on earth would you want some sergeant barking at you in the crack of dawn, I can't imagine."

Mom lifted the pot of potatoes from the stove with her round strong arms and drained the boiling water in to the sink, a huge cloud of steam rose up between the two of them.

"Give me the masher."

Mom started to mash hard like she did when she was mad, hammering the masher down into the pot. "Have to get up at 5:00 a.m. every morning and at night all those soldiers off duty."

"That's the whole point Mother, that's what Bess wants to see."

"Oh you stop."

"You know it's true you want to go because all the boys are there." Bess did love the boys and they loved her too, there was always someone on the porch.

"Well they are aren't they. Anyway I do not. President Roosevelt says everyone should help. I just thought it might be fun to see other places. There's nothing wrong with wanting to see the world a little."

"You can see it, look right out the window there, there's the world." Mom said. She was pointing out the back door where right then the green trees were bent over by a gust of wind that lifted open, then slammed closed, the screen door.

In the very next second Carl Ayers appeared, under the black walnut tree coming up the back sidewalk. Bess saw him and bolted out of the kitchen then up the stairs running so that he could still hear her footsteps echoing when he got to the door.

"Hello, Walt," Mom said pouring the milk into the potatoes.

"Hello, Mrs. Healy, I was just going by and saw your door open."

"Uh huh. You were just going by? Did your family move from Genera?"

She winked at me. She was kidding him; since they lived ten miles in the opposite direction, and since we were near the edge of town it was highly unlikely that he would happen by. He looked at the stairs furtively where Bess had disappeared.

"Well I can't stay."

"Well before you worry about staying, why don't you come in."

"I see you're about to have dinner so I won't bother you."

"You're not bothering me, yet." She glanced at me again and we tried not to laugh.

"We haven't started. We'll wait till James gets home with the little ones. Come on in. Can I get you a coffee?" she asked, nodding at the percolator she always had going on the counter. She put down the loaf of bread she was about to slice and poured him a cup and set it in a saucer on the table before he could answer.

"Sit a minute, tell us how things are."

"I'm fine."

The Protestants we noticed never said very much. Carl was a Protestant. He stood there in the doorway, with the summer green yard behind him, and his striped shirt and a crooked tie with it. I wondered why he was wearing a tie, since he worked at the grain mill, but I kept reading my book, and Mom kept working at her cooking. She was always cooking and talking. Put her loaf in the bread slicer and pushed it back and forth. She loved her bread slicer, left over from her restaurant days, but that's off the point.

I always thought Carl was strange looking, sort of a crooked smile, but he was easy going. His family were country people from over near Genera, Bess had met him at a dance. Now she was upstairs doing something to her hair and putting on lipstick I knew that. She was silly about men, it almost didn't matter who they were, she acted the same. Like she didn't know what to do.

"How are you Rose?"

I looked up from my book. "I'm good Walt, nice to see you around here."

There was a long pause with the sound of Mom stirring her lemonade with the wooden spoon in her big glass pitcher.

"I've been downtown and signed up for the Air Force," he blurted out.

"Oh is that right?" Mom asked. "Seems to be going around."

"I'm sorry?"

"Going around, I mean everyone wanting to sign up."

We heard Bess's footsteps on the stairs. She came in smelling of powder and acted surprised to see him.

"Oh hi Walter."

He stood up, "Hey Bess."

"Guess who signed up for the Air Force!" I asked her, I couldn't resist. She looked at me, and at Carl and back at Mother.

"I signed up for the Air Force today Bess," Carl said.

She glared at him fit to shame the devil. Pulled herself up and pursed her lips and walked right past all of us and out the back door and let the screen door slam.

He followed her out of course. They were engaged before the roast came out of the oven.

1942

*Blanchardville*

*Tomorrow we will leave by train from Toledo on our way to New York. The paper from the Navy says we can only pack*

*essentials since they will be issuing us uniforms and everything
else. Mother says we must have new underwear and night-
gowns. If Bess keeps coming in here crying one more time I'll
barricade the door. I'll play ball with the boys out in the yard
instead or step over to the church, I wonder how we'll go to
church there. Rusty is stationed in Massachusetts now too, so I
might even see him; though he says they're likely to ship out in
the next few weeks. I want to see New York but I don't know
what they'll let us do, they say there are soldiers from everywhere, and I'll be trained at Hunter College. I guess I'll have
to give up my dream of going to Antioch. I would like to go to
college, they always say I'm a good scholar, but I don't know
when I'll find the time now.*

*I'm taking the rosary Grandma Tindal gave me from the
Shrine at Carey in case I need a miracle, it was in the drawer
here where did it go, if I can't find that, oh no, and I might take
my collection of Dickens but not the ones I've read already, I'll
take Bleak House but that doesn't sound cheerful, or maybe I'll
take P.G. Wodehouse that's more fun, but books are heavy to
carry. Dad has agreed to let us join the Navy only because we
can go together, he doesn't like the idea of one of us wandering
around a military base at night he says any man in their right
mind would grab us, and it wouldn't be proper. We can't wait.*

## 1942
### *Baltimore, Maryland*

*My bunk is next to Genevieve Richel from New York. She
has a picture of her mother on the little table between the two
beds. I hate having to get up so early. Last night it was late
maybe one or two in the morning, and there was a fire alarm.
So we spring up out of bed, everyone's rushing, we're told to
take a blanket off the bed and go, and she turns to me and says,
"Rose, should I take Mama's picture?" And I say "No Genevieve, no. We need to go right now." Well it turned out to be*

*a false alarm but I never will forget her saying that. Should I
take Mama's picture. Marching makes me crazy. Get up in the
freezing cold and march around in a line. Down the field and
back, the most pointless thing I've ever done. Left right, left
right. I'm always falling out of step. My mind wanders.*

*My new job as store keeper is not bad. My typing has gotten
much better, I have to type out all the invoices for the payments
that go out to the soldiers tomorrow. And Lieutenant Winslow
called me into her office and asked me if I would mind being
photographed wearing the new Navy hats they've designed.
Said I was picked out from all the girls in the barracks for being nice looking. Makes me feel a little shy. But I have to go
on Wednesday, they're going to style my hair and all. I guess
they're going to put me on the poster for the new uniforms, or
something.*

*Letters this afternoon right after lunch. Roasted carrots and
corned beef hash. Ruth Goldblatt set beside me and I like her
because she talks about New Jersey and how they do at her
house about her Father who is the baker, how they don't like
to drink milk. I got two letters, one from Mom and one from
Rusty. Mom sends Holy Cards. Gotta read Rusty's.*

Dearest,

Talked with the Sargent, he did promise me a leave
before I go overseas. Its rather indefinite Darling but
whenever it is and wherever you are I am coming to
see you. I don't understand how the Army and Navy
can be so cruel about moving each of us at the wrong
time but they sure have done a good job of it.

I received a letter from Lowell Aller the other day
telling me about his trip to Texas to see Bill. It was a
swell letter and I sure was glad to get it. From his letter I find Bill is much the same old Bill and is taking
everything very well. Since I have more opportunities
and facilities for writing I am going to get back in the
groove of writing all my ol' buddies regular again. As

for you my love, I promise I'll write you at least twice a week, that is if you also cooperate and tell me you love me at least that often, and "darling" if ever for any reason you find you don't love me, please tell me then, and I probably won't but I'll try to understand. (But please don't say it).

Honey I haven't been to that photographer yet. I had an appointment for the 5th of January but I had to go to N.J. to pick up an A.W.O.L prisoner and I couldn't keep it. Since then I haven't had an opportunity. I will send you one soon as I can. Since you haven't got a picture I'll tell you something about this guy who is so very much in love with you. He's 25yrs young, 5'11½ tall, weighs 168 lbs (I gained some), dirty strawberry blond hair, has most of his own teeth, wears an Army Officer's Uniform, works hard and when opportunity permits plays even harder. Enjoys a drink only when alone or with somebody. His social life has been very dull lately and he <u>does not</u> like WACs but loves a WAVE. He sleeps with both feet under the covers and snores only when asleep. Financial condition very fluctuating. Highly recommended by all who don't know him. Do you still want a picture?

Darling I have to go check the guard so I'll bring this volume to a close. Please tell me about your new station and send me your telephone number. Also tell me all about your leave. Say hello to your beautiful sis for me and to the other little waves who are rippling around. Be a good little sailor and remember I love you more than I can ever tell you.

All my love, Rusty

Post Mortem #1

What store are you keeper of? I was just thinking I could use a good store keeper in the Mess. If you are interested in this job write to

Lt. E.L. Koehner

Bty "B" 491ˢᵗ AAA AWB Fort Devens, Mass

1947
*Cleveland, Ohio*

We were married of course right after the war. You've seen those pictures. I think the drinking started to get bad when he was traveling as a salesman for Diamond Match. He sold matches, not the kind between a man and a woman, but the kind that you light, well what he mostly sold was the advertising, the business name on the book of matches. Every restaurant, grocery store, oh and hardware store, or sporting goods store would order matches with their name on them in those days. People needed matches to light their smokes and it was good advertising.

Diamond Match was a big company then. They also sold restaurant supplies, paper straws and like that. So many of his accounts were in restaurants or hotels; those days the late 40's and early 50's most of the hotels were still downtown, and of course each one had a restaurant and a bar. So you can imagine.

What made him a good salesman was he was gregarious, he liked to tell a story or hear one, and he was a good listener, well as long as he could still hear, but that was only a problem later. So he'd get to a town, have two or three appointments scheduled. Youngstown say, a big steel town in those days. He'd meet with the hotel managers and so forth, he'd maybe know the guy after a few months on the circuit.

So one of them would say "Well let's sit and have a beer," while they went over the order. That would be lunch, and then in the afternoon, another guy "Can I give you a drink, have a seat."

"We got your toothpicks, drinking straws, and matches, you need anything else, coffee stirs we have those. And I need you to just sign off on this slogan for the cover."

"That looks good until next month. What about Ohio State this year, they gonna go to the Rose Bowl."

"No, John I think it's the toilet bowl they're going to."

"Who they got quarterbacking this year?"

"That kid Keller. But he can't throw further than the table."

"That whole throwing game is what it's coming too isn't it. My day, why we liked to run the ball, that way you always knew where it was, didn't take any chances. Course that was a while ago. Before pads, you know what I'm talking about. Did you play yourself."

"Yea, I did a little time on the gridiron, love the game."

"What position?"

"Well quarterback as a matter a fact. One year of college before the war. Now I could throw in those days. You say it's safe to run with the ball but you gotta remember you can always throw a ball a helluva lot faster than a man can run. So sure you gotta take a risk, but the payoff is there. I always gave it a throw to see if anybody would catch it."

"You like gambling in general?"

"Do I like gambling in general, well no, I like gambling in the evening."

"Ha I like that. A course I know where some games are, if you're ever in the mood."

"Thanks John I'll let you know. Got three baby girls I'm gambling on right now."

"Three women, you poor sucker. How old?"

"Let's see, the oldest is five, going to school, then three I think and two."

"You didn't waste any time getting to it. Did you go over in the War."

"I sure did, France and England."

"See the guys who were away they are always the ones who come back and can't get enough. Makes a man hungry for his own country, and American women. God when I was in Italy, I was in the supply line, I cried one day just thinking about Cleveland, not any one thing I could put my finger on, just being there or belonging there. Now it seems damn silly but at the time I was hurting."

"No, I know what you mean. I felt that way in Normandy, landing there wishing I was landing in New York."

"Normandy huh, what day did you get there?"

"Oh not until the third day, I wasn't on the beach, would never take that away from the guys who were. We were backing up the front line once they took Omaha, sending in the tanks to follow, stayed awake for three days but that's not so bad."

"Have another drink on us? Wilma, get this thirsty veteran a drink!"

"Thanks John. How about you, any kids?"

"One son, just one. I went right into college after I got out, accounting and finance. I always liked numbers. GI bill you know, you didn't go for it?"

"No, I had the girls right away see, so."

"Well a course. I gotta go to some god-awful meeting but Wilma is gonna take care of you here. Nice to see you Rusty, nice to talk with you. You take care now."

~

How many times can you have the same conversation?

Each night of course he had to stop in a new place. Which was all well and good until it got to be after dinner and other guys going home, and he with nowhere to go but upstairs to a musty little hotel room, with a bed and a chair, and a sooty window looking onto a dark alley. This was before television, you know. So he sat at the bar, for the company of it.

I suppose he would start thinking sometime after the second whiskey, that his life now, driving from Youngstown to Columbus to Detroit selling matches and toothpicks, wasn't the glory he'd counted on after liberating Paris and marching down the Champs Elysées. Then with the children coming pretty quickly. Our apartment in Cleveland crowded too, but I really don't think he minded that.

By the third whiskey he could talk to whoever was there, the bartender, the fat lady on the corner stool, make the hours pass so he could go to that empty room and not see it clearly enough to know where he was.

Course not wanting to face an empty room seems like a small obstacle after all, but sometimes it's that little thing that does you in. You know the story of Achilles. His mother Thetis dipped him in the potion of immortality, but that little spot where she held his ankle to dip him, that didn't get covered. How are you're gonna protect someone from every possible hardship. He did say once that the pressure of having to make the sales, since he worked on commission, weighed on him but the truth was he never had trouble selling anybody anything. Everybody who knew Russ liked him, but he wasn't used to being where no one knew him. He grew up in this town where everybody spoke to each other by name. He was a small town boy in that way. Then to be sleeping alone every night in a bed that isn't yours, in a room with only a number on the door to make it different from any other one. You're just the man sleeping in there, no one knowing your name or how well you could dance or how far you could throw a football, being anonymous like that.

Not that I'm here to make excuses for him. I just want you to think about what might have happened in his view.

～

A strange thing about that time, I always wondered about it; when we'd heard he got the job and I mentioned it to my mother.

She said, "Diamond Match he's gonna work for?"

"Yes, out of Barberton."

She said, "When I was growing up my Neuman cousins had a friend worked in Akron for Diamond Match. Well they worked in that factory, got paid hardly anything, but then well they all started getting some awful necrosis of the cartilage in their jaws. Turned out there was phosphorous in the matches and that's poisonous, it started attacking their jaw cartilage, was terrible, a whole town full of people with disfigured faces who couldn't eat or smile, and the owner, Columbus Barberton, didn't do a damn thing for 'em. Till someone in his company invented a way to make the matches without phosphorous, then President Taft said he had to make that patent public, to protect the workers and he did. But not without having his arm twisted. Now that must be a sin somebody is paying for, I wouldn't want my husband working for such a company as that."

"But Mom they don't do that anymore, you said so yourself."

"They don't but all those poor souls. Not being able to talk or eat. Who's making up for the sins of that company? For what they couldn't say, and now your husband, well he'll be lining the pockets of those shysters. I don't like it. I don't like that outfit at all. Wouldn't let mine get involved in a place that destroys people's faces, I just wouldn't. Sometimes if it looks like a frog it is."

"Mom he needs a job, he's not going to hurt anybody."

"I know he's not but it just worries me, if they treat people like that. Best not to get mixed up with the likes of them. God will punish them."

I thought of her later, when the loneliness of that job made his drinking become so obvious, he spent a good quarter of his pay before we even saw it. It added up $2 or $3 a night; in those days it was a lot. When he came home he was all right, oh he'd have a few beers at night but it wasn't a big deal, I didn't think, until later.

Summer 1953
*Cleveland*

We were living in that yellow brick apartment building on Fifty-first Street, about a mile from the lakeshore, called that neighborhood the Detroit Shoreway. Thank God it was a solid old building. You went there recently with your sister to see her old school St. Stephens, and to see what you could of my life before you were born. St. Stephens was a pretty old German church. Of course now like so many little parishes it's running out of people. Just old folks there now. But it's on the National Register of Historic Places, I read, I guess because we went there, hah. No, it's a beautiful Gothic church right in among the houses, a lovely carved walnut wood altarpiece, stained glass shipped over from Bavaria. Was the school still going did you say, I can't recall. Not much else there now I'd recognize. Same brick houses. Vietnamese groceries and Baptist rescue missions. Oh, after the War it was a crowded neighborhood, always kids out playing. Like I was saying.

I was taking a load of clothes off the clothesline on the back porch, we were on the second storey. I looked up over the roof-tops to that copper-colored sky, not an insect stirring. I felt the heat just settle out of the air and it was damp almost, you just could feel something coming. The older girls felt it too, they came running back from the playground down the street, came running up the back stairs. Your father was home for once.

Well just a few minutes later the siren at the fire station went off, that was the warning to take cover in case of tor-nado. And the siren started going just as hail started to hit the windows, hail the size of golf balls, was like the pestilence in the Bible, I thought it would break them sure. That's when I gathered the children into the hall.

You could hear it before anything. A terrible high pitched screeching noise, and a rumbling that shook the ground like a freight train pitching right down the middle of the street. Like the furies shooting out of hell it sounded, with a wicked dark-ness too. The girls were hiding under a blanket; I sat on the floor holding onto the smaller children there in the hallway, all of them quiet as ghosts for fear and trembling against my shoulder. I'm trying to hold onto all my children at once, try-ing to find a hand or ankle I can press under my arm, feeling fury at the wind that might take them from me. I can see down the hall to the kitchen window and branches blowing by scraping the wood, and clanging steel garbage cans rolling, glass breaking, and then dead silence.

The girls popped their heads out of their blanket.

"Is it over?"

"No," I say. "I think we're in the eye of the tornado. Don't you move. Stay right here." I waited. I knew the worst wasn't over. Never truer words were spoken.

But your father of course, the eternal optimist, he's watching it from the front room.

"I think that's the worst of it passed," he says. "Boy that was a big one, I never saw anything like it."

He's standing there watching in the eerie quiet.

I say "Rusty come away from the windows. I don't think this storm is over."

But he walks into the kitchen instead. Then whoosh the wind starts up again and right before my eyes a beam that was holding up the back porch roof comes loose, slams through the door into his shoulder and he goes down.

"Oh damn it, damn it," he's saying, "I'm all right, it just a crack damn it."

Then the roaring comes tearing through again, with a huge gust blowing through the open door, the cries of the children now ripped out of their mouths into the screeching wind. I squeeze baby Timothy to my chest, close my eyes. In a minute it's over. I hear it in the distance now. The children are clutching me, Mary's little fisted fingernails gripping my wrist so tight there's a drop of blood, but no one is hurt.

He's getting up off the floor. "I'm fine, I'm fine," he's saying, "just sprained my shoulder." He had a flashlight. "Oh its nothing," he said, made jokes to the children.

He was so good with children really, had M&M's in his coat pocket and calms them all down with the candy. We get blankets and sleep in the hall.

Was a freak thing, how that beam came through the door,

a miracle it didn't come down on his head. He has a broken collarbone, we find out the next day. Things are shut down for a few days but then he can't drive for a few more weeks, he can't work.

I had tried to tell him, this is the eye of the storm. But he didn't listen.

Was like there were two tornados that summer, one was that twisting wind, and then what followed.

Autumn 1953
*Cleveland*

*9:15 Good Lord, I can't believe they're here already this morning, I didn't even get a chance to do the dishes, well they're not taking the dishes as far as that goes. I guess furniture dealers don't take dishes or I'm sure they'd take the bowls out of my child's hands. Silver already sold, so no value there. Poor children don't know what to make of all this. Four big men clomping through the rooms. If he were here it would help, said he had to go make some arrangement, said he'd be back in an hour but he won't be back until tonight. He's too ashamed, I know. Too ashamed to watch what he's doing to us. One thing to sell my belongings to pay his gambling debts, quite another thing to have to be home to watch it. Becky's been hiding behind my skirt since the movers came in, what's she so afraid of. Maybe she's smiling, I can't tell. Oh the baby needs to be changed. Glad Mary's four now, she's a help.*

*But she's asking the men, why are you taking our rocking chair, taking the rocking chair I rocked my babies in, now Becky wrapping her arms around his leg saying, no no, mine, mine. Oh stop children it's hard enough. Why are they stealing our things Mary keeps asking. They are taking them to sell, we are going to a smaller place, we'll get other things. Oh never mind. Just never mind. Let's go in this room so you don't have to watch.*

"Come back here sit on the bed with me, sweetheart."

How many boxes do I have in here, seven, eight cardboard boxes, clothes mostly, hardly space to get to the bed to sit, oh it's a mess alright. It is a mess. I have to stay composed enough not to alarm the children, who are already excited with the moving men. Ostermans Moving, their van says, a brown van parked outside, they call each other Bud, are they all named Bud? The black man is kinder than the other two, calls me Mam. Tell the children to stop staring at him.

"Mam is this settee going?"

"Yes it is."

"Am I to take this silver Mam?"

*Yes, yes, I'm holding the baby Tim. Trying to keep the two girls out of the way thank goodness the older ones are off at school.*

*They're taking the grandfather clock away from the wall not that it kept time but it had been Grandfather's, and it is pretty. Used to have a matching art deco radio with a curved oak cabinet. Was just a nice set in a room. He's at the tavern, I expect. That night he said, we will have to sell what we can and move back to Blanchardville that's all there is to it. We have to do that or what, I ask him. Well it's just the way it is, he says, I'm sorry. I'll make it up to you. I'll get a fresh start and we can get new things. Or what, we have to or what? Or I'm not sure what will happen, the way he said that. What do you mean? I want to know what he means but he can't bring himself to say the words. Would they hurt him, kill him. I don't know. Over a few thousand dollars? Who on earth is he mixed up with? Cleveland mafia I'm pretty sure. Italians no doubt.*

*I said we had to keep the beds, and Grandmother's armoire to put our clothes in. I can't watch this, stay in the bedroom and close the door. Here is the pile of quilts that Grandma gave me, she had an interest in the old patterns. Wedding rings, log-cabin. I'll spread it out. Come on children up here on the beautiful quilt. Their footsteps sound so heavy on the stairs must wear big boots, coming up and down, it's better not to watch them taking what is being taken. Listen to it go. Sit here on the bed with the baby and my sweet girls. That must be my cedar chest they are sliding across the floor a wedding gift from my grandparents. Mom put in a dozen embroidered linen luncheon napkins decorated with roses, doesn't matter it's going. Gambling debts, he was gonna strike it big. Sure. Phone would ring, before they took the phone. Why did he close the kitchen door. Didn't want me to hear. Admitted he didn't have rent money. Pawned my engagement ring, thought that was the worst of it. Not too much to ask for a roof over your head. But I didn't see the depth of it; I should have seen this coming. But I didn't. If I talk it will calm the children. I should tell them a story.*

*"Would you like me to tell you where all the pieces of cloth in the quilt came from."*

*"Yes tell us a story. Read a book Momma."*

*"Well let's just look at the quilt. Patch a story together. That checked gingham, now this was the dress Mary wore to get her little lamb do you remember Mary's little lamb? This dark blue here now that was part of a flag that was raised after we won the Civil War, your great-great-grandfather carried it out of Shenandoah and they had tried to shoot it down, the flag, but he carried it up right while the bullets flew, he and the little drummer boy. Now this was part of a sail, this white one here, a sail on a ship that came across the lake in a big storm, Grandma found it on the beach. She did. Yes. Now look at their little fingers pointing here, here. This one, no this one. Don't fight. We will hear all of them. This striped shirt was the railroad man Casey Jones who drove the train that took the family to the enchanted mountain where the caverns were made of gold, but when he got there the brakes on the train wouldn't stop and it ran right on through to the other door, but everyone was fine. This, oh that green wool was the cape your Great Aunt Odeline wore when she came to this country on a ship, her name was Odeline and she wanted to go to school*

*but her mother said, no you have to stay home and eat cookies and ice cream all day and she said please Mother, can't I go to school so finally her mother said well alright. That dotted swiss fabric was part of a dress a little girl wore just before there was a frog that flopped down beside her and she thought it was a prince but he wasn't, he was just a frog. Good to hear them laugh. This blue velvet now that was part of the little girl's dress all the little girls had blue velvet dresses when I was little and we wore them even when we were sleeping because we liked the feel of it."*

*Mary's pointing now to Timothy, he's sleeping finally. Shsh. Let him sleep.*

*This is not a good day walking into the living room where there is nothing to sit on, nowhere to put down a book and he's at the tavern. The kids loved it though, they're happy with all the empty space dancing around the room that is suddenly so big. Got their tricycle from the back porch, the two of them riding it around the living room, I let them. I have some potatoes and bacon, and milk for the children but not much else, I have cigarettes thank God. It scares me to be honest with myself, these bare floors, and the echo of the emptiness. I'm scared what will become of us.*

*Anyway it is wrong to cling to worldly goods. Store ye up the treasures of heaven. Oh what's that psalm, hell I can't even remember.*

*Put the potatoes on to boil. Wished I had some green beans because that's a good dish, potatoes and bacon and green beans. I don't even know where we're going to stay. Mom just moved into a little apartment, she doesn't have room for us. I talked to Bess her husband is sick with Hodgkins disease, I can't trouble her. He said this morning he's making arrangements. He's sitting there making arrangements all right, where to get his next beer. I told the older girls that we were moving to Blanchardville so they would have more room to play outside, they should be back from school in a few minutes.*

*I have some coffee and if I could get the two little girls to take a nap I can sit down and read for a minute, and have this smoke. Now there, I didn't know my hands were shaking.*

## 1954
### *Locust Street. Blanchardville*

When we left Cleveland I had nowhere to go but to my mother, who at the time was in a little house on Park Street out on the South End. I had the five children. The older ones, Jane and Linda wondered why Dad was not coming with us. I said because he had to continue to work. But the truth was it was dangerous, the mob he got involved with. He went down to Texas to see his uncle because he had to get out of town. Well if he would have come with us they might have looked for him in Blanchardville. I think they did even go ask his mom where he was. Still don't like to think of it. Cleveland mafia I guess, though he never did tell me either.

Mom's house on Park Street was small, she was living there with my brother Tom. He was only about twenty-two, hadn't gotten married yet, he was working at the bar. They had only two bedrooms, well I moved into Mom's room we had three little single beds in there, Jane had one, we put the crib in the living room, while the rest of them had to sleep in the basement. It was a finished basement; we fixed up a room down there as best we could. I thought maybe I'd leave him then get a legal separation. He begged me not to, and the children said, "Where's Dad, where's Dad." That about broke my heart.

When he came back from Texas his brother got him a job at the sugar beet factory for a while. Then we moved to Locust Street. That was a nice house for kids, had a big yard with old trees in it, had some room, and it was close to Dinnell Pond and park; they spent a lot of time roller skating there or ice skating on the pond when it was winter. Your dad was always optimistic. "Oh" he would say, "it will be alright, we'll fix it up," and then he would paint the rooms and borrow ladders and climb around and work hard for awhile. We're gonna have a new start he would say, got a little off track and I would believe him and then the same thing would start all over.

That house on Locust had an old coal furnace and one winter well we didn't have money to buy more coal so we ran out. He would go to his mother's when things got bad.

It was the middle of winter and the house was freezing cold. So I put the kids in the kitchen where there were gas burners for the cook stove. I turned on the burners and we brought blankets and pillows and put them on the kitchen floor, or we would have frozen to death, we slept there for a few nights. Course I was terrified one of the children would touch the open flames you know get up in the middle of the night, but they didn't.

Losing the heat in winter was always a problem for us. You remember some mornings when there was frost on the inside of the windows. Those starlike crystalline patterns, like some magical but sinister emblem of the threatening cold. How did the cold get inside our house? Your breath on the frost, your mouth against the glass. Your lips will stick to it. By the late 60's they had a law, that you couldn't turn people's heat off in winter for non-payment. Well that was a boon to me.

He got a job finally selling men's clothes at a Britts department store, had to look good. So we would all be wearing hand me downs but he would always be immaculately dressed in the latest suit and tie. That lasted a couple of years.

So I never mentioned most of this to you when he was alive. What good would it have done. If wishes were horses, beggars would ride. You had a better chance in life thinking that your father was a reliable person than thinking he wasn't. Children need a hopeful world.

∽

1965
## *Pine Street. Blanchardville*

You must have been five or six, it was March I think, rainy and gray but not too cold. And your sister Carrie and you were bickering.

"I'm going to the Sundry Shoppe," Carrie started, "you can come but I'm not buying you anything."

"I wanna go" you said, "I have a dime Grandma gave me."

"You can't get Sweetarts for that much, they're fifteen now."

"So I'll get Pixie Sticks. They're only a nickel."

"They never have those."

"You girls quit arguing."

"We're not arguing, were going to the Sundry Shoppe."

You girls loved that little store just around the corner on Main Street. had things like felt and glitter and candy, greeting cards, two old ladies ran it, wasn't any bigger than a closet.

"It's Monday they're closed," I said and you looked about to cry.

"Come with me instead, I'm going to mail a letter."

I feel the memories you come back to, they are warm to me like a place where someone has been sitting.

As I said, I had a letter to mail, so we were walking out together to the nearest mailbox which was two blocks around the corner, past the Moores' and then through the wide school yard of Washington School. We walked in through the gate in the fence, passed the monkey bars where you often played and the basketball hoops around the side of the building, but no one was out that day. We walked past the wide windows of the basement kindergarten room where you all went before going off to St. Michaels on the other side of town. We turned and walked toward the mailbox.

It has just rained, and the rain has brought down the red buds of the maple trees, they are staining the sidewalk crimson and crunching underfoot. Grey clouds whip through the sky. The wind is threatening more rain but there is something else too.

Something worried in my face you see. You feel my worry; children do of course, its tangible in the air. We walk by the broad green lawn that stretches on one side of the school and there is a flagpole there and the flag is twisting and snapping in the wind like something caught. You take hold of my hand, as if to comfort me.

Why is Mother worried, you're wondering. What will happen now. It seems to do with father; it is the seeming of things that all children remember. He has a sickness that has to do with beer, so he doesn't always work. Last year we had gone to a large hospital with many old men who were missing legs and arms, to see him because he was staying there. They had all been in wars. Some were very old and they sat on a big front porch in wheelchairs and had called out and reached their hands toward you when you visited because they didn't often see pretty little girls come there. But that was not today.

You said, "What's wrong?"

"Nothing sweetheart, I'm fine," I said, but you went on.

"Why are you so worried?"

So I answered, " I was waiting on a check from the Veterans since your Dad's not working."

"What if this check doesn't come?"

"Well then we won't have money," I said, not really thinking.

"But if we don't have money to buy food what will happen to us?"

Then I realized how worried you were and I turned and bent to reassure you.

"You mustn't worry. Say your prayers."

We were at the mailbox.

"You can put it in," I said.

You pulled down the blue metal flap and put the letter inside. It closed with a clang. We turned to go home, but you kept on.

"But what will we do, what will happen to us if we don't have food," you said.

So I stopped again and I looked at you so you wouldn't forget this time, so you would stop worrying. I told you.

"God will provide."

There is a clearing in the forest of your memories where these words are planted.

"God will provide."

I think you were confused, to think that it was not me, your mother who would take care of things, it was God. A distant man you had never met, who lived somewhere in that grey cloudy sky. You thought well is God someone Mother knows? Has she met him, and talked to him? Did he know about us? Would we have to meet him? Just the weight of his name I think, made you look awful forlorn.

The wind blew. We walked on. You wondered had the letter been sent to God? Was that why your mother seemed so confident? Was it true, would God provide?

Well I hadn't meant to frighten you by invoking the presence of God, but eventually you came to see what I meant. Didn't you?

Everything that can't be known for sure, every chance that was taken, every journey you took where the end wasn't known, God provided. Call it what you will.

Maybe my reassuring you like that wasn't the best thing after all. Gave you a confidence to run into the world without the fear you should have had to protect you. But He did provide didn't he. All the risks you took, hitchhiking, flying over volcanoes, wondering the streets of New York all night long who do you think was watching?

That was a memory I left you, that sentence strung together like an heirloom necklace of precious jewels. God will provide.

Words that make a person brave; and that part worked on you. But I'm not sure you ever stopped to ask what it was you wanted God to provide exactly. Then again maybe you shouldn't be asking him at all, better off to ask yourself what you want to provide for you. Be your own mother.

1967
*The Trestle. Blanchardville*

Religion was a help to me in my life. Kept the mystery present in my mind, and so I lived in light of it. Of course just getting to church was an ordeal, none of you very willing.

Then too, it would have been easier for us to get from the house on Pine Street to St. Michael's school and church if the river had not divided one from the other in such a crooked way. The swale wallowed out to the west of us, so we had to take the Cory Street bridge; a good three or four blocks out of the way since none of us could walk on water, far as I know.

I always told you children, stay out of the swale. It was all wild in there, full of foul-smelling mudflats, reeds beds and willow bush left from some wild oxbow meander the river had taken just out of spite, I think, to upset the order of streets on our side of town. There were pockets of quicksand in there too, and one of you could get caught in there you'd never get out. Of course if I said stay out, well off you'd go, straight there. Hoodlums hanging around in there too, racing motorcycles around and drinking beer. I will say the swale was a good place to collect insects for biology class. You'd make a butterfly net out of a wire coat hanger and a bit of old sheer curtain, mayonnaise jar with lighter fluid, and catch all kinds of things back there, tiger swallowtails, praying mantis, golden beetles, and a walking stick I remember you showing me, a little brown twig with legs, just fascinated you and you tried to keep it alive in a shoe box. You loved just collecting insects, finding where the different ones lived, how each one had a flower or tree they called home, a whole world of homes out there.

The ground shifted there every spring when the river was high, so nobody built there until a few years ago. They filled it in now, made it into four big softball fields with lights and all, granddaughter Jessie plays out there, she's quite the softball champion, gets all your brother's attention, while he ignores his own son Daniel who isn't athletic. Goes around comes around.

But now my story is getting all bogged down in the wilderness of the swale; well there's nothing wild around here now, but what I wanted to say was how the straightest route to school would have been the route the railroad took; not Cory Street and the bridge.

You had to cross the tracks before you got to the bridge. I always worried about you children crossing the bridge because I knew the trestle would be a temptation. Of course I shouldn't talk about the danger on account of that one time, or maybe two.

That one morning I walked to school with you. It was rare that I would, but I had a job interview at Manpower over on Harding Street just two blocks from the school.

~

*I have to sit for a minute to curl my hair. Missus Ursalitz said 9:00 a.m. but I'm not sure how I will get there. If it worked. Say a prayer it would at least give us some income to rely on. Can't sit here hoping anymore. Can't but try. Said they needed someone who could run a switchboard, and I can do that. Probably all new equipment though. What kind of test would they give for that. Wonder if I could get away without wearing stockings it's warm and all. Oh I guess I better, maybe one of the older girls has a pair of pantyhose, they'll complain about that, God I hate those things, garters are more comfortable but you can't even buy them now. I hope he stays sleeping. Who knows what time he came in, kills me that we have to have the*

*bed right here in the room next to the living room, where you
can see it from the front door almost and now with the mat-
tress on the floor cause of his back being thrown out, gives him
another excuse. Wish I had just a bit of privacy to get dressed
without someone walking through, oh well. That's a cardinal
out the window, that flash of red, seems early but some winter
over. Ms. Ursalitz said they needed someone ten to six. Well
that's not so bad. I know a lot of people in town so that might
help, as they need contacts she said. Poor Mary Queen of Scots,
that was a bad deal she got. Cardinal out the window made me
think of it, blood red cardinal. I never met a cardinal but I met
a bishop. Maybe I can stop at the library too, get another in
that historic series. Father Fleck said I could ask for a legal separation if it gets any worse. Might be but a few hours a week,
won't amount to much. Hope I can stop and see Bess on the
way home, maybe she'll have a cup of coffee, course the little
one is gonna be home from Kindergarten. I don't know if his
father will still be here or not. Wonder if Bess is better off with
her Carl gone, and five children left to do for. She doesn't have
much but that regular social security check, and that pretty old
house. I smell something burning.*

"Steph are you burning toast?"

"No, Mom Joseph did it."

*And Carl was always so jolly. Course she said she could
barely pay for the heat last winter. Did they each get a bologna
sandwich today, four bags, I guess so. Wonder if I have fifty
cents for a pack of smokes, looks like. Better try and get back by
noon. I don't know if this watch even keeps good time, seems
to be ticking.*

"Children, are you ready?"

You remember that morning I walked with you to school
because it was so rare that any adult would presume upon
your territory. You all seemed happy at the novelty of it. You
wanted to hold my hand. I felt like a queen had come out to
greet her subjects.

We were running behind but I didn't want to be late for the appointment, so when we came to the railroad crossing. I looked to the left where the tracks angled direct toward Hardin Street and said, "Shall we take the trestle?"

It was you two youngest girls and Luke and Tim, five of us. You looked at me like I was from the moon, then you started elbowing and shushing each other because you didn't want to say that you took the trestle half the time, though I'd warned you against it.

"Sure if you think we should," you all stammered like fools.

Luke smiled and ran ahead down the tracks. I don't know why but I thought of Anna Karenina, losing her child and throwing herself in front of the train, which always seemed like a stupid thing to do as there would have at least been some hope of seeing the boy again. I was glad my children were with me. Maybe Tolstoy had that one right that it was worse to lose your child than your husband, usually men don't understand about children but I think maybe Tolstoy did. Of course he didn't treat his wife very well either, gave all their money away.

We were almost at the start of the trestle now, you were chattering away.

"Luke said little kids like me could fall right through the ties into the river below, so it's best not to look down. Or if you don't fall through you can get your leg caught. You could be stuck there trying to get your leg out while the train came. When you cross the stripes tie, water, tie, water it can hypnotize you if you are not careful. If you hear a train whistle you have to run back, but they don't always whistle. If it came fast you would have to climb over the black iron railing and jump into the Blanchard below, and you'll probably die."

"Oh now don't be morbid. Watch what you're doing."

Our feet echoed across the wooden ties, the smell of creosote sharp in the balmy air. The trees were not in leaf yet, though the light of the year had risen high. *Lead us not into temptation and deliver us from evil amen.* Birds sang, in the trees, in the river below a fish jumped.

"Step carefully children."

Luke was walking along the top of one rail holding his arms out like an airplane.

"Look I won't step on the ties the whole time."

"Stop that you'll twist your ankle, quickly now, hold your sister's hand Steph."

"Are we supposed to do this?" you asked.

"Well I don't think it's illegal," I said, "and there's no point in being put off by a slight danger if the risk is reasonable."

"Ah, Mom wait, I'm caught."

"Sure you are" Carrie called back "we're not even looking."

Well I turned and sure enough there he was, the poor kid on all fours with his foot between the ties and my stomach just sank. Oh God, I thought, if it's broken I won't be able to carry him, let alone get to the interview on time.

"It's stuck, it's stuck," he was squealing frantic already like a little fox in a trap.

I bent to help him, he just needed to turn his foot the other way and it came out.

"Now see? Didn't I tell you not to play like that?"

"Stupid Goddamn railroad tie," he said as he wiped away a tear.

I guess I shouldn't have taken the trestle. You don't think how everything you do is going to affect your children at the time. I didn't think, oh if we walk the trestle today you'll all grow up to take the dangerous back routes through life; I was just trying to get to my appointment on time.

Maybe it is true in this family we're set on going. Thinking of the trestle reminds me.

～

1964
## *Pine Street. Blanchardville*

"I want to go on a train" you said, pulling at my arm as I sat in my chair at the table in the dining room on Pine Street. We were home together that year, had your baby brother, but the rest of the children were in school.

We had a big wooden table in that dining room, where we all could fit, with Grandma's old buffet running along the back wall, several of its doors missing now. There was a tall window there and since it opened into the side yard I never put a curtain up, so the light was strong. I think because your sister had read you one of the little Golden Books we had, *The Little Engine That Could,* you said.

"I want to ride a train. Can we ride a train sometime?"

"There used to be trains here," I said, thinking of the trains Grandpa Healy worked on, "but they don't stop anymore."

"Why not?" You frowned and put your head on my shoulder as if the news was a great tragedy. I wanted to read my book and have a smoke while the baby was napping and the others in school, but I saw you needed some attention so I roused myself.

"We can make a train," I said. "I'll show you. Get all the chairs and line them up here." We pushed the dining room chairs across the brown linoleum. Old wooden chairs we had mismatched, but high backed and strong.

"Line them up," I said. "No not side by side sweetheart, seat to back, seat to back, in a line see like this."

"Wait there a minute," I said, and I climbed the stairs to take a white bed sheet off your sister's bed. I came down stairs, tore a page off the Reader's Digest on the table.

"You'll need a ticket, to give to the conductor, when he asks. Here's your ticket. Now get on."

You sat on a chair your legs crossed in front of you.

"Now then, close your eyes and I'll make a train."

I shook the white sheet in crackling billows overhead, you looked up as the sheet came down over the backs of the chairs, making the roof of the train and each chair a separate compartment. You were inside a train now.

"Are you ready now?"

"Yes. You come too alright."

"No, I'll stay here, in case the baby wakes up."

The train took off with such momentum that you were pressed into the back of your seat; you marveled at the speed this train traveled, so fast. You were not sure where it was going, or if you were supposed to know, or would it be allowed, but your heart thrilled and you were happy. Traveling on a train, there was snow outside. Outside the train windows you watched the snow covered mountains passing, across the aisle there were foreign-looking strangers and they wondered why one so young was allowed to travel alone, you wished your mother were with you, you can ask her you would say. You pretended not to notice them. The conductor was coming to collect tickets. You thought this is what it means to travel; this is what I have been waiting here for.

I went on reading until about half an hour passed and the baby woke; you finally said:

"When will I be at the next place?"

"Soon enough. You want to take your little brother along too?"

"He can ride in the caboose," you answered, ducking under the edge of the sheet to fetch him. Even while the train moved slowly along, you pulled his chubby bare legs up onto the last dining room chair.

"Stay," you ordered him, running to get back to your car.

"Where does this train go to anyway?" you asked, peeking out from under the edge of the sheet.

"That's up to you," I said.

The train gathered speed again. I stood there and watched you go.

You can never tell ahead of time how one little event will effect things to come. I think of that day now when you're moping around about your leaving home so prematurely. Occurs to me now that you seemed headed in that direction from early on.

Well you're a big gardener, so you should know. Watching a child grow is like looking at the flower on the seed packet then waiting for them to come up. They can't be some other kind of flower.

1967
## *Pine Street. Blanchardville*

One winter, must have been the week after Christmas because you were still out of school. We didn't have any money; had run out of bread. Maybe you had seen the last piece get eaten from the brown kitchen counter or looked in the long plastic bag for it yourself. I remember saying it, "We're running out of food, I don't know what we're going to do." You watched me standing in the living room, I went to the window that opened onto the alleyway and pulled the curtains back, as if there might be something there to help but there was just another view of snow and icicles leaking from the eaves.

One loaf of bread was 35 cents then. It's not much unless you haven't got it. Your brothers were going out to see if the field around the corner where they played hockey was frozen over. You took your mittens from where they were drying on the cold linoleum in front of the black gas heater and went out with them.

You always liked to walk around the neighborhood anyway. You'd spend an hour just watching the snow fall, and the mysterious winter light that was always blue somewhere. Along Pine Street the broad maple tree trunks lined the sidewalk like pillars in an abandoned palace. Overhead their bare black branches etched the sky in ever smaller lines, like veins in someone's hand. You felt that the spreading branches were reaching toward something you couldn't name, an expectation of something about to end or begin. Half your childhood in breathless anticipation of what?

It was getting on twilight. You followed your brothers toward the field, a low yard behind the grocery store. You walked by the Weakes house, on Clinton Street. You fought with those kids, called them the Weaklings. But one day in the summer they had just hung a star in the window, which meant that their son had died in Vietnam, and a few days later rumor went round that the house was haunted by his spirit you could see a window blind moving up and down on its own in the upstairs window. Children came and stood on the sidewalk outside the house and waited to see something. But nothing happened.

That same street had a Methodist church on the corner, where it intersected Pine. One Sunday in spring, in front of that church, a dark car had unloaded a small white coffin, and it had been covered with yellow daffodils. Why is it so small you asked, it is a child's coffin I said. We watched them carry it inside, you asked me who it was and why the child died, but I couldn't answer. I didn't know them. Must have been a baby I said, it happens. Say a prayer.

Now the snow had melted back enough to leave the limestone sidewalks bare, and dry. Your brothers went on, you kept walking around the block. You were thinking that the twilight was coming, days were so short it would be dark soon, you were thinking of the problem of the bare branches reaching overhead, and how would we would all eat.

And then it was there in front of you on the sidewalk. A blue vinyl wallet, dry and cold. Remember the crispness of the vinyl as you picked it up. First you looked around but there was no one. You took your mitten off to unsnap the change purse pocket on the back and found the quarter and the dime that made 35¢ for the loaf of bread, and you knew that God was with you. You opened the fold; there was a five-dollar bill. There was no name inside.

Your brothers caught up with you just then.

"I found a wallet, look five dollars and thirty-five cents."

"Where'd you find it?"

"Right here on the sidewalk."

"I saw that first give it to me."

"You didn't just find it laying there."

"Yes I did."

"It's probably stolen. Did you steal it?"

"No I found it right here."

"Sure, you did."

"Let's go to the carryout and get some pop and chips."

"No I'm going home to give it to Mom."

"She'll make you give it back."

"To who, there's no one around."

The lights were dark at the two houses nearby.

"There's no one to ask here. Plus we need it. I'm taking it home."

You were sure that the wallet would change everything; that everyone at home would finally be happy. You ran toward the house, racing around the corner by the church, you ran into the street, and when I heard a car screech on its breaks I went to the window to look, but you were still running into the yard now and you jumped over the two broken steps and pushed the door open into the living room and gave me the wallet. We both knew what had happened. God had provided, just as I'd said he would. Usually.

1970

*Blanchardville*

*I've known Mildred Walsh for ten years and I never did like her. Knew her when I was working for the answering service over on Lima Avenue there, she was the front desk girl. Could never stand the way she smiled and nodded her head when ever her husband Frank said a word, with her tight little curls and false eyelashes, has an eagerness reminds me of a poodle on a leash. I don't like women who are overly fussy with their nails and such, hers are bright red, pointed like daggers. Frank was a bricklayer but then he got some county job laying sidewalks out in the new subdivision, she got her job with the county from someone he knew on the sidewalk committee, that kind of thing.*

*Rusty's been out of work all summer, irony is he's sober now, but lost so many jobs that he can't just walk into a a-nother. Lucky if he ever works again. Couldn't even pay the rent this month and six children to get ready for school, I don't have money to buy a piece of notebook paper, let alone shoes. I don't know what else to do but go to the County so I call and just my luck get Mildred. Talk about adding insult to injury.*

*Well wouldn't you know the County office was there in the old phone company building on Hardin Street. It's all been redone to where you couldn't recognize it. I don't know what I expected, some trace of the old switchboard, or the offices above that which used to look out over the floor, but not a trace of anything left from the time I worked there.*

*Bell starts ringing when I come through the door, sounds like a warning, what a dark little waiting room and who should be there but Mr. Doolittle, sitting there in his overalls with his head against the wall snoring. Bell woke him up, I guess. He's sitting up, grinning at me with his three remaining teeth and his no remaining hair, keeps nodding, well he's feeble minded there's no doubt. I've never seen him sitting down before, Doo-littles are usually walking around downtown, he and the wife and six or seven children all in a line like refugees on a forced march down Main Street. One has Downs Syndrome, one's in a leg brace, one's cross-eyed and I'm not making this up, poor things. Whole family of misfortune. Just my luck to get in there with Mr. Doolittle. All my girls think the family is named Doo-*

*little because they do so little, sit around and wait for help, or that they're related to the guy that talks to the animals, but they're just simple minded, it's not their fault.*

*Oh I wonder who the receptionist is, looks like one of the Lynch girls.*

"Hello, I had an appointment with Mildred Walsh."

"Was that in Family Assistance?" *She says it like I couldn't possibly remember.*

"Yes it was."

"Mildred's in the first door on the left, you can go ahead in."

*Wasn't this hallway even here when I worked here. What ugly wood paneling, and cheep framed pictures of the County Commissioners and the Mayor shaking hands with LBJ. Must not have known LBJ was a Democrat. Door's open, of course she's doing her nails.*

"Hello Mildred."

"Hello Rose, so nice to see you. You come right in here and sit down. You must be awful tired."

*How would you know what I am Mildred, don't dare say it of course.*

"I'm fine thank you."

"So let me get your file out. You're here to see what we can do in the way of county relief. Well I can imagine with all those children this must be very difficult for you. Now how's your husband Rusty? He's such a nice man. Haven't seen him out at the golf course lately, you know he and Frank used to golf together."

"He's fine. Has had some trouble finding work."

"I see that here on your form. Now you haven't paid your rent this month?"

*Says it like I'm a misbehaving child.*

"That's right."

"How much is it you normally pay. When you do pay I mean."

"Two hundred dollars."

*"Goodness gracious I didn't know you still could rent a house for that price."*

You don't know anything Mildred so I'm not surprised.

*"I guess it isn't much unless you don't have it."* Best try to be light or I might turn on her.

*"I understand. Now how many children exactly do you have?"* she asks me gripping her pencil in her blood red talons.

How many children exactly? Like I usually just estimate, or like I might not know.

*"Seven still at home."*

*"That's right, that's what it says here. Oh I bet you have your hands full, that must be hard with three boys too."*

Have to bite my tongue not to turn on her. What is hard, Mildred, is my having to sit here and share the difficulties of my life with the likes of you who has never read a book in your life and can't think beyond your fingernails. It is hard to sit in this chair across the table from you in this building where I used to manage fifteen women and be asked asinine questions, while you sit there like Lady Catherine De Bourg in Pride and Prejudice, *like it's* your *money you're giving away. I know it's not charitable. I'm sure Mildred tries but it's just about more than a soul can bear. Doesn't see Rusty at his golf game. If he would sell his golf clubs we could get a week's worth of groceries but the idea would never cross his mind.*

～

What amount of money they gave I forget, but it had to be spent so much on each child and I had to bring receipts, you little girls were excited to have a new dress; you picked out a little green cotton shift with bright yellow and red embroidery across the top; even if those clothes always seemed sad to you later when you wore them, and then some months later avoided wearing on account of the associations they brought.

Now this was before food stamps, this was earlier and we were given an amount of credit at the grocery store, and then we could go buy what we needed. But each item had to be written down, on a yellow legal pad, and then why there would be a balance at the end or not. I had them send it to the Food Center which was a little further away from us and not as good a selection as Food Town which was right down the alley. Food Center was up there on North Main, past the piano store where you kids used to get the piano boxes and turn them into hideout forts in the back yard, one block further up next to the Sundry Shoppe and next to where in later years your sister's husband would have a pizza place. Food Center was smaller, a little slower so everyone didn't have to see our situation. Wouldn't slow up the line so much.

It was more of an old-fashioned grocery with the high ceiling fans and black-and-white tiles on the floor. I know I shouldn't have, but I used to send you children to do the shopping there, I couldn't always face it. I would send a list with you, they had a good meat counter in the back, made their own Dutch loaf and pickled pimento spread I bought for sandwiches.

You were always allowed to pick out a treat for yourselves, you and your sister would push the cart along the aisles, peanut butter, miracle whip, a box of powdered donuts or Kool-Aid and chips or what have you, sometimes it was hard for you to reach the goods on the top shelf.

The two of you little girls would go through the list and wander around in there, then go up to the checkout line. You'd argue about who was gonna say it.

Carrie would say, "Oh you have to tell them this time."

"No I told last time."

"Well I'm leaving then." Always so stubborn, she'd start walking away from you.

"No, don't go, I'm leaving the cart right there then, I won't do it."

"You have to do it."

"I'm afraid."

"Oh just say it," and then you would blurt it out all at once. "We have a food order under Koehner."

The clerk would look down at you children barely able to see over the counter, and the expression on her face would change from the numb common-place of her cash register rhythm, her eyebrows would go up and there would be either interest or pity, and sometimes a sort of pulling back as if the fear of hunger was hovering around you. The older women, the ones with dyed hair and cigarettes in their apron pocket, were the best to get. They understood and reached under the counter to where the yellow legal pad was kept and got it out, and started the process without a lot of fuss. But some time you would get one of the college girls and she'd get all flustered, frown and look around for your mother, then ask the other cashier.

"Do you know what they want? What's a food order?"

Or she would say wait here a minute, and she would have to go get the manager who would come down in his short sleeved shirt and tie and explain it to her, and during all those long minutes other people waiting in line or just staring, so that was the sort of uproar you wanted to avoid if at all possible.

You stood by the cart and you watched their faces carefully, as they wrote each item down on the yellow pad of paper. You wondered if the yellow pad were evidence of some beneficent being who had decreed that you would not go hungry, even if there was no money at home, a being who controlled all the women and the store too. Was it like the story of the *Little Lame Prince*, one of your favorites, who was given a magic carpet to ride around on because he had trouble walking. You felt something illicit in the whole transaction, a sense of what shouldn't be that was, and hunger so much stronger. You remember the taste of powdered donuts.

～

Sometimes in the fall, when we lived on Pine Street, I used to sit and watch you and your sister out the dining room window which looked onto the side yard. You'd rake up all the maple leaves from the front yard and the neighbors, too, the rakes scraping rhythmic through the grass until you had a good big mound of scarlet yellow leaves well above your waist, the dry broken smell of the leaves coming in through the open window. One thing I have noticed, children love the world around them. They naturally do, if you watch them, they are designed to love and understand all they see and touch.

I'd watch you then take big armloads of leaves and shake them out of your arms into long lines about a foot wide and thick, one coming behind with the rake to help form the line, going back to the pile for more then shaking them into lines, then turning at a right angle and making another row until I could see the outline of the house that you were drawing across the yard.

Making one room, then another inside the larger outer square, then raking doorways through the rooms. A breeze would sweep in and the leaves go swirling away in a little red cyclone no sooner than you placed them down, but you'd go back and repair the breach, until all the borders of the house were set clear and straight.

This construction took some time and your sister would tire of it and go off, but you would stay in the yard adding another room or hallway. It took you a while to get clear in your mind who the characters were who would live in the house, what were they to each other, what did they do and want? This was the exciting part, but always it seemed that darkness came before you could answer. So much time taken up with the physical construction that there never was enough time to inhabit what you had made, and this left you a feeling of longing,

I wonder if you aren't still doing that, walking around the perimeter, wanting to go inside.

But at that time I didn't see a problem. I saw you walking in the yard living brief half-imagined lives around a house of leaves. A house without walls or a ceiling or whose walls and ceiling were clear and weightless as a child's mind.

1966
*Blanchardville*

Usually I tried to behave as if I weren't in the center of a tornado even when I was. I tried to maintain some forbearance and humor, as I thought that was the example you children most needed; but I must admit there were times I failed to see the point of it. I know you remember some of those. One day I had been downtown to get my hair done, I think I'd just gotten the job at the Paper. I was all dressed up, had my good shoes on. It had been a nice autumn day with the maple leaves blowing red and crackly around the sidewalk. The paper's office was next to the courthouse at that time, right around the corner from Aunt Bess's, so I stopped in for a cup of coffee at about three. Bess put the percolator on.

Mother was living with her then. Always sitting in her brocade armchair there in the parlor on the left as you came in. Well that helped Bess some as Mom could contribute some of her social security. Was nice having my sister and mother in the same house and that parlor was so pleasant, Bess always had a huge vase of lilacs there in front of the fireplace in the springtime or waxed leaves in the fall, her place was so clean and elegant. So we were visiting, when a huge peel of thunder came down from the sky, startled us, and a downpour followed.

"Good Lord that come out of nowhere."

"Raining cats and dogs now."

"Those kids will be soaked to the bone, catch their death of cold out there."

"There the umbrella sits," I told Mike, "take the umbrella, but you'd think I was talking to the door."

The rain had caught you children enroute home from school and you all came running up onto the porch squealing with your hair plastered to your faces. Bess said stay in the vestibule there, and don't drip all over the wood floor, she got some towels and we spread your wet books and whatnot out on some newspaper to dry and toweled you off. You and Bess's daughter Kat were just a few months apart weren't you, well you two went upstairs to play. We used to just sit and visit in that big old Victorian house, talking of the news and who said what. The rain just got worse and worse and I wondered how we'd get home. I sat and had the coffee and another one but it didn't look like it was gonna let up. I called your dad, of course he wasn't there. Well, Bess needed to start making dinner, so I called the Vets Cab.

We all piled in, you and Carrie and Luke while I sat in front. Could barely hear over the wipers, going like mad and hail pounding the top of the car like a tin drum.

"Nasty weather isn't it," the driver said. He wasn't one of the fellows I knew. I knew a few of them.

"It sure is," I said. "Not fit for man nor beast. 122 East Pine, please."

A few minutes later, just as the rain stopped of course, he pulled up in the alley beside the house. I said go ahead get out to you children, go on now, while I get my purse. Now what's the charge, he turned the meter over to $2.50.

"Oh dear I need to get some more change, I'm sorry let me run in and get that for you."

"Uh huh" he said, but I saw the fellow's face fall then. So I stepped out and walked up the stairs to the inside and locked the door behind me.

"Now don't you go to the window" I said.

"Why what's at the window."

"Just do as I ask."

Taxi driver waited a few minutes then started honking his horn, honk, honk, and you children said. "Why is he honking the horn?"

"Never you mind."

"What does he want?"

"He wants to get paid, but I don't have it to give him."

"He's going to come and get us," Carrie yelled and you and she hid upstairs with the excitement of it, peeking out the upstairs window down on the alley where the green taxi waited like a hungry reptile growling and squawking, blowing his horn, and the rain starting again.

~

Not that being inside a house really ever saved us from anything.

One January your brother Luke was sick with strep throat and I didn't have money for the doctor, so we waited an awful long time seeing if he wouldn't get better. Got so he couldn't swallow anything, well I feared scarlet fever of course, so I finally found a doctor I didn't already owe money to, he was awful sick by the time we took him. I moved him downstairs into my bed so I could watch him. Drifts of snow up to the windows. He had been restless all night but the penicillin was working now so he was sleeping and I was dozing finally in my chair.

Well, in my dream it seemed like someone was hacking at my front door with a giant axe, swinging against it again and again, was like the Huns sweeping out of the North and I knew the best thing would be to keep away from whoever it was that was pounding like that, knew that I shouldn't open that door, not under any circumstance, a terrible aversion I had to that sound I can recall to this day.

But one of you girls, I think it was you, woke me, pulling on my sleeve said Mom, Mom, somebody's knocking on the door, I said see who it is and tell them to come back another time, people are sick here, I thought thinking it was a damn Jehovah's Witness or some such.

So you opened the door and I couldn't quite hear but then heard a man's voice I couldn't place at first, and you came back and said Mom it's Marcella Santini, and Bill, and I thought well what does she want with us, they lived way out of town. But it was sub-zero cold I couldn't very well leave them standing on the porch, so I said to let them in and they walk in the living room each of them carrying a couple of bags of groceries.

"Hi Rose, I heard Luke was sick, and well I thought maybe you could use some extra groceries, I didn't know if you could get out." Marcella said.

Well I wondered why Linda had told her, our business didn't need to be known by the whole town. Linda had just gotten engaged to Bill. Of course they had to get married because she was pregnant, it wasn't her first choice, she had had a journalism scholarship all lined up at Ohio State for the coming fall and now that was done.

I said "Oh Marcella you didn't have to do that we're fine." I felt like maybe she was checking up on me.

"Oh well I just thought…" she said.

Marcella looked more worried than I did.

"How's he doing?"

"Oh some fever but doctor gave him a shot of penicillin that should help."

She was a good Italian woman from Cleveland, she knew what it was to want, I guess, but it was hard for me sometimes.

"Well I picked up some ice cream I thought if he couldn't eat it then one of the other kids could. "

Then Caroline came in, you could both see there was ice cream and cookies sticking out the top of the bag.

I wanted to ask her in to sit down, but there wasn't a clear place to sit. Bill was still holding the groceries.

Trying to smile at you girls, trying to get your attention. "Hi Steph, hi Carrie."

I didn't like the way he was friendly with you, I didn't like anything about him.

"Is there anything else I can do to help?" Marcella asked.

It's not charitable, I know but I wanted to say get out of my house so I don't have to stand here in front of my children taking charity from you the mother of the boy who got my daughter pregnant when she never wanted to marry him in the first place.

As if that wasn't enough trouble. And Bill would cause our family plenty more trouble in the future. I don't need to tell you that. So when his Marcella comes standing at the door with the two bags of groceries, I know that there is a lot more in those bags than orange juice and chicken noodle soup; a lot more to make up for than simple neighborly help. I wished I could have just said "woman mind to the sickness in your own house and take your groceries back with you." But then there is always someone else isn't there, another child standing there looking up at the ice cream.

Don't think I've forgotten what happened. I've been thinking all this time, while we've been talking, I've been thinking, maybe I'll never know what would so propel a person out of a town with all the energy you put into your leaving, but maybe I do.

~

Luke got better a course, but when your dad was sick and dying everyone came to visit but not Luke. He was so solitary as a child, didn't like school at all. I used to send them all off to school but Luke would crawl back into the house and hide behind the couch until about noon. He just couldn't go along.

I never will forget one summer day, must have been the same year, it was hot and all the sudden the screen door slams and the kids come running into the kitchen saying, "Mom, there's a police car Mom the police are here!"

Well I think to myself Rusty fell down drunk again. He would come home with a bloody ear or eye now and again. So I go to the door and see two police cars pulled up in front of the house, with the sirens going and the lights flashing.

Back door opens on one of the cars and there's Luke coming out, fat cops on each side. He couldn't have been more than nine or ten years old. Well he's white as a sheet of course, looking at the ground and crying.

"We're looking for Missus Koehner"

"Yes, I am she."

"Is this your son?"

"Yes it is, officer." They're still holding onto him one on each side.

"We found this boy and another, set off an alarm at Foodtown and we were called on suspicion of attempted robbery."

There were three or four officers there, and one of them had his hand on his gun as if we were common criminals.

"We didn't break anything," Luke said. He had a tear going down the dust on his sunburned face. "Howard dared me to kick the door, so I just kicked the ball against it, we were just playing around there."

"They say they just kicked the door accidentally, but this is very serious. Does your son have a record of this behavior? Mam, they may think they were playing around but I call it running from the scene of a crime, had they been two inches taller we would have had to fire."

Can you imagine the officer saying that? I was so mad I was literally dumbstruck. Stood there with my mouth open.

"Yes Mam, if this boy would have been two inches taller, we would have fired."

I thought you malicious son of a bitch. Made me so angry, I was fit to be tied. I wanted to say oh no you would not fire at a child, at a boy running around on a summer day. That is my child, my son, not something you kill you damn fool idiot. That is a child that came from a woman; that is my baby or some other mother's that is not a suspect. You can see who he is and what he is. And you have the nerve to stand there with your hand on your gun and tell me, tell me you almost killed my child. What did you think I would say. Think I'm gonna stand here and say what. Say thank you?

Oh, I have half a notion to call the chief of police right then, but I can't 'cause your father owes court fines and speeding tickets.

"Doesn't seem like a huge offense, officer. They're just boys," I manage to say.

As if I didn't have enough trouble. Oh he was trying to imply of course, that I wasn't watching my children, and was his father home. No. Don't think I don't know that they look at the house, my other children outside, the falling down porch and talk to me like that. Think they'd go out to the country club and say that to a mother? No I don't think so. And the lot of 'em no more educated than a pig in a poke. Shoot at some barefoot boys who are playing in a parking kicking a ball around. Make some claim so you can use your gun and feel important, well I hope you rot in hell the lot of you. I kept thinking, I don't know why exactly, of the *Grapes of Wrath* and how Ma Joad hides her son Tom after he hits the policeman. John Steinbeck knew something. But don't start now comparing me to Ma Joad, please. Still, after that I took the side of the kids if any trouble came up. Especially with the boys cause who else was around to stick up for them?

1968
*Cedar Point. Port Clinton, Ohio*

*This summer has been hotter than any I can remember, but maybe I just don't remember, it's too hot to think. August after all, like a steam bath. Rained last night a little, just heated it up more. Not a breath of air moving through this dining room. Called time and temperature this morning said 98. More than two weeks it's been near that, all over the Midwest. More headlines about the old women in those Chicago high rises, dropping like flies. Poor things. Fact that the bars are air-conditioned doesn't help him. At least I'm working. Heat makes me determined to get to that lake. Been thinking of when we used to go to Grandma's cabin. Always a breeze there. Well just once it would be nice to have a family outing. Doesn't seem too much to ask. These weeks seem to drag. Tired of say-*

*ing no to the children all the time, we can't go there or here, can't have that or this. Just once it would be nice to not have to deny them. All this summer children coming in to wherever I'm sitting, here at the dining room table reading and having a smoke. They're begging me, can we go to the lake, can we go to Cedar Point. But they keep asking can we go somewhere, and I say yes you can go outside and play. I give them credit they walk out to the pool almost every day to swim and we have the tent set up in the back yard so they can sleep out, but that's all.*

*They need a little treat occasionally. The weight of his disease shouldn't weigh so heavily on them. The older children especially, I worry the boys will start to despair before they've even had a chance to try themselves out in life. What with their sisters' husbands over in Vietnam, everyone talking about the Kent State killings, such a terrible tragedy. They need something to relieve that. What's there for a young man to look toward these days. Maybe I worry more than they do, make do with what you have only goes so far, Pollyana. I don't know. What was it Pangloss said? Everything happens for the best, in the best of all possible worlds, I used to believe that but anymore I don't know. Candide wasn't it? French aren't practical. How does it end, after he goes around and loses everything, "tend your own garden" does he say. Stay home and tend your own garden. Like to see him do that in this heat.*

*They've wanted to go up to Cedar Point since school let out. Well it doesn't help having all the neighbor kids come up here on the porch and talk about going up two or three times already, talking about the Blue Streak and the Needle Drop every kid in the neighborhood bragging and little Luke just nodding. Thank God he won that Green Bay Packers football uniform in the Gatorade mail sweepstakes he's been happy ever since that, well he tore the box open and started putting it on in the yard here before I could even get it in the house. We never won anything before.*

*I never had any interest in amusement parks but it's nice*

*being by the lake, and cooler. Better take the trash out. It reeks in this heat. Oh is it lunchtime already must be there's Mr. Cramer next door back from the dairy. Now whose sled dog is that running down the alley, poor animal probably trying to get back to the Arctic, oh lord it's pulling its chain and the stake on the end of it.*

~

"Hi dog, you look hot." Oh it's the Stones' poor thing, why they would keep a Siberian husky in this climate I'll never know. Belongs in the Arctic, like *Call of the Wild,* those blue eyes are striking though.

"Go home dog, go home." Don't want it bothering the kittens in the garage, mother cat comes here you'll be sorry dog. Franky Stone there chasing it.

"Come on Blue, come on boy."

"Lost your dog Frank?"

"Pulled the stake right out of the ground, if Skip gets home and he's not there I'll be in big trouble, there I got him now, come Blue."

"Luke Roy Koehner I hope you're watching that your Mother had to take the trash out herself because she got so tired of asking you to do it."

"We're in the middle of a game Mom."

"You shouldn't be playing football in this heat anyway, you'll have a heatstroke."

~

*Might as well save my breath as talk to those boys. Too hot to insist on anything.*

*Food Town has a special discount this week, buy $20 worth of groceries and get a family pass for only $10, about a $20 dollar saving is what it amounts to. I can just about swing it with what I got last week, paid early because of Labor Day coming up next week but he doesn't know. I'll buy it I just have to get him to drive us tomorrow. I mentioned it and he didn't say no. But he'll take issue with it anything I suggest. He'll find fault*

*with. That's him pulling in. See how drunk he is before I talk
to him. Well he's stopping to throw the football with the boys
in the backyard there so maybe he isn't so bad off.*

~

"Hello."

"Hello, how did the spring get pulled off the screen door
here? I wondered why it wasn't closing."

"It's been off there for the last month, it needs a new hook
for the spring to go into."

"Well what the hell happened to the old one?"

"Who knows, things break. Are we still planning to go to
Cedar Point on tomorrow?

"When?"

"Tomorrow, Wednesday?'

"Wednesday, well why Wednesday?"

"Well that's what you suggested, I don't have to work."

He knows I work Monday, Friday Saturday, those three af-
ternoons a week he drops me at the paper's office. I wonder,
has the drink gone now to his brain?

"Well I don't know how we're all gonna fit in the car to go
that far."

"Well the older girls don't want to go, they have other
things, so it's just the youngest six."

"Well with us that makes eight."

"Yes so four in the front and four in the back. I can hold
little Jo."

"Well I suppose. If that's what you want to do."

"It's not what I want to do, the children."

"Well it's not just the cost of the tickets you know it's everything else when you get up there like how are we going to
feed them and that?"

"We can pack a picnic lunch."

"Oh you know they'll be asking for this and that won't
they."

"Well let 'em ask."

"All right I'm going to see my mother, told her I'd mow her lawn."

~

*Go ahead. Go see your mother. Think she'll give you money for the bar tonight, well maybe she will. I don't know where you get it. Her with her neat little house and her cooking. Why can't I be like his mother that's what he thinks, why don't I stand around all day ironing, and making pie crusts, her with her sixth grade education, and her incessant pedal-powered Singer sewing machine. Oh her peach pies, he says. She can cook. Never occurs to him that the oven here's been broken for a year, or that she has a washer and dryer so she can iron the clean linen all day. Married at fourteen, right off the farm well she's a good woman but God forbid you'd have to ask her a serious question, she'll clap her hands together and say "Is that so!" and smile no matter what you tell her. Course she can't hear and he's getting hard of hearing too. It's congenital. Never occurs to him that it might be harder to keep a house clean with eight children in it. Oh let 'em sit there and talk to her damn parakeet. He's not to be relied on, not in this state. But I'm hoping.*

~

Do you remember this event? I walked over to Food Town with your brothers Tim and Luke, I told them we might be going and they danced around. We're going to Cedar Point we're going to Cedar Point; we're going to tomorrow, are we going? Yes, I think so. We'll see, I have to say that see, what if he's out drinking all night and then to say no to them. The two boys were barefoot, and they had just tarred and graveled the little alleyway that cuts from Pine Street over to the grocery. But they were walking right through the tar, look it's so soft and squishy and their little feet leaving footprints in the tar. Now you'll never get that off your feet, I tell them, and my shoes too, getting black tar all over my shoes, and them sticking to the ground.

Well we got ham for sandwiches and some Oreos and chips, some treats like I said, so we won't have to buy food there, and milk and potatoes that I needed anyway. The boys pushed the grocery cart home. They were all excited now. I asked them to please take the cart back to the grocery, well it's two blocks away, but no it sets there by the porch and five of them walk by it and it doesn't happen unless I beg them, they have no discipline see, discipline comes from a father.

Later that night he came home and he wasn't in too bad a shape. I thought well now he knows the children are watching him, waiting for him, maybe that will straighten him up a little. He even had the nerve to scold me about the groceries, didn't like the way I had bought the groceries. Oh well that's not gonna be enough, he said, you didn't get cheese for the sandwiches, and what are we gonna carry this all in? Well what's wrong with a paper bag? I say, and he says, now we're not going to walk around carrying a paper bag all day, oh he's always worried about how something is going to look to the outside world but doesn't even notice whether his children have enough to eat. You didn't get anything to drink he says, they can drink water I say. And you children stood around and watched us arguing wondering if that meant we wouldn't go, but I knew his arguing meant that we would.

Do you remember how it started out? Well we got up early and I made the sandwiches, we packed up a bottle of water with ice, and all, get all the kids in the car.

The car was parked there in front of the garage. Dad starts up the engine and oh there's a terrible squealing sound and a big burst of fur comes wafting out of the engine, like a huge storm of dandelion fluff in the wind, a terrible cloud of it right out over the hood. I recognize the color, but I don't say.

"What in the hell," he says, turns the car off.

"What was that, what was it?" all you children are yelling.

He goes and opens the hood and you children start to get out.

"You just stay in the car now." He's yelling and cursing, "Oh for God's sake."

I knew. I got out to see if I could help him. Well when I heard the squeal I thought it sounded like a kitten, and sure enough a kitten had crawled up there into the engine and when the fan belt went on, well, you can imagine. It was terrible. He went and got a grocery bag, and the dustpan and scooped up the poor little torn body, and closed it. I thought we should bury it but he said a dog would find it so he wrapped it up in newspaper and put it in the garbage can with the lid on tight. The kids had the windows rolled down in the car, the boys saying, I want to see. No you're not, he said, just stay in the car. That was how the day started. You and your sister were crying for the poor little kitten. Which one was it, you wanted to know, was it one of the black ones with the white paws, or the calico? But we couldn't say right then.

"Well now don't cry, there wasn't anything anyone could do, it was an accident, that happens, God has his plans."

I hadn't seen mother cat, but I worried for her when she returned to the dark garage and tried to count them up.

We went up Rt. 68, I used to drive that way with my father when he went up to the lake to fish, or in earlier years when the Healys had the cottage there and we were small children.

"Are we going to see the beach," you wanted to know. You were set on seeing a beach. Joseph was on my lap in the front and kept crawling over into the back seat and then back it was hot of course though we had the windows down. We had gotten up early, so the boys slept, and Carrie read her Nancy Drew book.

When we got there of course the older kids wanted to go one way and the younger kids another. They weren't tall enough to go on the bigger rides. I can't quite recall but that we all went in different directions, I had said let's make a point to meet back here in two hours, at this picnic spot, and they all said yes.

I remember you and I rode the gondola that carries you over the park, and how I held little Joseph worried that he was small enough to fall through the bar that holds you in place. And there was the new ride, the Log Run where you're in a boat that slides down into a pool of water and everyone gets wet, and we did that several times. But somewhere around there you were lost with your sister Carrie. The two of you wandering around, looking for the beach, which you finally found, but it was on the other side of a chain link fence, and no way to get to it. By the time you got back the lunch was mostly gone and the cookies all eaten. So all summer you had been waiting for this day but when it came, you ended up pressing your face against a fence and walking around hungry and thirsty, or so you said. We spent a little time in Frontier Town just you and I, together. They had crafts people making soap and candles. There was a blacksmith and a glassblower twisting big globes of liquid glass, which you liked, and I reminded you that your grandfather was a glassblower.

Meanwhile your father had gone off to have a look around, and get a cold beer to have with lunch. Of course he didn't stop there, and by afternoon when I saw him again he was unsteady on his feet. By then it was getting to be around five and everyone was getting tired and hungry again. So we get in the car.

Patty always had to have the radio.

"CKLW Motor City Music, Bringing you the Motown Sound with the Sizzling Sound of the Summer Countdown…"

"Do we have any cookies left I didn't get any."

"They're all gone."

"I'm hungry."

"It's gonna be 'Light My Fire,' *try to set the night on FIIIIYAAA, yea'…*."

"That's enough of that. Now turn it off it gets on my nerves."

"Mom I got sunburned look at my shoulder."

"I told you to wear sleeves and you wouldn't listen."

It took forever to get out of that parking lot as I recall, we sat there in a long line of idling cars, had all the windows down, still our legs were sticking to the hot plastic seats, packed in against one another, and I could see that your father was looking sleepy already.

I said, "You better take the smaller roads, so you can take your time." I knew he wouldn't have to go as fast, seeing what condition he was in, so we did go down through Fostoria way. He would be OK for a minute, but it was awful hot and muggy, was like the motion of the car was putting him to sleep, and a few times he drifted side to side. We got into Fostoria, you know that's a railroad center, and we stopped to wait for a long train there, well he started to doze off at the crossing. I reached over and took the keys out of the ignition. He didn't even notice when the train had passed.

I said. "Alright we'll just stay right here and the cars behind us will have to go around." And they did.

There we were at the railroad crossing with him asleep, literally at the wheel. Oh I never wished so much that I could drive as I did right then. Bess and I were going to learn to drive when we got out of the Navy but we never did, I know I must have been the last woman in America didn't know how to drive. I thought now what am I going to do. Evening coming on and still thirty miles from home, stuck at a railroad crossing, police will come and take him to jail sure as hell.

Tim was about 14, he said, "I'll drive, I'll drive us."

"Now nofody belse needs to drie this car," your father says waking up.

"Oh yes they do." I said to him, I was angry then. "I have the keys and you're not getting them. I'm not gonna sit here and let you kill us all."

"Now relax. For God's sake now there's nothing wrong with me."

"Sure there isn't, you just try to take these and I will get the police here. You can roll it over to the curb there, just take a nap then, or get some coffee somewhere."

"Now just gimme the keys."

"No I won't." I wouldn't do it.

Well you little ones in the back were starting to plead and cry, I want to go home, how are we going to get home. Little Joseph had been sleeping against the door woke up and started crying.

And you piped up shouting at me, "We never should have tried to go to Cedar Point to begin with, then the kitten wouldn't be dead and we wouldn't all be stuck here."

I thought you might be right, I thought now God's punishing me for trying to put pleasure in our lives when the fates had ordained against it. Why I couldn't seem to learn that I don't know.

"I'll drive, I know how to drive," Tim said.

"No I will," Rebecca argued, "I'm older."

"But I've practiced more," Tim said, "but if the police stop us what are we going to say?"

"Well, I'll just have to tell them what happened. He's not fit to drive, if he doesn't kill us he'll run into someone else."

"Alright now Russ you scoot over."

"Now I don't need him to drive."

"Let him drive, Dad, don't, you can't." Carrie and Luke are crying, and then little Joseph half hysterical screams, "Dad let Tim drive!"

And so he did. Always did whatever little Jo said.

I gave Tim the keys.

"Go slowly Tim."

"I will."

We got onto Route 224 and went along pretty smoothly.

"Gas tank's on empty but I think we have enough to get home," Tim said.

It was starting to get dusk, and lights were coming on in the houses along the road. The big red Bonneville cruised along, you children were quiet. It took us awhile but we got home. Pulled up under the maple tree out front, and the doors on all sides opened, we jump out like swimmers off a sinking ship. Left him there sleeping in the front seat. I carried little Joseph up the creaking porch steps.

*First fire-fly out there by the garage, the green light against the grey, I've never thought about it but it's interesting that their light comes and goes without sound, just a lighting and a darkness and a quiet around it. Yet it has a kind of music.*

It was sad for the children, but they joked about it in later years. I had hoped to make a treat for them, but it seems like I had gone against the nature of what our lives were then and that just made things worse.

I thought of that day when Dad won the horse race so big, the same day his mother went to her deathbed.

So after that I didn't try too much to make our situation seem more promising than it actually was. I don't know if that was a good idea or not.

# V

## VISITATIONS

### 1981-82
### *Northern California and Oregon*

WHEN you live in the same place for a long time and don't have a chance to travel, it doesn't occur to you that you're in a place at all. You never see the edge of where you are to realize you're in the middle of it. You don't think, "Oh I've been living in Ohio," until you get out of it.

I remember so clearly that first time I went to California, to see your older sister Jane. I arrived very late at night into San Francisco. Just as soon as we stepped outside the air was so different so cool and invigorating, then we were on the freeway, everyone driving so fast and the lights on the hillsides draped around in all directions, we drove across the Bay Bridge so high up above everything, I felt like I was crossing over into some other world entirely.

Jane lived at that time with the Italian boy from Michigan, Frank Murello his name was, and I liked him. Well everybody I met there was from somewhere else. New York, or the Midwest it seemed. I could never figure out why they weren't at work all day, but they all seemed to have odd hours. They had a big old cedar-shingled house in the Berkeley Hills, which they shared with another couple, do you remember that place? Anyway, they lived together despite not being married. I didn't object, why they were both plenty old enough, and I was used to you children going against the church by then.

First morning I woke up in the upstairs bedroom of that house; the sun was shining in and a soft wind was lifting up the curtains with a wonderful scent I had never known before. So I went to the window to look out into the yard and there was a jasmine vine, growing up the whole side of the house with huge white sprays like ruffles. Must have been early April. I had left our frozen yard in Ohio where there was barely a crocus poking up to this. And there was Jane down in the green grass in a nightgown, brushing out her wet blond hair, and shaking it out in the warming sun.

"Well good morning Lady Godiva," I called down.

"Good morning Mom, you ready for some coffee, I'll bring it up."

"Now you don't need to do that, I can come down soon as I pull myself together."

Well no sooner did I start to dress than she was at the door with my breakfast tray, coffee, fresh croissants, giant strawberries, and little vase of that jasmine. Never will forget that. Such a lovely morning, and the light there so vivid and crisp, it seemed like another sun shone there altogether. Everywhere you looked there was something to see, hills everywhere. All the young people out walking, or running. No one ever sitting still. Getting away from home, from your dad and brothers lightened my spirits of course, but I hadn't expected how beautiful it would be, I felt so free, like a girl again.

We spent some days looking at San Francisco, drove across the Golden Gate Bridge to Mount Tamalpais. I'd never seen a view like the city of San Francisco from there, like a little toy model of white blocks on a green cloth.

I thought now in Ohio we never get what you would call a view at all. No high ground to look out from. I wonder if that makes people different, that they never get up and away enough to look back on where they are. Until they get to the point I'm at. But you know what I mean.

Well I didn't know then that I'd be spending so much time visiting there in years to come, that I would have three children living there. But that first trip I never will forget because after that I had a picture of where you all were, and that was a comfort to me. I could go there in my mind and be closer to you.

You were living in Oregon at that time. Remember you drove down with your old friend Lisa, the one who sang in the all girl country band. The plan was to take me up to Oregon, so I could see Highway 1, and your place of course. Lisa had a big old red convertible I remember, she pulled right up to the front of the house and you both jumped out like rabbits, so excited about everything. We drove up Highway 1, taking the loop through the redwood trees. It surprised me the way those little pullouts off the highway put you right into the forest. We stepped out of the car into a circular grove of old redwood trees with sunbeams floating down through the spiraled branches like kaleidoscope, golden pollen hovering in the air. All somber and grand it was, a little like things are here. I'd never been in a forest like that, giant ferns everywhere and the ground so clear and soft underfoot with layers of needles and moss. Maybe quiet on account of the age of the trees, maybe time has a kind of weight, I don't know. We didn't even talk there, what could you say? Seemed like the inside of a church or cathedral, or did John Muir say that? Of course I had read John Muir, and Jack London, but somehow it didn't prepare me for the size of things out West.

We started to pass the lumber mills up there near Eureka. Huge hills of bare logs all stacked up and waiting to be cut into lumber. And the mills there spewing steam, like they would boil and slice up the whole world if they could get their hands on it. Oh and not just one, but miles and miles of those stacks all lined up, the logs sorted by size, just waiting to be cut up. It seemed like enough lumber to build the world over again; boggled my mind that there ever could be that many trees in the world.

Well Ohio had been a huge forest before the settlers came, but it that had been 200 years ago. I thought how the felling of the forests had marched across the country until it got this far west and I was looking at the last of it. Which isn't quite accurate I know, you have to account for the Great Plains but other than that it's true. You were up in arms about the clear cutting they were doing up in Oregon. "They're shaving whole mountain sides off and bulldozing the streams, just to get at the lumber." And I said well of course they would, you can't stop progress, if there's a buck to be made someone will go take it. Sometimes I think you don't have a practical bone in your body.

You said you were living in a cabin out in the country in the Coastal Mountains, but I couldn't picture it. Lisa was from around there wasn't she that was how you had found it? We went down a little winding mountain road through solid ever-green forest, big stands of Douglas fir and giant cedar, rivers every hundred yards. Was like following the *Journals of Lewis and Clark*. We turned into a valley lined with green pastures and evergreen hills rose up and spread along that side of the valley like a curtain.

We drove up a dirt driveway to your little wooden cabin; it sat on the hillside, with a little porch looking out, there was a white cat on the railing that jumped off. There was one room downstairs with a wood cook stove, and a ladder up to a sleeping loft.

"I'll get the fire started," you said, "and make some tea." I thought well all this traveling and we haven't progressed at all in these years. But that's another story; oh I seem to be rambling here. Where was I?

∼

*She keeps saying it's Lisa's twenty-fifth birthday we have to all get ready for the big party. I guess nobody here ever does go to a job. Been here two days and no one's spoken of one. This morning I saw a couple of boys walking down the road carrying big machetes scared me half to death, turns out they were on their way to trim the Christmas trees in that field. Apparently you need to trim them fairly often, they all walk around with a big machetes, wonder they don't cut their legs off. Party is to be in Jerry Cotswell's pasture, wherever that is. I enjoyed meeting him last night. Big burly fellow in suspenders, merry blue eyes, everyone here looks like a character out of an old Western. Says he's the great grandson of the man who originally settled the valley, came out here on the Oregon Trail. They have two or three homesteads dotted along the valley here small white houses and those immense silver barns. Told me he loves living here, never wants to live anywhere else. All these young people out here building little cabins in the mountains, growing gardens, one of the girls' husbands does horse logging. Girls this morning talking about blackberry jam recipes it's been some years since I heard that.*

*God how my parents tried to get away from all this and here they are. Stephanie gathered eggs for our breakfast from her chickens, wants me to come to the quilting bee at the WOW hall tomorrow. Woodsmen of the World, never heard of it before. Apparently every little town has a WOW hall. Oh those goats are bleating again, neighbor woman was milking them last night, makes cheese out of the milk. I didn't trust the cheese she offered, none of it's pasteurized of course. I don't know what they have against having some convenience in their lives.*

*Seems this party is a big to do. Wants me to sit out here and spread some blankets out. They brought me a chair but I can sit on a blanket. Asked if I could help them set up the table but they seem to have plenty of people to help. People coming in from Corvallis, and Eugene and Newport, come for the whole day of course, and well once you drive that far. I've never seen so many VW vans in my life, and pickup trucks. Boys digging a pit to roast spareribs, have a whole pile of firewood there. Those other boys are setting up a raised stage at the edge of the meadow. I guess they're the local band Ramblin Wrecks, she was all excited about them coming. Who's watching those boys running barefoot through the meadow, now one of them's on top of the barn, throwing sticks, he better come down from there those boys are up to no good I can tell. I see those other men smoking marijuana over there by that truck, that one with the beard looks like Moses, even older than me, well I'll look the other way.*

～

You were worried about what I might see as if I hadn't seen all that before. During the Depression men used to smoke Jimson weed we called it. Though it was nice to have someone worrying about what I thought of things, not that anyone at home ever did. I think you found Oregon more unusual than I did; maybe there were parts I didn't see. But you were eager to introduce me to everyone, like I was evidence of the New World or something.

"Steph is this your mom? Oh I am so happy to meet you. Did you come all the way from Ohio? Well your visit is just another reason to celebrate. I made my famous rhubarb pie, did you taste this homemade mead?"

"Mom this is Polly, OK honey I will."

"You must be Stephanie's mother. I'm glad you finally made it, she has been talking about you coming for the last month or two."

"I know it's awful rare that we get to visit."

"Better get a plate before they're all gone. I gathered this green salad from plants in the woods and make sure you taste that salsa and beans that's Melon's specialty."

"What was your name dear?"

"I'm Melon, well Mary Ellen but they call me Melon."

"What a nice shoulder bag you have, the needlework on that is just beautiful."

"I got it in Oaxaca. We go down every winter. When it starts raining non-stop. You know."

"Stephanie talks about you so much I thought I just had to come and meet you."

182 ～ BARBARA ROETHER

"Well I'm glad you did."

First time I can remember us sitting on a blanket together enjoying music, but you keep asking me if I need anything. What would I need? Wanted to sit and listen to a song, see something new in the world just like you do. Wanted to look and listen to where I was. Living out in the country is more like living always was everywhere. Maybe everybody does, feel less separated when they're out on the land.

We ate from the long table of potluck dishes that were set out. Fresh greens, sorrel and lambs quarter gathered from the woods, lots of flowers in the salads, nasturtiums, borage, pansies; oh there was salmon, and crab and watermelon, brown rice and bean salad. Introduced me to some young man, who caught the salmon from his boat off the coast of Newport.

The afternoon wore on. The music kept playing, all you girls kept dancing; all dressed like gypsies spinning the little children around by their arms, gonna pull their arms out of the socket like that I thought. You were so excited for me to know about everyone you knew, trying to talk me into your world. I do recall that woman lived next door to Lisa, she came by to talk her name was Helena, fine boned and small, very shy. I gathered she was a Chicago heiress who had decided to be a hippie instead of a society matron. She had the goats and a little cheese shop in town; which sort of shocked her family in Chicago who owned a famous department store; but she never mentioned their name. If you met her you wouldn't know where she came from, well she spoke nicely that was a clue, a course you don't have to be poor to want to get away. Some years later she was the one gave Lisa her farm house then moved to France, was so generous to everyone you said, and then went one day went and drowned herself in a river like Virginia Woolf, put stones in the pocket of her rain coat and jumped off a bridge. Terrible tragedy. But that was some years later wasn't it? Where was I?

It was nearing dusk. Your friend gave us her toddler to

watch. A fat little boy named River, so she could go play her guitar with the band. Come sit, you said and the boy sat on your lap.

I always remember that day, it seemed like just one day when we were in the same field sitting together, and the springtime sun was warm. Watching the women dance, clapping the babies' hands together.

I was happy maybe in a way you had never seen before, or remembered seeing, because we were away from what troubled us; there among children and music and the warm fresh air. Someone had just given us plastic glasses full of homemade beer, and we were laughing and singing on the blanket.

Tall tongues of orange flame shot out the loft door of the barn all at once. And a trail of black smoke went into the sky.

"Uh oh it looks like the barn is on fire!" I called out.

"Oh no it looks like the barn is on fire" and the call went out, everyone started to say, "The barn is on fire!"

"Where are the kids?"

"Tell the band to stop."

"Find Terry and tell him."

"Oh no, it's catching the grass."

"Quick get the hose."

"The barn is on fire."

There was running and shouting, mothers worried to find their children. I carried the baby toward the road. You ran to find Terry. In a few more minutes flames were licking out of the top of the barn. Somebody said to call the volunteer fire department, but it turned out they were mostly already there.

"The truck's coming but it will take twenty minutes."

"Make a bucket brigade, bucket brigade from the creek."

For a while we stood in line and passed buckets to the man behind us. But there was no use. By now the flames were engulfing the barn and the new summer's hay inside. The flames covered the outline of the barn perfectly neatly; walls of flame rising into the gathering darkness. The entire barn was sheathed in transparent orange flame.

There was not much anyone could do.

The fire swept across the field in places, where embers landed, sweeping here and there with the wind, we all scattered toward the road, the flames at our heels.

I held onto the baby, though I should have taken the blanket, it was a pretty old quilt, I should have grabbed it.

It was left behind and burned.

Sharon came to find me, "Oh my God I saw Stephanie and she didn't have River I thought oh my God, but she said my Mom has him, thank you so much."

She took the boy as if he had been in some terrible danger, of course I wouldn't have let anything happen to a baby.

We stood and watched the flames continue with roaring and power enough to light the faces of those of us who sat in the field. Watching. Watching the glow spread to the green hills behind like the sun was setting a second time.

People stood in rows by their cars, or vans. Some packed up to leave. One mother was a little frantic; her boy was one of the older ones. The boys were found hiding in the woods. One of them had matches. No one said very much, once all the children were counted.

The roof fell in and a shower of sparks lit up the sky like a scarlet snow. It was still burning red and glowing when we went home.

What a shame we said. His grandfather's barn; was the oldest building in the valley.

"Lucky he didn't lose his house."

"That's for sure. Everything's so dry."

～

Seems like the warmth and happiness of that day, was connected to the fire somehow, burning down that beautiful old barn? Was like the impact of our two worlds meeting up sent up a spark that flew up and caught the nearest fuel to burning. I have often wondered what omen that was. Must our pleasure always be tainted with worry and loss?

Later that night we stepped out onto the porch and could still see the smoke curling up to the sky at the end of the valley. Very next morning, you woke up with a fever of 103 and I always thought it was some coincidence. Burning hot you were with a dry heat that seemed to be coming from deep inside, awful sick, looked like strep to me but we couldn't get you to the doctor until the second day. Well when we finally got you in the clinic they took your temperature, had a fever of 104, said they didn't see so many people who walked through the door with a fever that high, so I told them we came from Ohio where extremes of temperature were the norm. Oh they laughed. Turned out it was strep and that fever went so high that clumps of your hair fell out, you had terrible bald spots.

All our clothes, and the rooms smelled of smoke for days after that. As if we too had been through some fire.

∼

Some years after that, there were five of you living out on the West Coast. Horace Greeley said 'Go West Young Man.' Well mine certainly did. My brother Jim said I had the most fiddle-footed crew he ever did see.

You didn't come to Luke's wedding in Portland when he married Martha, that was a nice affair. Your dad and I flew out for that. Then they had those two beautiful little girls looked just like Luke, blonde blue-eyed. Regan and Keely, they must have been five and six when she left Luke for the rock and roll drummer if you can imagine, told Luke he wasn't exciting enough. Well the man worked as a carpenter laying floors all day, and he was tired when he got home; but she wanted to go out dancing. A'course the drummer left her after a few months and she went into a downward spiral, had to sell the house he had worked so hard to get for them, gained about 100 pounds, not to make snide comments about a woman's weight but in her case. I don't know what she was thinking, not thinking about anyone else that's for sure. Never seen the like. And he never could get over her. Oh he kept talking for years how he thought they would be getting back together. I think he really loved her.

Seems to me hardly anybody gets what they deserve. Falls short one way or the other. Always something.

Around the same time your sister Jane married the famous symphony conductor and they got that house in the Hollywood Hills, that wonderful old Mediterranean style house, with balconies everywhere looking over the lights of the city. Huge place, and just the two of them in it. I never knew why Jane didn't have any children, I guess as the oldest of ten she had enough of children. At any rate your father never liked to go and stay there you know because he worried Vladek, her husband, would think we were freeloading, or taking advantage of him. He didn't like to be taken out to dinner to places he couldn't afford to pay his share, he said, but I think his tremor embarrassed him too, that his hands shook at the table. A couple of times we did go but he was always uncomfortable.

Jane was certainly always generous with us. One day the doorbell rang and it was the UPS man with a big box for me. I wondered if it was a mistake because it wasn't Christmas or my birthday and a big label from Saks Fifth Avenue on the carton. But I opened it and inside was the most beautiful hand stitched Italian nightgown and a floor length blue velour robe. Remember that robe? I wore it for years it was so warm. Well inadvertently the price tag had been left on and your sister Linda and I had to laugh, as the price equaled both our weekly paychecks combined.

But we were happy for her. Vladek was a good man, escaped the damn Communists in Poland and worked his way up in the business.

They built their place in Big Sur a few years later. Have to have two houses of course. Last place on earth I'd imagine living but it is so beautiful. Worried me to take children up there, one false move and somebody could go over the cliff. Well we talked once to her neighbor Ray the surfer. His house was sliding down the cliff into the ocean. Did you ever go down and look at that place. His doorway is all catawampus like a child's drawing, and the garden he planted, grapefruit trees and all, can you imagine grapefruit trees, well they are about ten yards further away than they used to be. But he stays on.

Things were certainly easier for your father and me in our later years, once we retired. We were never rich mind you but he had a good pension from the county, and I had my Social Security so we could afford to travel a little and that's where I was going with this. Big Sur.

What's the name of that beach down the hills from where their place is? I know you used to go down there a lot. You and Jane were always close. Jane got married on that beach as I recall, we had the wedding party later in Hollywood but I think they had the actual ceremony right on that beach.

Pfeifer Beach, we took your son there when he was a baby. I remember that trip when I came, it was soon after he was born.

1994
*San Francisco, California*

*I'm gonna call her up in San Francisco today. I wish she were married, don't know why she doesn't get married, if he is divorced, why they would want their child to be born out of wedlock is a shame, they seem to like each other. Well it's not my business but I don't want Aunt Marybelle to know, well she spreads the gossip all over town. Whole town will know. I could help her though if I go out there. Leave Earl here by himself. Linda comes over once a day from the County office around the block, she can check on him. They always got along better than anybody.*

*It's her first and I never did really get to go stay with any of the girls when they were having babies. I'm seventy-four by God. Who was it in the Dickens story where the woman is doing the wrangle and had all the little children that she sort of ignores in order to take care of the orphan children, Ms. Wrangle? I'm gonna call her up.*

"Hi it's your mother."

"Hi Mom."

"Hi honey, I was trying to make some plans here, I'm thinking of coming to stay after you have the baby. I was planning I could come around April 30th, what do you think of that?"

"That's great."

"Plan to stay for two weeks. That alright?"

"Yes" you said, "of course."

But you were worried, you had just gotten together with Paul, it would be more crowded. You worried that you would have to take care of me as well as the baby. You worried about my heart trouble, my trouble with stairs, about the long flight up from the sidewalk to your first floor Victorian. And you were worried about having such attention focused on you. We had never had the chance to talk for two weeks and it frightened you. When I got there you wouldn't let me do much, I offered to cook.

"What do you mean you don't know how to make a pot roast?"

"Well I never cook meat."

"You need to eat some meat if you're nursing, need the protein."

We sat in the little garden that you had made out the back door. The back stairs to the two apartments above yours came down there. In a narrow strip of yard there was an avocado tree and lots of potted plants.

We were dressing him.

"Put the pretty clothes on him now because they grow so fast, you won't get a chance to use them, they certainly won't get worn out."

We dressed him in a French-made white suit with a ruffled collar, there were small green leaves embroidered around the edge.

"You two could go out. I'll keep him."

"Maybe later."

It was another day, we were in your kitchen eating burritos, you had bought around the corner.

"Let's bathe the baby, bring him into the kitchen. I thought we could bathe him right here on the table."

"Alright but I usually do it in the tub, but OK, I'll bring the tub out there."

"Well I thought I could help if we did it here on the table I can't bend over too easy."

He had a small blue hot water pad that was to be filled with warm water to lie on as we washed him so he stayed warm. You made the water awful hot I thought, thinking it would quickly cool off but it turned his skin pink.

"He's awfully red honey I think you have the water too hot."

"I think he is alright he likes it," you turned him to see his warm red back, thinking that it was good if he could sweat.

I still thought it was too hot.

"Best to test it on your own skin first. I'll finish up if you need to get some work done."

"Alright."

"Don't you have some baby shampoo."

"Yes here."

"Always be careful of the ears, you don't want to get water in his ears."

The light came through the stained glass windows that covered the bottom panes of the two windows in the kitchen. The windows looked right into the neighbor's little yard, where a woman named Maria grew herbs, she handed us a bunch of herbs one day, she said for stomach if we had any problems. The windows had a flower pattern of pink and yellow tulips against a background of green. All full of light.

I washed his head thoroughly with my expert attention, into the crevices of legs and buttocks.

"There, there, handsome boy, there, there."

I took his two ankles in my old wrinkled hand and another hand expert behind his head and lifted him from the bath water. Then changed the old water to clear.

~

*How many babies have I bathed, did it at the kitchen sink in later years, wrapped them in my apron as I took them out. A boy baby will urinate on you from the feel of the water or the cool air once they're out you have to be careful, but they like the bath, because that's where they've been the most in the warm water, they go back to where they came from.*

*I never saw a baby who didn't like water. Course I want her to do it I don't want to seem to take over anything, she needs to get confident herself. I enjoy this part as much as any, when there is the bath and cleaning and the wrapping up and then it's done, for the child you've done what was needed. It's so hard to do that as they get older, what they need is so ongoing or unfinished and not so close to hand. Not what can be worked out of an ear with a twisted corner of a washcloth, or smoothed over with some baby oil. Not the oil that you can massage into the scalp gently, mind the soft spot, to get rid of cradle cap, of course the bath does make me think of getting him baptized.*

*I do wish they were married. I could take him to a local church maybe some kind Mexican priest in the neighborhood would baptize him. I could stand in for him. I don't remember who stood in for Stephanie. I wonder does soap remove the sacrament of water from the water. And then too I know in baptism the water is supposed to be running, so the soul is washed, washed in the blood of the lamb.*

"Here little lambkin, so you like the bath, well yes, yes you do. Oh there's a smile already."

*I would like him to be baptized to protect him, but I don't know that he isn't already. Maybe each child is baptized in the water of the womb, or getting born is baptism enough, from the darkness into the light. It is a painful journey isn't it little one.*

"Don't you cry now. Is him cold?" *A little more hot water there, there.*

*Babies cry when they're cold, but they just cry too. They cry in the afternoon especially if it's overcast. I've heard it from my ten, and fifteen grandchildren, for no reason you can find. They just cry I think for the general suffering in the world. They cry ahead of time at what's in store for them. Just sounds like to me that they know it's coming.*

*I don't know about original sin. If it is there. And if it is, can it be taken away by the hands of a man the baby has never known? Not that there aren't some holy priests, oh there are. I'm not contradicting the Pope. But if this fine boy has original sin well it might be that I'm the one to chase it out here with Ivory soap and water. Maybe don't even need the soap. John baptized Jesus, not the other way around, to show that the power of grace rests in the common man. Or so I take it.*

*Maybe that's the only kind of baptism there really is anyway, what some other human being can do for another with love and kindness, without our asking. That's the real blessing not having to ask for it*

*I guess this child is my disciple. Child of my child. The resurrection of the flesh and the life of the world to come. Never truer words were spoken than that. All children are the life of the world to come.*

*See your eyes still stained with the blue of the sky or the robes of Mary mother of God. My tiny disciple I have flown a long distance to see you to know you so I could rub my big old hand here on your tiny chest; over your chest where I can feel your heart beat quick against the bones, beating like wings, like a moth that you catch in your hands to put outside, the strum and flutter of a moth cupped in two hands. The beating of your eager little heart. All children are eager. They are eager for life.*

*But there's no hurry little one. No hurry.*

*The sacrament of baptism says we die into the water to be born into life everlasting. By joining Jesus in death, we join him in everlasting life; or that's the catechism and it has a logic about it. If you need logic, well men need logic. That's who thought that up. For a mother, now, logic doesn't always answer what we see and know. A baby tells me children are where you find everlasting life and that's where they came from.*

*Maybe every woman's womb is the cave where Christ was laid to rest, to rise again, I have always thought but must never say, such a sacrilege.*

"What blue eyes you have, little man, what blue eyes."

"Oh it isn't raining rain you know, it's raining violets isn't it yes, it is."

*Well it also says in the catechism if there is no priest around and you are a Christian you can baptize by reciting the Trinitarian formula. Can't hurt. Over the forehead three cupfuls, I hope it doesn't matter that it's poured from a blue plastic cup.*

*The first one, I baptize you in the name of the Father, another, in the name of the Son, don't cry now, in the name of the Holy Ghost, amen. I'll anoint his head here on the temples, as Christ was the anointed one, now you are like him, marked with chrism of the chosen.*

*Try to get the lid off that calendula oil without letting go. I don't want to let go.*

*Three cups of water, and the oil, now you are baptized.*

*What is this original sin anyway, just some man saying that what comes from a woman can't be all perfect. God just being jealous he can't have babies himself. Original sin I don't know. I think that those of us here on the earth already when the babies come are the original sin, the sin they come into. And it can't be cut, not like the umbilical cord is cut at birth, the cord that carries blood and oxygen between the two of us, maybe cutting that is the original sin. The theologians say that original sin represents our share of human suffering except that*

*that would make it seem there was an equality to the suffering*
*and we know that's not true.*

2002
*Blanchardville*

Was always a sadness to have my grandchildren so far away.
Remember you came to Ohio to fetch me that one year. Your
sister Carrie wanted me to come out to Sacramento for her
daughter's first communion. It was March I think. Not a good
month anywhere. Well she had to work and I wasn't well
enough by then to travel on my own so you came to Ohio to
fly back with me. For some reason, even before you arrived
back you were a nervous wreck and I couldn't find any reason
for it. You didn't have too many children, I think and you
didn't work too much, you were doing freelance work. I wondered if I made you nervous for some reason, but you said it
was just that Paul didn't have work and so on. But it occurred
to me that you didn't have anyone to talk to close by, I mean
no one who really knew you. No one very close except your
husband, and that's always fraught.

Anyway you were helping me pack. You were helping me
pack as if the two of us could be taking off to somewhere new
and better, even if I was just going to visit my daughter who
lived a few hours from you. We sat upstairs in my room.

"Well get the middle sized suitcase out of the hall closet
where your dad kept it." He was gone by then.

"Oh maybe I'll need the larger one if I'm to stay two weeks."

I opened the door and you took it out of the dark where
a few of Rusty's old sweaters were still hanging, I had given
most of them away but it seemed wrong to give them all away,
just in case. Just in case what he needed them? I don't know.

In my room we opened the suitcase and put it on the floor.

"Now let's see. What do I have hanging there?"

"You want your blue suit?"

"Guess I better take that for church huh."

"It's nice."

"Then honey can you get down there and find the navy shoes, that go with that, they're just sling back, those are they."

"How cold is it there now?"

"It varies, its warmer in Sacramento than San Francisco."

"I know it is. Well get that green pantsuit out for me will you. The cotton one. There's a sweater that goes with it. Do you see it? Would you like any of those blouses hanging there, please take some I have so many.

"No Mom I don't need them."

"Well I have too many things. I want to get rid of things."

I was packing to go to California where I was going to visit but it occurred to me that you were doing the same. You weren't going home there any more than I was.

～

How long have you lived in San Francisco now, and I wonder why you still don't feel at home there. Oh I was awful worried about you after the quake of '89. Sat all evening watching on TV and not knowing how or where you were, and other people calling and asking me "How's Stephanie?" and I'm saying "I haven't heard, I haven't heard". You were living alone then, it was before you met Paul and I thought well who's going to know if you're OK or not? Sure there are corners and blocks that are familiar like that one at Twenty-second and Mission but they're not yours. That Victorian apartment building in the Mission, fifteen years you lived there. It's fresh painted now, but still white, the two flats on each floor with the black wrought iron railings winding along the stairway in the middle. There are dozens just like it in the city, and the only thing different is your memory of what happened there.

Wonder how fifteen years you could live and a child raised there but not any sign of that now, or of the curtains with blue sailboats that hung there when he was small or his little hand pulling them aside to peer down at the sidewalk where his father might be coming home. Not a soul who knows you there now, isn't that strange, and a whole city like that, or a country where people's memories are left behind in places they never see?

San Francisco especially, I think, it being so hemmed in by water doesn't blend away at its edges into the countryside like Ohio towns but drops away to the bay or the ocean. Was it ever your home, though you live there still? Well you spent some years away in New York, in Africa, but you keep going back to San Francisco, so I wonder what you find there.

∼

Turns out you had been in the publishing office down near Jackson Square, directing a photographer how to photograph the baseball game when all the sudden the building shook and shook the red brick walls, and after the shaking that went on and on there was a thin red cloud hung in the air. And then the handsome young husband of one of the girls you worked with ran into the office and took her in his arms saying "Natalie, Natalie you're OK." He worked further down Montgomery Street in the Wells Fargo building, and in the minutes after the quake he had run down ten flights of stairs and run at full speed up the crowded street. But no one was to come and look for you, you felt that sharply. No one even asked how you were getting home, your own fault for always seeming so capable. And so you went through the streets. *"Through half deserted streets and muttering retreats",* well it wasn't a wasteland but that comes to mind.

You walked outside and so many windows had shattered, was like a sprinkling of snowfall of glass on the streets but not much more really a few fallen bricks here and there. Passersby said they were closing off Market Street, they said not to walk down Market, and so you went up through North Beach to Telegraph Hill, then up Nob Hill, where groups of frightened tourists were standing in the square, they'd been evacuated from their fancy hotel rooms and were bunched together and afraid to move while waiters from the Mark Hopkins served iced drinks from trays.

Sirens whined in the distance. You kept walking, uphill and down across the city, then turned down Polk Street.

Only the addicts went on with their normal lives, sleeping in urined doorways, dreaming of older disasters then this one. You passed a narrow apartment building where some years earlier a boy named Brad had lived, he was a good poet but took heroin too, you had spent a few nights with him there in that building, and the memory found you as you walked by. Storekeepers stood in front of their shops watching; radios played. You stopped in a corner-store for a bottle of water, there was no power inside it was dark, the Indian man couldn't open his cash register, he showed you by gesture, he didn't speak English, but you gave him a dollar he gave you the change, his fingers touched the palm of your hand. It was calm in the dim shadows you stood and took a drink of cold water.

A few blocks more, then the golden dome of City Hall rose into view, shining bright over the Civic Center square where the network news trucks were clustered like giant insects, with antennae and flashing lights for eyes. You stepped carefully over the thick black cables that led to the cameras that were broadcasting images of your besieged city to my living room in Ohio, but still I could not find you or know if you were alright who walked past the cameras unnoted, past the noise of what is broadcast into the silent obscure story of your own going-onward walking.

Thinking, I am a woman walking home, if my home is not there I'll keep walking until I can stop somewhere. The wooden building on Duboce you had just moved into was likely to be fine, you thought. It was. It was all fine. You got home and called me to say you were all right, since you knew I'd be worried.

～

After you were married and lived in the Mission you had such a beautiful garden; all kinds of flowers, jasmine, bougainvillea, avocado trees out back. You told it had been paved over soon after you left. That's what a city is I guess, layers on layers of events and memory covered over and accumulating, depending on how far back you want to go of course. That block where you lived was the end of the streetcar lines in the early 1900's there were stables all around. One still stood on the corner, below that big blue Victorian, now rented out for cars. You can trace the circular turn around tracks left in the cobblestones there, and if you kept going back tracing what had been covered over you would get to Mission Creek that flowed a few blocks north where Mariposa runs now, where the butterflies came to drink.

～

It's not just what's covered, it's the way things go on just as they always have that covers us over too, things that happen whether we're there or not. Remember when Dad and I were visiting one spring and came to the Carnival Parade that passes on Twenty-fourth Street. We all walked down there from your place on Twenty-second, oh that was quite a show all those feathers and sequins I've never seen the like, and of course your father liked the naked girls on those trucks,.

"Oh that sure was something," he said as we walked back to your flat.

Mexican fruit stand around the block where you went is still there too, I went with you there sometimes, Maria's Frutas y Verduras, right on South Van Ness, always sort of dark and dingy in there but you could buy warm tortillas and tomatillos with the light green skins still on like paper, and strawberries in bulk, Maria herself there in her high heels and makeup every day, "Oh que lindo nino," when she sees your little blond boy.

He wants a helado from the cooler, strawberry too, milky

and fruity at the same time, always a fresh bunch of cilantro just for the smell, good on eggs.

But now someone else lives there. You never even walk down that block, why would you. Maybe on occasion you pass close by on the way across town and it seems for a second that you're going home but you're not. Yet there's something of you that's left there, as time is always left in some place, believe me I am in a position to know about this. You leave some of your life as leaves are left on the ground under a tree. Mornings playing with your baby son, the first heat of your marriage, the white rabbit that you kept in the garden. Now if that place were always in your life, even if you didn't live there anymore, why, you'd come back to it, or someone you knew might live there and that time would be near, not hidden from your notice. There is always something we leave.

So many places you left. First place you lived in the city on Ashbury Street at Frederick, you can barely pick that one out anymore. A big three-storey Victorian, the ones around it look exactly like it. 17th and Arkansas, so many nights there with the boy before Paul. Had a back wooden stairway, rickety stairs a slanted wooden floor, the smell of the Anchor Steam plant, its sour barley mash cooking through the neighborhood air, birds would flock to the empty baseball diamond there. To get to work downtown you would take the bus along 3rd Street before it was developed into condos, the big concrete factory was there and the rusted ruins of the pier, and rotting hulks of ships left from the war. Later your son went to nursery school across the street, and so you played in the park there with him, on that same corner and a hundred other places but none of them really yours, or any more.

～

And when you were in all those other places, in India, in Morocco, Spain what did you find? You found Leila, for one. Your brightest high school student in Morocco had a sister and her mother lived in that little university town there. And her father came and went from Paris, had other wives, was planning that Leila with her English and French and degrees would help his businesses grow, but she did not want to leave her mother did she. And what advice did you give her? Her mother who spoke only Berber who could not read or write, in her djellaba and scarf whom the girls were almost embarrassed for in public, you drove them to the wool souk one day, you saw how it was, how they were all so tender with one another laughing, touching. So Leila asled you if it was worth it to go to Paris, to leave that unwritten language her mother spoke. And what did you tell her? Leila was not a fool, she saw further than most. Saw that the love she wanted and acceptance was there already. Go across the world and meet yourself. Do you ever keep in touch with her?

⁓

Wasn't the last time, but almost the last time we spoke on the phone you were in the High Atlas Mountains in Morocco. Way up at the top of the range a mountain called Jebel Toubkal, all snowed in, there was an old casbah, dark brown stucco building covered with snow, had been a military lookout now a hotel of course, mules met you at the foot of the hill and carried your bags up, it was Christmas Day. No cell phone service, there was a telephone in a little wooden booth by the gatehouse, a phone booth and an old man who attended it, didn't speak any language you knew. He was toothless, his skeleton fingers were stained with something blue. You were putting coins in and they were clanking right out through the bottom, but he helped you. Showed you that each coin needed to be warmed by rubbing on his dirt-blackened coat then blown on with his warm breath, then put in the slot to keep my voice there. Hello Mom, its Stephanie. Merry Christmas we are in the mountains you said. But what you couldn't explain was how in the building down the hill a little boy with a stick sang as he tried to herd his cow into the stable under their house where the animals were kept for warmth. Or how the toothless old man was helping you with his gnarled hands and the breath from his toothless mouth--working frantically to help you as if he sensed the distance you had to go. I couldn't smell the charcoal cooking fires starting up for lunch in the street below or see the two young girls with long black hair, with a blue robe around them, their horse was white like the snow that fell around them and when they saw you they pointed and laughed then galloped into the mountain pass. The old man kissed more coins with his wheezing breath and you put the coins in the slot, each time one fell I could hear it. I was sitting on the couch over at Linda's house watching reruns of *Upstairs Downstairs.*

So now you live in San Francisco again, in the Outer Sunset. Course you never would settle just for the Sunset, have to be the Outer. Now you've gone as far as you can in that half of the world, put yourself right up against the edge, a bleak block from the ocean and it is never out of your hearing. Well does that make you feel better? Having gotten to the very quivering end of this country you are from the middle of.

～

I'm trying to think now how old you were when your father finally stopped drinking. Thirteen or fourteen I guess. He started selling hearing aids during the day and working at the courthouse as the maintenance manager, at night. You could drive down Main Street after dark, see John Hancock's statue standing there on top of the big gold dome of the courthouse. See all the lights glowing in the windows and your father's silhouette, mopping floors and waxing and buffing the hallways between the judge's chambers.

Used to have his dinner and then go in. From seven to ten, I think something like that. Fact that it was at night meant no one had to see him do it, and that saved his pride. He hated wearing that uniform, because he had always been such a fancy dresser and now wore that green uniform shirt with his name written above the pocket, carried a big bunch of keys on a ring. He didn't mind the work so much as you'd think. Would come home and brag about how shiny he got the hallway floors in the courthouse with his new buffer. The hearing aid sales weren't so reliable, he always joked because most of his customers couldn't hear what he was saying to begin with. You're selling what?

You know how bad his hearing was. Like his mother Hazel, she didn't hear a word anybody said for the last twenty years of her life, she just sat in her rocking chair nodding and smiling regardless of what you said. You kids used to tease her say "Grandma Luke's been run over by a car!" and she would say "Well isn't that nice!"

Made communication such a chore.

I have to say your father got some determination somewhere and just decided to quit drinking. I don't know what changed exactly. He saw his last son growing up, thought he had one more chance with that son and that did it somehow. Said I'm quitting and he did. He started working two jobs and finally the city offered him a job managing the city landfill. Well I know, not a very glamorous position by the sound of it but he liked it. He ran the office, took the money, kept the books.

He drove us out there one time you were visiting. It's out on County Road 214, out by Trenton Ridge. You asked him how he knew which road to turn at amid the endless grid of brown stubble fields and empty farmhouses, but he knew, had known those roads his whole life. He drove and talked.

"There's a lot more to it than digging a hole in the ground and filling it up. A lot of engineering goes into how to get all that stuff into the earth, back into the ground. Landfill is what you have to have when life progresses, progress goes on and things are used up and discarded. They have to go somewhere. Even after you don't want it or it doesn't work anymore there is still the thing itself. The problem of the weight and shape of the material thing itself, you can't just wave a magic wand and get rid of it. It's gotta go somewhere. And we make it a place to go. It's a principle you can apply to different areas."

There was a green corrugated metal building near the entrance where the trucks pull up to check in. He sat behind the window that slid open, to have them drive onto the scale, take the money, give them a receipt. Cost depends on the size of the truck, the number of axles. You got to ask each trucker if any of them has hazardous waste because that costs extra, and has to be put in a different place.

"The hell of it is, a lot of them hide the hazardous stuff down in the bottom of the truck, then say oh no we don't have anything hazardous. Course then they dump stuff out and there it is, well that kind of thing, asbestos, what have you, can poison the ground water and you have a mess on your hands.

"You have to watch out for fire. A fire burning under there could go on for weeks. Have a big problem on your hands. That's why you can't put rubber tires in.

"The Cats dig a big hole, as if you're making a lake almost, now the thing is you can't have the dozers tipping over, and it's hard to keep a smooth edge to it. First you need to excavate a big area. Couple of times you'll hit a pocket of natural gas, or even a water spring. They're all over. You'd be surprised. But that's just the start of it. I'm in charge of which holes should be filled in and when it's time to dig another."

We stood there at the office as the noise of the trucks and the scrape of the giant bulldozers drowned out the sound of his voice trying to explain.

"See how the layers are spread down and then the bulldozers drive over, and then the compacters. You have to fill in with sand sometimes to get it smooth. Now take a guess how many cubic feet of material we get into one of these pits, 1 million. Can you believe that?" We all feigned interest to the degree that we could.

"Eventually if all goes well, after forty or fifty years you'll be able to grow corn over the top again. But it takes a while."

We used to kid him when he got up to go to work, we'd say to the dump, to the dump, to the dump dump dump. You wouldn't think it, because it was only digging holes and filling them up, but he loved that job, it had the shape of a grand big undertaking that he had always looked for somehow, had machinery and action on a large scale. He did that for about six years, driving out on the slippery county roads in the dark to get there by 7:30 a.m.

After being the hero on the football field, and then the battlefield, was like he was always looking for something grand; some great American undertaking, some grandiose project involving vast miles of land and machinery, something of depth and complex layers, something that would never end and always be needed and he found all that at the county landfill.

# VI

## MALADIES

### 1985
### *Toledo, Ohio*

Y OU didn't ever come up to Toledo with us when your
brother Joseph was in the hospital did you? Damned
highway's always under construction. Thirty-five years we've
been using I-75 and there's forever a place they're still working on. Every time we drove up I couldn't help but think of
driving up here in '65 when Rusty was in the hospital, talk
about history repeating itself. He doesn't remember coming up here that time, he sure wasn't driving. I forget who
brought us up must have been his sister, he was certainly in
no condition to drive, I don't think he sobered up until a few
days later. Veteran's Hospital is up by the waterfront. This
place where Joseph went is right in the center of the old part
of the city.

*It's a little gloomy and run down but St. Vincent's was a
good hospital in its day, wasn't surrounded by all these liquor
stores and abandoned buildings. What are those kids doing
there with that bicycle, looks like four of them are going to try
to ride it at the same time damn fool kids, someone'll get hurt.*

*Nothing looks good on this kind of winter day, red bricks
and the concrete parking garage, bare trees and garbage cans,
nothing looks good. They say if he completes the six week
treatment he can go back to work, disability only pays for that
much anyway. Course his father is still making excuses for him,
he feels so guilty about it to begin with.*

*Well Hooper Tire pays for him to be in the residential treat-*

*ment facility they have there, Union pays for it. He's a good union member volunteered to be the officer for his group at the factory, the men who work the machines that stamp out the treads. I don't know what you call them. I doubt they call them tread man, or tread mill, well it certainly is a treadmill. They say if he completes the five weeks of treatment he can go back to work.*

*His father was still trying to help him find an excuse for why he ended up there.*

*"Oh he just had a few too many drinks and shouldn't have been driving. Forget the other list of DWI's and the blackout and the cocaine possession. "Just had a few too many beers one night," Rusty says but he's been doing that since he was 16. It's a miracle he hasn't killed himself or someone else by now with his driving. Get calls at 2 in the morning, "Oh Joseph's in jail, picked up after ramming his car into a tree out on Rte. 224." We're almost there.*

"Aren't you gonna park here in the garage?" I ask him.

"What?"

"Why don't you park in the garage it's only two dollars?"

"We're not gonna stay long."

"Well they say it's a family meeting it's gonna take a few hours."

"Oh hell alright."

We waited a long time it seems, oh they finally came out. All the families waiting. Sitting in this plastic orange chair so long my legs start to fall asleep. Feet are damp from stepping in the slush getting out of the car. At least he doesn't have any children yet. Oh the male nurse is gonna talk to them, talk to everyone.

"Oh Joseph your parents are here, anything you want to say to your parents?"

"Just that I love you and I'm sorry to put you through all this worry Mom, and I'm sorry to disappoint you so much, I know I never lived up to what you wanted Dad."

"Now I've been where you are son and it's damn hard, though no one can help you. Truth is you gotta go on and decide for yourself. You gotta do it yourself."

"Is there anyone else would like to speak. No. Well let's say goodbye to our families."

"Hey son, keep at it, I know you can beat it," Rusty says.

"I'll pray for you," I kiss him but he seems sleepy, and doesn't look me in the eye. I don't know if they give them some kind of drug to calm them down or what.

No one ever talks about it, but all the men in the factory drink, what else can they do. Bone tired when they're finished. My niece's husband works there has a drug problem too, think of spending your day at the end of a huge machine pulling a lever, week after week. Use a hundredth of your brain but you have to pay attention to the gauge, open the door, lift another load of material into the machine, close it, pull the lever. I think the machines make them drink. Factories want something from a man he can't give and that's to be a machine himself. Mary's husband works as an engineer for Hooper. Jo says they keep redesigning the machines but they never ask any of the guys that run the machines what would work better. That kind of thing demeans a man's work; to not be asked about what you know, and year after year, like you're not even there. Day after day, you and a piece of machinery. Say it gets up to 110 degrees on the stamping floor in summer, but its better in the winter when it's still fairly warm. He's only twenty-three there's no reason he couldn't still go to college and get a different job if he wanted to.

It's sad about the men who work in factories. Never have the satisfaction of mastering a craft or working through a profession, so how do they have the sense of growing. They don't, they're the same at twenty-five as they are at fifty those factory men. Well having children, that makes a change for some, but for who they are, what outlet do they have?

"Goodbye Son," your father said, and we left the building

walking silently to the garage next door. Tears my heart out to see the two of them. None of his sons ever lived up to being the quarterback, or the army officer, but the drunk he was, they all lived up to that. He's Willie Loman if there ever was one. Willie Loman to the bitter end. They all are these poor men; expect too much so of course they're disappointed.

"Remember what floor we left the car on?" I ask him.

"Who's carrying on?"

"No, what floor we left the car on," I repeat it.

"What?"

"Where's the car?"

"The car's right in the next row."

"Should we stop at the Big Boy on the way home and get a sandwich."

"You want to get who a toy?"

"Should we get a sandwich. Food. Eat?"

"Well God damn it I don't know. You want to stop. Where?"

*He can't hear anything by now, oh it's tiresome having to repeat everything three times and so loudly well it makes me not want to say anything at all. There's no way to have a conversation now. Would like to have someone to talk to. But we're left with just the necessities of life, meals, transportation. You want to go now, or not, 'bout all I can say. Any kind of conversation, did you see such and such in the paper, or that was a pretty garden, I don't bother trying to say and that gets lonesome after a while; when talking is such a chore.*

*Sitting in the room earlier listening to him talk about how he stopped drinking made me wonder if I wasn't better off when he was drinking. It's a terrible thing to say I know but once he quit I had to listen to all his criticism about how I keep the house, and how what I cook never suits him. I don't iron his shirt cuffs right or how I wasn't disciplining the children, nothing suited him anyway so why try to please him. About the day he became sober, his eyes fastened on his youngest son and I let him take him.*

He told me, "You never mind, I'll raise this one."

And I said, "Fine, I'm sure you can do better!"

Was insulting to me that I couldn't raise my children right, but I took him at his word and I never interfered between them. Maybe I should have. Well Joseph then got all the attention he never noticed how the other children felt neglected. He would buy Joseph a new mini-bike for Christmas and the girls would get a sweater it wasn't equal at all. But they never complained really. There was nothing he wouldn't do for him and we all just accepted that was the way things were.

Child became his raison d'être. Got him on a kids wrestling team and took him all around the state wrestling. Once there was a tournament in Cleveland and we went with them, do you remember that we took you and your sister. That was a big trip for us, stayed in a nice hotel downtown and did some shopping and sightseeing. You had just turned thirteen and he was ten or so.

Talk about wrestling with demons. All those matches, wasn't your brother it was your father wrestling, trying to twist his way back into the contest of life through that child, and he never gave up. He never stopped thinking that he could get up off the mat and pull a surprise reversal, and his son was how.

Poor boy, was so driven by someone else's dream that he never got a chance to learn who he was. Had a father who drove him, then he had a factory that drove him, and the man inside has yet to take over. I feel like I let him go too easily, but he never held it against me.


2000

*Cranford Street. Blanchardville*


I could tell by the way he was acting that he didn't feel good. Always took a walk after dinner but then stopped taking his walk, started falling asleep in his chair. Hadn't been feeling good all summer. Said he felt pain in his chest and so they checked out his heart didn't find anything wrong. Well, early August it got really bad and they finally took a chest x-ray, well, why they hadn't done that in the first place I don't know, it's a podunk hospital.

Now we come to find out it's lung cancer. After he quit smoking all those years ago. Said he might as well have gone on smoking for all the good it did him. It was spread pretty far by the time they found it, no way to operate. They could have tried radiation or chemotherapy but the doctor didn't think the chances were very good, and your father wanted to be the tough guy.

"Oh hell, it's gonna happen one way or the other, might as well be this way." I was surprised by the way he accepted it. And then pretty soon after hearing about the diagnosis he began playing the part of the dying man. Started using a walker, wearing his pajamas all day, he had never done that before in his life, had you go out to Penney's and get him an extra pair of pajamas when you came. He just started staying inside, wouldn't even go for a ride in the car on a beautiful autumn day. Moved himself from upstairs to downstairs for sleeping and eating but that was about it.

~

Linda and Cathy told me we're going to home hospice, that's what he wanted and when you sign up it means you're going to die at home. You're not going to the hospital at the end. That's what he wanted. I thought he should go to the hospital when it got bad so he could be taken care of, but I went along.

Anne had come from Texas, and Tim from Oregon and you came back in October to take a turn, and say goodbye. At least you were still in the country then.

Well it was the afternoon and time for you to head for the airport to catch your flight and you knew it was the last time you were going to see your father. He was sitting there at the round table in the dining room on Cranford Street, beautiful autumn day and you couldn't put it off anymore.

"Well Dad I have to go."

"I know you do honey."

You sat looking at each other and holding hands.

"I love you. You were a good dad."

"Well I hope so."

"I love you, you take care now."

Tears in every eye, but you have to stand up and go.

I always was grateful to you for saying that to that dying man. You hadn't planned on it, but when you sat there and you wanted to give him something to go with, you said you were a good dad. Even though we both knew it wasn't true. And he knew it too. Said I hope so, meaning he wished he had been. Or did your saying it to him, at that very last minute, make it true? Made it true between you is what I saw. There wasn't any easy thing like that I could say.

～

*Know it doesn't sound charitable but I don't want to watch him die, would have been better if he went to the hospital. Girls all think I'm being mean spirited, that I don't want the inconvenience but it's more than that, do they think I don't have any feelings at all. To watch him degenerate right before my eyes. Used to walk so fast no one could keep up with him, now he totters around all stooped over who stood up so straight his whole life, drinking out of a straw like a child. A body I knew like the back of my own hand, black cinders under the skin on his knee where he fell on the track in high school, freckled forearms in a sport shirt, the body I had children with. Watching him go makes me feel so pressed, my life going with his woven together as it is can't quite put my finger on it. What I loved. But love did not spare.*

Like I said the home health care nurse came every few days. But we still had trouble getting him in and out of the shower, none of us girls could lift him. We had the shower chair and all but he still needed help.

Well brother Joseph seemed to be avoiding us altogether, I think he couldn't stand to see his father suffering like he was, he was in a lot of pain. But one day, I think you might even have been there, I said I'm gonna call Jo and get him over here. Well he didn't have any problem coming once I asked him, and he had something specific to do, drove his truck over before work.

It was October, a beautiful day, the whole season he was dying was just lovely. Wouldn't you know.

"There you are, your dad's upstairs waiting for you, there's towels there on the hall table."

I left them to it, but I could see through the door slightly, Earl sitting there on the shower stool slightly hunched over and his fair freckled skin still smooth over his arms and chest. The water ran down his back.

"How's that feel?"

"Feels good."

"You wanna wash your hair."

"If I can, hurts like hell when I raise my arms like that."

"I can do it for you."

"Alright."

Took the shampoo and lathered it in his hands then onto his father's thinning old head, and rubbed it gently, lather rinsed down over his face so he closed his eyes. His son's hands mixed in the water against this skin, "I'll wash your back too," Joseph said. And he took a washcloth out of the little basket there on the edge of the tub and soaped it up then rubbed his father's back.

"That's good. I'm ready to get out now."

"OK." He turned the water off.

"Let me get a towel down on the floor."

"OK ready."

Joseph took his wrists in his hands and pulled him naked from the chair where he sat into a standing position and
leaned his shoulder against him as he lifted his leg over the
edge of the tub. Then he stood for a moment dripping water
and leaning against his son.

"Let me catch my breath," he said.

"Sure" Joseph said "no problem, here's a towel." He put
the towel around him, and pulled the toilet seat cover down
so he could sit.

"That's better. Say, could you help me shave."

"Sure."

Earl lathered up his brush with soap as he always did.

"I can do this if you hold the mirror for me."

He held the mirror but it kept steaming up. Joseph would
wipe it with a towel every few minutes and when he was done,
he took the towel and wiped away the bits of white lather.

"Want me to get your robe now?"

"Nah, I want to get dressed. Might as well go ahead and
get dressed."

He put on his khakis and his grey cashmere sweater and
Joseph helped him get down the stairs, and he sat in his chair.

Jo went off to work but seemed happier, I thought, for being near what it was he was trying so hard to avoid.

⁓

*His children all going about caring for him and I'm spookin'
around here thinking how we have been struggling hope
against hope all along. For what?*

*Maybe some irrational hope that what wasn't said or given
will be made right. Then that hope dying right in front of me,
but is resolved by dying too. Have to watch the horror of his
dying along with everything else I've had to watch him do.
Hear his breath rattling in his throat, or watch them give him
ever more drops of morphine, one then three then four doses.
The home health care nurse well she finally came and gave him
a dose I think that was what did it, they don't say oh at a cer-*

*tain point we'll give you so much morphine you'll die from it
but in essence that's what happens. And Becky sitting there beside him saying Oh Daddy it's all right like we ever called him
Daddy to start with. Could he hear her? I had to go upstairs
at a certain point. To the very end more than should be asked.*

~

One summer you were home soon after Dad died maybe
five, six years ago, I don't know why it comes to mind now,
because Dick Dougherty died I guess, they had his funeral recently. You wouldn't know him but he was the bandleader for
the concerts out at the band shell at Riverside Park. Remember you took me occasionally when you came in the summer,
your father never wanted to go, well he couldn't hear it for
one thing; but I always thought it was pleasant out there on a
summer evening. I always thought the music chased the mos-
quitoes away, I know it sounds crazy but it's true. We were
walking along arm in arm passing the time.

"Playing 'Green Eyes,' used to be my favorite. Old band
shell looks pretty in the sunset, pink to the west tonight, pink
sky at night sailor's delight, and they just painted the band
shell pink too. Was quite an uproar in town about the color of
course. A lot of people thought they should stick to white. Nice
and cool here though under the tall trees, shady, and a breeze
off the river. Quite a crowd here tonight. 'Tuxedo Alley,' gets
my feet moving, I can sing a little no one will mind, well there
aren't any seats left we should have brought our chairs well
we can sit here on the benches. Gonna Taaaake a Sentimental Journey. I don't know why I'm whispering like, the sun is
behind the trees, going down. Poor old folks in wheelchairs
pushed up to the front so they can hear, and look, not a one of
'em is awake, all bent forward like wilted flowers.

"I'm telling you there are an inordinate number of old wid-
ows in this town, look at them lined up one after the other in
their chairs with their matching blue hairdos, and all dressed
up, well we are obviously underdressed. Course I don't know

a soul here, except Dick well he used to work at the paper. I'm glad you came. Your father hated in his last years to go out in public he was so self-conscious about his tremor as if everyone was looking at the fact that his hands shook, but no one notices anything really. Yes that retarded man you're looking at goes to our church, I know his mouth is open and he's drooling, now I don't know his name, he's so overweight that doesn't help him.

"He's mentally disturbed, but he goes to church so maybe he's a holy man. Well once I was in church you know that half pew right inside the front door, well he comes back from communion and just starts to sit right on top of me, like he didn't notice I was there, I moved over as soon I could.

"I think that's the last song. 'Stardust.' Oh it's nice to walk here by the riverfront. Might as well wait till the traffic clears out. Did you see the new platform they put over the water, you can sit up there, oh I can barely climb the stairs to it. Look there on the water, seven ducklings are following their mother, oh see how flustered they get when they can't find her. They say so many people have been feeding the ducks they stay when they should go south and then freeze to death when winter comes. People ought to let nature take its course.

"Now what was that just surfaced out there, muskrat maybe, or a big carp, remember that time somebody dumped a giant carp, must have been three feet long onto our front porch one day, and nobody saw who did it, well one of the older girls had broken up with some boyfriend and she thought he did it maybe out of spite, but we never did know who did that. Well who would do such a thing I don't know, it was hot and that fish smelled to high heaven. You never know who you're getting mixed up with."

～

Worried me that you were mixed up with that William when he had a wife, and I know you said it was just a Green Card marriage so he can stay here from England but I didn't trust it. He was so much older than you. Oh sure he made it to Cambridge from a coal miner's village in Yorkshire and you liked him because he seemed a rebel to all that, sort of the rough explorer type, tall and weathered. I don't know, what did you see in him? You could talk about poetry, he could show you London, take you to his old rooms, or quote Wordsworth, but I could do that. *I wandered lonely as a cloud. I gazed—and gazed—but little thought, What wealth the show to me had brought.* Took you years to figure out what I already knew first time you brought him to Ohio.

You were on your way to one of those travel assignments out West, you and he were doing those for several years writing for the Triple A, and stopped to visit.

I had him sleep on the couch in the living room. But I heard him come up the stairs several nights to wake you, heard you two go down into the basement so you couldn't be heard, and then go sneak back to bed. Like I didn't know. Lust is one of the seven deadly sins you know. Looked on you as some kind of amusement I thought. Wanted you to be faithful to him but he never had any faithfulness to you and you let him, he was never going to take you seriously, or you didn't take yourself seriously, I don't know, he used your body is all I saw. But you can't see that when you're young.

～

You gave so much away that you could have kept for yourself. I don't know why, and you gave it away so easily. Like it wasn't worth so much, but plenty of other men would have thought it was, if you had just taken the time to look. You gave away always more than you had to, and went further away than you had to. You always thought I didn't see how things were, that you were in some world so different than mine but that wasn't really the case. Anyway I'm glad you chose Paul in the end, he's a good man, and Irish too.

Anyway that evening in the park we saw a great blue heron on the other side of the river. "Look at that. Can barely see it against those grey rocks. Look how still it stands. Wait let's see it moves. I want to see it fly. No it's just standing there, standing on one leg like that for how long? Let's wait for it to fly. Could be hours. I guess. The dam looks awful low today. You know your dad's childhood friend drowned there, was a terrible tragedy. 'Bout nine years old, boys from over on Lima Avenue, used to come out here to swim and fish. Well one day the group of 'em, came out to swim and then rode home only to discover that Les had not come with them, and they found him the next day under the dam there. I think your dad always felt a little guilty about that."

You kids practically lived all summer at the park here, swimming, didn't you. Walked out here almost everyday, from Pine Street down Clinton and then along Center Street to the pool. Center Street wasn't so run down in those days. There were just long streets of solid Midwestern houses with front porches and swings, and lawns getting mowed and kids with their bicycles and bigwheels out front and little wading pools in the yards, and teenage boys washing Mustangs. Now I swear you go out and don't see a soul. All inside in the air conditioning.

The park was different then too, you used to have the roller coaster and the bumper cars, cotton candy, and the taffy man. You would come out of the pool for a break, put on your rubber thongs and get a 15¢ bag of popcorn, to last you the whole afternoon, popcorn stand stood in the center of the concession stand, was decorated with stars and stripes and filled with white and gold warm popping. That old stone shelter was filled with picnic tables and kids in bathing suits eating hotdogs and fries running to the playground to swing on the rings, those ring on a chain on a pole, you loved to hold onto the ring and spin high into the air, around and around like you were flying.

Pool's still the same. You kids would go swimming all day in the vast blue of the pool, diving off the boards, then diving again. All day diving, and working your way up the platform to the four feet, six then ten. Took courage to dive off the ten foot board. Then too you had to be able to swim a certain distance if you wanted to play in the deep end.

## 2005
### *Cranford Street. Blanchardville*

Boo Radley, that's what I called him in later years. Remember the man who never comes out in *To Kill A Mockingbird.* Well that was your brother Tim.

This was when he came to live with me after Dad died. Just after the funeral he went back out to Portland to settle his affairs then drove his truck back here. He didn't leave much behind there, had been renting a room in a house, had handyman jobs. But he functioned you know. Or it seemed as if he did, oh I was glad to have him come home and help.

Your sister Jane said well she would pay for him to finish up college at State here, he only had a year or so left. So that's what we did, and it all seemed like a good idea. He went to State up the road and that was working out well, the first summer he even had a summer job, and was working construction until they just didn't call him back one day. Well we didn't worry 'cause we thought once he got his college diploma he could do something else.

We all went up there to the graduation. But he never worked after that. Months went by. Linda and Kathy would come over.

"Hey Tim you send out any resumes?"

"I'm going to."

"Did you call the employment service at school?"

"I called them last week."

"Supposed to call them every day."

"My professor said he might have an assistant position."

"Tim that was four months ago."

"He's probably going to call."

But of course no one called. He never pursued it, see. He thought he ought to be given a job right off running the whole department.

Well, it did come to weigh on me that he couldn't be budged. For one thing he was obsessed with George Bush. Hated him with a vengeance, well we all did but he spent everyday on the computer, just following every move Bush made.

He'd say "Oh I know what's going on, I see what they're up to. Most people don't know, but I've read and I've put it all together the whole voter fraud thing here in Ohio; I've tracked it down but nobody does anything."

"Well I know you do son."

"Well it really bugs me that he gets away with it, you know what he did yesterday?"

"No, son."

"Well he took those machines and…" then launched into another a rant. Well sometimes I thought if I listened to him, if I paid attention to him he would get it out, but that never seemed to be help.

"Well I know Betty Maloney who has always run the Democratic Party here in town, the 100 democrats there are anyway. Well if you hate George Bush so much go do something, go call up Betty and campaign."

"I'm going to, somebody has to do something."

He would talk about it. Then the day would come.

"Wasn't this the day Betty was having a meeting, at the headquarters."

"I know but not until six o'clock."

"Well it's five now so why don't you go get cleaned up?"

"I will."

Then forty minutes later. "I thought you were going out to the Headquarters?"

"Oh those meetings are stupid, I don't want to drive all the way out there. Doesn't do any good anyway."

Got so he just ranted about George Bush to Linda or Dave when they would stop over with the kids.

"I've just printed out the reports see, about Iraq, I've put all the sources together here you should read this. I got it all right here in this binder."

Would sit there in the dining room, cursing at George Bush on the computer screen. Or playing that damn fighter jet video game, for hours on end, shooting down fighter jets on the computer screen, *put-a-put put put put.*

Got so Joseph and Linda wouldn't even stop by 'cause they just fought with him. Said he shouldn't be living off me for free.

I begged him to stop. We all begged him.

~

One night a long time ago, Tim must have been about ten, I was listening to Walter Cronkite on the eleven o'clock news, I hear footsteps. Think, who's that coming down the stairs, it's Luke Roy.

"What is it, why aren't you asleep, it's almost midnight."

"Tim won't stop talking. And it's so hot up there. He makes us turn the fan off so he can talk. It's fun for a minute but he never stops. He talks every night when we are trying to go to sleep, telling movies over and over again, last week it was *The Blob*, and this week it's *The Fantastic Voyage*, every single detail, we don't even want to listen to him, but he won't shut up."

"Tell him you want to go to sleep."

"We do Mom, he won't stop. Come here, listen." Luke was pulling on me, "Come and listen to him."

I went to the foot of the stairs and heard Tim talking on. He was telling about the *Fantastic Voyage*, that film I guess where they travel through the human body.

"But by then see their boat gets too close to the heart, and with each beat there is a huge tidal wave that goes pulsing across the blood ocean and they almost tip over and they worry, see, is the next beat going to suck them in, because it's like a vacuum there in the cardiac cavity, there's a pulse outward but that pushes everything to one side see and that's when the boat will slide down the wave and get sucked in, like into a whirlpool and if it does, into the aorta, when that closes, comes down like a giant steel garage door well they'll be crushed by the valve, and then there's no going back, see. So they have to time it just right to ram the boat in there between the beats, and the one guy says it's too dangerous he wants to go back through the veins, see, but…"

I walked up those creaking wooden stairs to the front bedroom where you younger children slept under the slanted roof, two boys in one bed, two or three little girls in the other, was a big room. I said, "Timothy that's enough now, you go to sleep."

He said "Not yet were just into the lungs, and it's not half over."

I said "It's over for you, now I'm gonna have your dad up here with a belt if you don't mind me."

"He's not even home."

"He'll be home, so let your brothers and sisters get some sleep for heaven's sake. And I'm turning the fan on, you'll all suffocate up here without some ventilation."

"Good Night."

~

So there were some obsessive traits early on but every child is different. I didn't think at the time. Course your father never encouraged him. Well then he started to play Irish music here and there, like the flute and the penny whistle. Well, the penny whistle was not a very impressive instrument for your father. Whenever Tim would visit he'd be practicing in the basement, and your father would say, "Damn it he's on that goddamn whistle again. Gonna have every dog in the county over here." He was joking but it hurt Tim's feelings I know.

Well it worried me those last years of my life that the man

couldn't seem to make a life for himself. I thought for the first few years that a mother's patience and understanding might cure him of whatever it was. Thought maybe he wants someone to take his ideas seriously, so I listened to him, and listened to him, but it just seems to make him spin deeper into his own obsessions and his conspiracy theories.

It was all building up inside him, all that he didn't do, or try, and that was starting to weigh him down. I've seen it happen to others, a burden builds up in the soul when there's too much we haven't done or attempted that we should have, and then the burden defeats us. You can use your brothers and sisters to learn from. Don't go down that road. I've often wondered what you were waiting for, too. Pacing around instead of sitting down and taking a crack at it.

But I tried everything I could think of for Boo Radley. His sister knows people in the County who could get him an office job but he won't even apply. He was the final worry I was to have in later years. Another man to worry and pester me. But what was I gonna do. Can't turn him out onto the street.

December 2004
*Cranford Street. Blanchardville*

*Can't get him to do the simplest thing. Asked him two hours ago to take me over to the store, he said give me fifteen minutes. Well I've given him fifteen minutes four times over. Now I'm all dressed have to put on so many layers in this cold, boots, coat, hat scarf, gloves, with the wind-chill they say ten degrees, now he doesn't come. I'm sitting here on the back porch for fifteen minutes now said he was coming, not like he's doing anything just sitting at that damn computer. I'll call him again.*

"Now what's the holdup Tim, come on."

"I said I'm coming I just need to finish this...just wait a minute."

*Oh, no point in trying to reason with him. Let me get a whiff of fresh air there oh, it is cold, at least it stopped snowing, doesn't look too windy. Just wanted to get a piece of meat and a few things for dinner, he's the one who'll eat it after all.*

*Hell, why should I sit here and wait on him. Been sitting and waiting on some fool man to do something my whole life. Probably could carry what I need, it's only that block down the alley and across the parking lot. Only reason I don't walk is the snow on the ground and the cold makes me short of breath. I can wrap my scarf over my face probably be fine. Gonna be dark in a few minutes, wanted to be back as Julie said she might drop by.*

*Oh, I'm gonna go ahead. Put my purse over my shoulder, so I can hold onto the railing. Step down carefully first step. Doesn't look like he shoveled here like he said he would. One more step, oh it's ice under there.*

～

Next thing I know I'm slipping, put my hands on the garage to steady me no, but it was too far away, I was pitching forward like something pulled out from under me and my glasses go flying off, put my arms down in front of me to break my fall, and my palms scrape open on ice and gravel, then my chin hits.

*Oh the ice is hard. I'm laying on my glasses. I think I'm laying on my glasses. Blessed Mary Mother of God pray for me. Try to push myself up but it hurts.*

*Must have pulled my shoulder. Oh I can sit up. Can't hardly catch my breath, heart's racing. Don't want to die here alone in the driveway. Collect myself for a minute here. "Tim, Tim, can you"... Oh there's a little bit of blood must be coming from my chin, scraped my chin like a child, "Tim can you help me." Oh he's not hearing me, hell.*

*Now I'm crying. Tears will freeze on my cheek, crying isn't going to help. Shock of it, the ice cold the broken glass scattered around pain so fierce in my old bursitis shoulder joint, and my jaw, looking at the grey concrete blocks at the foundation of the house; the handle of the unused snow shovel sticking out there to mock me. Oh I've fallen, the earth and the air conspiring against me, breaking through my body, this coat to no avail. Cold pouring in now, fright of it the worst part, feels like I was mauled by a giant grey wolf flying out of the winter from nowhere, all claws and teeth against my soft old flesh. Call him and he doesn't come and I'm crying like a baby when I've had better reason a hundred times and never shed a tear.*

*Whose car is that pulling through the alley into the dentist's office next door, oh it's one of the girls that works there I better stop crying, it's too pathetic, I've seen her car before, oh she's stopping, thank goodness, window going down.*

"You need some help?"

"I slipped down here."

"Oh dear, should I call the ambulance?"

"Maybe you could just help me up, first." I'm embarrassed but I'm crying right in front of her.

"You poor thing," she said. She was getting out of her car.

"I don't think anything's broken."

And she came, her name was Janice. I got to my knees and Janice helped me stand up. Was a relief to be standing I could tell then nothing was broken, blood from my chin all over my camel hair coat, I was shaken but I could walk alright.

"My son's home there if you could get him."

Well just then Timothy walks out the door, looks horrified.

"Your mother fell down the stairs," Janice said.

"Why did you go, I was coming right out. Why didn't you wait for me?"

He actually stood there and said that, why didn't you wait for me. Oh I wanted to take up the snow shovel and hit him over the head. But my shoulder hurt too much. It never was right after that.

~

1974
## *Blanchardville*

It's hard to believe what some men can do. Or people can, I guess I should say but it does seem men are self-centered in a way most women I know aren't. Thinking of Tim, though, I did start to wonder about mental illness, he was alright as a child. I guess mental illness has its outbreaks just like flu.

Certainly your brother-in-law Bill was mentally ill; but we didn't see it until after the damage was done. We should have been more careful about letting you stay over there, but life is much easier in retrospect.

I thought your sister Linda really needed the help with the two little boys is why I went along with it. Leo was just in Kindergarten I think, Vince a toddler. She was working the graveyard shift at RCA, and Bill was working the six to two, so they had a cross time problem, one had to leave before the other got back as I recall. It was just going to be for a few weeks and then they'd move her onto the same shift. She asked me could one of the younger girls sleep over at her place and I wanted to help her. You were in what eighth grade I think. Carrie was already in high school, she always had so much work to do and got up early to do an extra class or something.

Anyway they were willing to pay you $25 a week, and that was a lot for you in those days. But it wasn't so much the money as we wanted to help her out.

Well, in retrospect Bill had been acting a little strangely toward you, like that night he asked you to ride to Columbus with him to order a car part. I don't know what we were thinking, he said he needed someone to ride with him to keep him awake. We sent you down there with him a rainy dark night, you waiting for him in the dark car, as he went into the highway rest stop and stayed a long time. You sitting in the car in the dark alone. And didn't some man yell at him as he was coming out of there? Say pervert or something? Am I just imagining that? Well he was your sister's husband, we had no reason to suspect him. He was quiet and artistic, liked to paint pictures. I never liked him as I said.

He said something to you that night didn't he? But you didn't ever tell me about it. You didn't think to tell us, it just seemed strange to you. When he came out of the rest stop sat down in the car seat next to you and he said, "Can I kiss you?" And you said "No." And that was that. You didn't think so much of it, maybe older men were strange like that.

What did you know, or if it was some temporary insanity you aren't a person to tattle. He drove back and dropped you at home. When the other event transpired a month or so after that, then it seemed important and obvious but it didn't at the time.

I can see now what you didn't tell me then, see it affected you in a way I didn't know.

You were sleeping on a bed in their little sewing room upstairs. Heard a light knocking in your dream did you? Like I did that one day.

No, I think he just shook your shoulder, woke you in the middle of the night it must have been near 4 or 5 a.m. He said, I can't sleep. I'm going to swallow these sleeping pills and kill myself.

He said this to you waking you up, he said the sleeping pills are in the pocket of this bathrobe, and he gave you the bathrobe, as if you should put it on, he said can we go downstairs so we don't wake the boys.

What I can see now that I couldn't see before are his hands. His hands wrestling you to the floor. Why? What did he want? He didn't want to kill you. It wasn't clear to him what he wanted.

～

He was raving. He said, I like you, I'm depressed, I've always liked you. Can I kiss you. He wrestled you to the floor, you tried to get away didn't you. You tried to get away but he didn't want you to scream. He didn't want you to wake the babies, so he put his hand over your mouth. Didn't want you to scream, but the problem was, there wasn't just one problem, but one thing it seems like such a small thing, such a little detail, like Peter Rabbit trying to climb under the garden fence but getting his coat caught on a wire, a little wire sticking out that catches in the fabric and you're finished no matter how fast and strong, or smart you were, because you couldn't breathe.

He put his hand over your mouth to stop you from screaming, but you had a terrible sinus infection you couldn't breathe through your nose at all, so when he put his hand there you couldn't breathe, and you struggled to pull his hand away trying to tell him you couldn't breathe but that made him think you were trying to scream you weren't trying to scream but he wouldn't give you a chance to tell him. I can't breathe you tried to say I can't you pulled with all your might, you gained a breath or two but you couldn't get his hands away and when you struggled then fell to the floor and he pinned you to the floor and held his hands over your mouth and you started to faint couldn't get a breathe in and at that moment you saw, saw your own spirit rise in the room, imagined, as you fell away, that it had started to leave your body.

Saw men in blue uniforms, there was an ambulance outside, there was a question, people were asking questions, there was your sister, your brothers, your father, I came in to find how you had died and the light was dim there it wasn't morning there, they came from the driveway came up the few back stairs that led into the kitchen through the kitchen a dark square of shadow, there on the floor in front of the love seat you were, and a reporter from the newspaper of eternity came and said it's clear now there was something missing. What belonged to you.

It's better that I tell this story, you should never have to tell this story to yourself or to anyone again, you can let me tell this story my dear daughter, I can tell this story for you though your fingers could type the words they will not be your words nor the man behind them any longer, no.

∼

You had gone beyond and seen ahead, beyond the event of your own dying to the news of it spreading from there and spreading to me. And in widening circle you felt the time that had been taken from you, the missing days, oh a good many days as you were so young. All the depths of the days stolen from you poured into the room with the dense weight of absence, an element like plutonium, or some laws of physics I don't know, what they call a black hole, where your days were pouring out of that room, out of the future where they were to have been, the force of it pulling the walls inward and the door off its hinges into the center of the floor where you lay still under the gale force of it, in the deep magnetic graphite of that dream before his hand felt your stillness. And lifted.

Through the ten thousand days that had been taken you returned. You returned to the floor, and gasping whispered to him. So that he would not mistake it for a screaming, whispered. Please when your hand covers I can't breathe, I won't scream. He seemed to hear or was it that he simply had grown tired and went upstairs to sleep. Leaving you to sit huddled on the couch until your sister arrived.

She put on the coffee pot when she came in, and you told her what had happened, she seemed too tired to cry about it. Was there penetration she said, because of course the possibility was she might need to take you to the hospital, but you said no not like that.

It wasn't rape, in a purely anatomical sense because he wasn't able to. But of course there was a penetration of another kind, as light penetrates a pulled drapery, or a penetration of knowledge glimpsed before its time, something out of order. Well he is sick, your sister Linda said, he needs a doctor.

In years to come I watched you writhe to breathe under that invisible hand like a fish out of water, watched you fight off everything that came near. Now I see the effect that had. Violence can penetrate a child easily. Upset the whole order.

Then again the fact that there wasn't intercourse, made it so we didn't have to take you to the hospital. That was maybe good, or bad, I don't know, I think you didn't have your period yet. You were fourteen but that wasn't unusual in those days anyway.

Linda brought you home, she phoned I think, I can't quite remember it was a school day. Your dad had already left to drop the kids at high school. Linda said there was some trouble. She came in and we talked a minute, you were there you didn't look bad, you looked tired. Your dad came back, he didn't say anything. He needs to see a doctor we said, but did not offer one to you.

I asked if you were going to go to school, and at first you said no, but then the thought of staying home all day thinking about what had happened was too much. You said you wanted to take a shower. I talked to your father, we tried to decide what to do.

"She seems alright. Now what happened?"

"I don't know," I tell him. "He grabbed her. Threatened suicide."

"He what, now?"

You know he couldn't hear, it was so hard to say anything, especially if it was hard to explain, or contained any kind of subtlety. You didn't look terrible.

Of course we didn't see your body, in the shower. We didn't see the fresh bruises as you did, standing in the water that could not wash them away. You saw them for the first time. Bruises just now darkening on your young body. Bruises where you had fought him and he had held you, around your ribs, on your upper arms and shoulders, and even your legs though you could not fathom how they had been bruised, and you cried in the shower for your young body, that had been so marked and damaged.

You went to school late, you were still at Center Junior High. There was a drama class performance you didn't want to miss. And you wondered if anyone could see any difference in you but you did not tell anyone or say anything. You pretended nothing had happened. You watched yourself on the stage.

～

Walking down the school hallway, lockers opening and slamming closed, the painted yellow brick walls just after lunch. You had gone down to the counselor's office and you thought maybe you would talk to him because everyone liked him he was a young man, and friendly with the students even the hoodlum boys liked him, but there was a line waiting to see him. Kids you knew, you didn't want to be asked questions. It was possible to make an appointment but you had to go to the office you had to have a reason and you didn't want to do that. But if the counselor had been there to talk to just right then, you would have told him and that probably would have helped. But there was only that moment, you might have talked and then it was gone.

I don't know what consequence that would have had for us. You wanted to tell somebody, and then what? have them take him away, have him punished, but you never said that. Or maybe you didn't know that.

～

Nothing was done. You went on. Pretending that nothing had happened.

But now I see. You had given up on us then. You saw you were on your own. That year, that summer you started smoking marijuana, drinking. By ninth grade it was regular. It wasn't just the smoking marijuana, I know that's not such a huge deal. Reading about Carlos Castaneda, new age crazy people, shamans, birds, people flying, and Kurt Vonnegut, it was the 1970's, it wasn't a simple time. Everything was in flux. Moving.

And you were going away, away from your body. Things went on as before but not for you. You saw that you would not be protected, there was no protection for you, the world would come and you would have to fight it off by yourself in the middle of the night and no one would speak of it. You'd felt your own life being taken from you, but you'd fought and gotten it back. Must have been terribly frightening for you. Oh there was sadness you felt for your own life too, what you had lost that you couldn't name, and that was an awful lot for a 14-year-old girl to feel. Why did it happen to you, you wondered. Why was such difficulty saved up for you and not others. Course every adolescent gets a little grandiose like that, they're all the center of their own universe. But it certainly made it worse in your case. That's when you made leaving your specialty. Mississippi was just the first place you ran away to.

The way you would talk to people was terrible to hear. You'd put down everything, say, "So what's the big deal in that?" Almost anything someone said to you, you'd answer with some version of, I don't care, I don't care. Or it doesn't matter, it doesn't matter. Oh sure there are plenty of kids get that hard shell to protect themselves, and yours might have been harder than others. The shell protects you but it also causes goodness to slide away before you have a chance to savor it.

～

Bill and Linda stayed on as before. You saw him at family dinners, events. You said hello, suffered his limp kisses at the door on holidays. He was always a reminder for you but we soon forgot. Did he know what he had done even? He was sick. Well, that showed even more later. At the time she had those two little boys Leo and Vince and they depended on his salary, they were trying to buy a house. What would have happened to them if he had been arrested, or to you, to have to say all that, to all of us? Would have been a terrible scandal. A terrible heartache on our family and her. So instead we gave that heartache to you to keep, we gave that to you to carry.

I'm not saying it was right but it's what we did because we couldn't see to do otherwise.

~

It wasn't that month or the next, but you soon saw it. You saw what you had been given to carry. In how things are organized in this country, maybe every country, though I wouldn't know, someone has to bear the burden for the sins of the other. Someone has to absorb what is wrong so the others can go on. Usually those who do it are those who are able to. You and I share that quality. You were invincible. You could carry that burden, and lift it so high no one even saw it. That burden you carried, but it wasn't one you chose. And I was wrong to let you carry that. I didn't know what else to do at the time. But that doesn't make it right. No one else should decide what we carry. And no one else should think that they know the story that defines us, that's just another kind of injustice. As if we couldn't speak for ourselves.

That lightness he took from you. Or did he? It's so easy to jump to conclusions. To make one event the catalyst for every other. I think it's hard to fix the blame on a permanent point. Him, or me or your father or God, take your pick; I certainly couldn't in my own life. Find a clear point of blame I mean.

If there is divine retribution it certainly did find him. Now his grandchildren don't even know him. I don't know if he even knows that Leo has five children, or if they even know his name. Well, he left Linda some years later, told her he wasn't fulfilled. Just to make it more palatable, right. About a year later he moved out to Texas and married a born again Jesus woman, named Tammy. Well, that fell apart and then he was living on the street pretty much, his brothers tried to help him but he wouldn't get help. Later his son Vince offered that he could live with him if he got psychiatric help but he wouldn't do that either. I guess he has a cabin in the mountains somewhere in Oklahoma, all littered with broken cars and mewling cats. So we don't have to worry about him anymore.

Of course I still think of all that you could have had for yourself besides running forward like the hounds of hell were on your heels. What you might have found if you weren't writhing and struggling to get out from under those hands, running away from those for years to come.

But maybe, I'm not trying to make any excuse here, but don't we all end up in the same boat wrestling some demon or other? It's the Bible but I can't quite recall, *we wrestle not against flesh and blood but against the rulers of darkness* something like that. Or maybe, because I love you, because you are my daughter, we never left the boat to begin with, rowing in this same boat all along, fighting the same demon all along. Maybe there is only one demon waiting in the deep, and it waits for our bodies; our bodies are the vessel of our going as we float on this wine dark sea.

# VII

## FAREWELLS

### 2002
### *Tiffin Glass Museum. Tiffin, Ohio*

IT WAS summer, the last summer we would have but we didn't know that then, you were visiting from Morocco.

We had your brother Tim drive us down SR 224 the old highway you used to use to come visit from the East when you lived in New York. Came that way. Catch it in Akron and it cuts straight through the middle of Ohio past those red brick farm houses standing tall and skeletal against the onslaught of time, that two-lane road, seems to run right through the front yards on through small towns with complicated inter-sections and railroad crossings, with roads angling in from the countryside in every direction to get to the grain elevators along the tracks, mostly unused now. You used to mark off those towns in order Greenwich, Bloomville, Willard, Tiffin and then our town.

But today we're driving east toward the Pioneer Mill Restau-rant one of my favorites in Tiffin. It had been a mill at the turn of the century, not that any of the rivers near here flowed fast enough to turn a mill wheel, but where nature was lacking the determination of locals made up for it. Some pioneering soul had decided to just build a huge damn on the Sandusky River to harness the power from the falling water and he did, though the mill burned down several times, fire being a constant in this part of the Sandusky not far from where the hapless In-dian fighter Colonel Cranford, anathema to the Wyandot and Pawnee peoples, had been captured and burned at the stake by the Wyandots he had sought to exterminate. The famous frontiersman Simon Girty looked on but didn't try to help, or did he, he was on the Indian side. Well I think you should take whatever side seems in the right regardless of where you come from, so I don't blame Girty. Well then that friend of your sister Susan's wrote a book about Girty in California, and it was a friend of his who turned out to be her future husband. So that's a connection. The Wyandot had loved this area near Upper Sandusky, teeming with game they said in the history books, fertile and lush. You had been canoeing on that river when you were a child at the Girl Scout camp, you loved being on the brown river with the green banks just down the river from here too, and my oldest granddaughter had married a boy from Tiffin too, you see how the road and the river, and the people that had lived along it and what had happened to them, was known to us as if we moved within a story that was already partly written, or written over in different hands.

Lunch at the Pioneer Mill was good, we had roast beef and pie, sitting among the old hewn beams where the giant grinding stone had once turned, gears and wheels along the wall.

I said, "After lunch we'll go to the glass museum."

"Is it downtown or what?"

"Oh we should have gotten directions, we'll never find it."

"It won't be hard Mom, I'm sure it's right downtown."

We found it, a low brick building in the center of the old Main Street. It was cool inside. The glass that had once been Tiffin's main industry was arranged in cases by periods; dishes and containers with forgotten functions, candy jars, cordials,...

"No one's cordial anymore," you joked.

You held my arm lightly as we peered into the display cases.

"Hideous, that one."

"Oh you don't like the purple?"

"Sometimes your great-grandfather worked over here, we might see something he made, who knows? Well, see those glass dinner sets—you know, before the 1940's glass plates and saucers were much more common than china or stoneware. The plates are a lovely shade of blue and deep."

"But there are miles to go before you sleep and miles to go before you sleep," you answered.

"Stop being smart," I told you. "You like the simpler shapes better, with clamshell edge? They were so popular in the 1930's. All the different patterns had names, my mother used to collect vases, well each housewife had her patterns, they always gave them romantic names like Versailles, Regatta, Montego. No one wanted to collect "Ohio," women wanted to think of somewhere else. Well they used to give dishes away at the Friday matinee movie, was like a special raffle ticket. Mom used to go, and get her plate or sugar bowl. You see this stemware they made here and supplied to Sears and Roebuck Company."

We continued looking into the oak cases moving from the 1920's into the modern decades where the abstract twists of Tiffin "art glass" had made it into the 1970's.

"Now that is just hideous isn't it?"

"Can you imagine having that on your table?"

"No I can't, it makes me irritated just to look at it."

"You know they kept the furnace burning here for almost a hundred years before they finally let it go out in 1980, well you can put down the real end of glassmaking in this area to that time."

You feel my arm trembling as it holds onto yours, feel me swaying a little unsteadily. You hold on.

We keep looking.

"Never liked the yellow, champagne they call it, and there's the frosted, no I didn't like that either."

You can hear my labored breathing.

My body is quivering, but I act as if I don't notice, as if nothing's the matter because nothing is. You wonder why I don't say anything.

"Are you alright?" you ask.

"I'm fine. That orange color was very popular in the seventies, one of the girls had a set like that at their wedding."

You grip my elbow tighter, I lean my hip against yours. Your strong body feels my body weakening.

You look at my face so closely to see if I notice what is happening, I turn away from you.

I sense only a distant fluctuation separate from my thoughts and feelings. I want this afternoon with you my dear daughter away from the living room and the constant TV, so it's more important that I'm with you. Can ignore the pain if I choose to.

We go on.

I'm swaying each time we take a step, but act as if nothing were the matter.

"Are you alright Mom you seem unsteady?"

"I'm fine." I did feel fine.

But you could feel my body giving way, swaying under what was coming. Oh I was done with the doctors at that point, whatever happened to my flesh was of no interest to me; four years of nursing, fifteen pills a day, injections, and the doctor every few weeks, but I was done with it.

We came to the molded glass.

"Now that was the molded or pressed glass, used to make a set of molds now those were very valuable, because they were each unique, and once you had a good one you could make hundreds."

You offer the strength of your young body to steady mine. Hold me under the elbow, lean your weight against mine to straighten my balance. Hold me upright, steady where I shake.

You begin to understand me, or your body begins to understand mine. You look at me with some kind of wonder, like you might look at a Hindu sadhu who can put his feet behind his head or a Russian saint without shoes in the cold. In this quivering in my arm, this swaying you realize that my body stands now only by virtue of my will, and spirit. You

know then that this has always been true of me, that I have
been present by the will of my spirit alone. You wonder, looking into my eyes though I can't answer. Is this the truth of all
of us?

You hear the air of my breath speeding up slightly, then
slowing down.

You feel that I'm no longer in the arm you are holding, and
it frightens you. Like holding the tether of a balloon, someone floating overhead you think, your body feels that mine is
empty, your body feels the truth of mine.

How I'm willing myself to stay, you feel it. Oh but is it
love or denial, love for you that makes me want to stay warm
against your arms, bones, my child, or am I being stubborn
and ruthless, refusing to give into what I'm feeling. Is it the
spirit in me that refuses to yield?

Until finally, after sometime after thirty minutes or so I gave
way, faltered.

For that afternoon anyway my body won out, I had to sit
down.

"There's a chair here by the door, sit down." You're eyes
were wide with fear, glaring at me. You saw sweat come out
in beads on my upper lip, you gave me a tissue. "Mom you're
sweating."

But I was cool inside.

You watched the color drain from my face, saw the grey
around my mouth.

"You're getting awfully pale."

But I felt happy. My breath was wheezing so it was hard to
say what I wanted.

"Mom, just rest."

"I'll be fine in minute. Get the nitroglycerin out of the bottom of my purse will you?"

The nitro always helped.

We had planned on going to tour the old factory, but I
couldn't manage it.

"We better go home," you said.

"Yes, I'm awful tired now," I said, and you drove me home.

~

Maybe this all boils down to you wanting to be known, is that it? Is this a test for me you coming back here. Knock knock. Who's there? Daughter. Daughter who? Daughter who never comes home. Well then how could you be knocking? Shouldn't talk nonsense. Did you ever leave? Where was our home any of us, where are you?

Seemed we were all racing forward into some future where we would finally get home, out in a storm at night like that Thomas Hardy story, I forget the name of it, where the visitors come to the house, the convict is escaping one way in the storm and the hangman is coming from the other way, when both take shelter in a house in the middle. The hangman has never seen the convict because he's coming from a distant village, so the convict listens to the hangman tell his story, even sympathizes with him. Then says he has to leave. Later the guards come to say the convict has escaped, but he is long gone by then.

Why did I stay with your father, week after week, watching him drink, and not even trying to get away. Because I had to hold the baby right then, or try to boil some water for spaghetti, or I just wanted to read my book. Why, why, why we ask the cat, or the wind or the doorbell and there is no answer except what we did yesterday, those moments we did them, tomorrow.

The time we spent together, was enough after all. Wasn't it? Full enough in its own way, if not as attenuated as other relationships.

There is some way that people in stories are never alive in the same sense we know living people, by something more than what we see or hear from them, we know them as they resonate in the stream of our own being living. Or in the realm I used to say of the Holy Ghost, but I'm not sure one ghost is any holier than the other now. Not from this angle anyway. I guess I'm talking about presence. The unspoken weight of all we're aware of.

Why do we all agree to say less than we know? Women especially. Who is deciding what we can know or not know, and what are the means to our discovering it? There is another world in this world daughter, you know and I know. Its boundaries are not crossed by airplanes or skin. I never did when I was alive talk philosophy as I saw fit to leave that to the church, but the church proved small in the face of all that I saw. Relations upon relations, and I don't just mean cousins, I don't just mean blood but something like blood shared between now and then, you and me. Used to read those science articles in *Time* magazine, scientists discover new theory of wave and particle, headlines like, "Can one thing be in two places at once?" That sort of nonsense and always wondered if those men were alive enough to notice anything? It was so self-evident, I thought, to any mother.

1960
*Pine Street. Blanchardville*

*Ninth child by now I should know what I'm doing, try to nurse her for a few days if I can. I can't do much longer than that with all the others. Snow blowing from the east. Can't hardly hear anything else when I have a baby in my arms, but I need to keep an ear out for what the other children are up to. Can't hold her little head up, isn't that something the weight of her bald head in the cup of your hand the way one just fits inside the other, and those blue eyes like a summer twilight. See her little heart beating right there in the soft spot on her skull. She's not finished none of them are finished at this size I feel her come to life when I nurse her this warmth filling my breast and flowing into her mouth, like an electric current almost. Breasts are solid and swollen today. Oh that's a good letting go seems immodest to think of but where does it come from really where does breast milk come from. How does the body know all that it does? Comes from somewhere or some other source I'm the fruit of. Is it the milk of human kindness my mother always mentioned. What is in us that wants others to live? Yes little one there you are. Need to change sides. Is that Theresa getting up from her nap? No just the cat jumping. Sound of a baby nursing is unlike anything else I've ever heard; full of animal hunger and happiness at the same time. Hunger growing to satisfy itself and the satisfaction and the hunger humming together. What you might hunger for later on and what weeks you might wait for it to come we can't know now. Sitting listening for certain footsteps or searching the winter sky for a shred of warm sun or God forbid hunger in your belly, but this is America that's unlikely at least. More likely there will be a longing in you for somewhere else. Hunger for the world roots up in little children like a stray prayer.*

*For now though, what it needs and giving it. Baby wiggling and arching its back stretching its mouth to the breast as one body, how she was inside me now part of my body inside hers. Seems like just looking at a newborn is a way to hold them, she can feel my eyes on her like a warm hand. Sometimes I've thought they need you to watch them for them to grow, as if a mother's gaze has some kind of mineral in it.*

*That tastes good doesn't it. That suckling sound like bees swarming in trees. We live in quiet country, mother and infant, one always listening for the other. Husband snoring or another child's nightmares or a honking horn, none of that heard but when your baby cries you hear it. Blessed nuanced language a mother and infant know, gives rise to all the others.*

∼

Sometimes I've thought that it's just when a child learns to talk that she leaves her mother for the first time. She leaves her mother for the world because with words the world becomes hers. The first syllable, *ma*, coming down the hallway, ma they say, but you know it means "I'm leaving soon." Thirst has a feeling, the feeling is water, water comes and turns into the word, wawa, and a ball rolls up and becomes "ball." They say ball and brother rolls it back. Oh it's the concept they know at first, they know the door opens, they say go. Go they say and you take them, and then they are gone into the world, calling to the world in the words everyone knows, and no longer yours at all. Yes, I think a child leaves her mother when she can talk.

2007
*Toledo, Ohio*

Gathering your bags from the carousel at the airport in Toledo, bleary eyed from the long flights; you straighten up to look out the tall glass window. Your heart sinks at the view, and you have to steady yourself against the luggage cart. In the vast half-empty parking lot dirty piles of snow wait under that bleak January sky. Beyond the lot only a flat featureless landscape of white; leafless trees like a gray fuzz on the distant horizon. The harshness of it threw you. As if you had landed in the land of the dead, it seemed. Everyone deals with winter in their own way; but you were busy cursing the entire Midwest with words I'll not repeat. As if my dying were the particular fault of the landscape. Now that landscape had changed for you, I know. There was no longer a promise of warmth in the winter no longer the soft music your mother's arms make for you in any world. No longer color or cheer in this place where you had landed dozens of times in the happy apprehension of my presence.

As raw and mean as your grief the landscape was, and to think, you said to your husband, that your mother had lived here her whole life, in this frozen wasteland. All the places you had been, the streets of Paris in springtime, a Mexican beach swept through your vision in their richness, and to think you had left your own mother here in this unspeakable plainness while you came and went from her world like a tourist. You felt the shame of that.

Standing in line at the Hertz rental car counter, you were thinking of a house you had visited near Guanajuato. A big square house painted turquoise blue, built around a courtyard, there were agaves in pots, a long scrubbed wooden table under the arcade. In the center a tree, with a fountain running at its knees. There are hummingbirds with their beaks in the center of magenta hibiscus flowers, a lemon tree in the corner, even poor people live in such houses, mothers grandmothers. We could have too, had you lived your life differently—to make yours part of mine.

You offered once to take me to Mexico. Remember you and Paul were going to go live there. You suggested it. I was all ready to go. What, you didn't believe I would go. Ask your brother. I talked about it all the time for months, told the other girls we were going to go live in Mexico that year. I even took a Spanish tape out of the library and started to practice. But then you changed your mind, went to Africa instead. Well you can see it now, how it could have worked out, the job choices or connections, the plans that you might have followed. You saw the choosing that had been going all along. Nothing had to have been how it was.

～

"Mom's really crying again," Whitman said to your husband, he looked up, but knew there was nothing he could do but drive.

The road was icy coming down I-75, it was slow going. You only made it to the viewing at the funeral home for the last few minutes. Your cousin Nick was leading the rosary. He's practicing to be a deacon of the church, which is like a lay priest, you do everything but say mass, and consecrate. But it was a comfort for you, you all grew up with Nick. His daughter was there, eight months pregnant even though she was only seventeen and a good Catholic, no one knew who the father was, or she wasn't telling. I know what kind of comments you're thinking about the church but you can keep those to yourself. Nick arranged the chairs in a circle so you could all face each other, and rolled out the Hail Mary's. Aunt Bess knew the rosary by heart and croaked it out loud in her cigarette hoarse voice; ...*Mother of God, pray for us sinners now and in the hour of our death amen.*

Had you gotten to the funeral home a little earlier you would have seen Harold. None of you had ever met him so it took a while to figure out who he was. A lot of people came whom you weren't quite sure of at first but most introduced themselves, old friends and family that we hadn't seen in 20 years, and you could place them finally. But this older man was wandering around there looking a little strange, in an old sweater and boots, dressed like a working man. He glanced around at the other people like they were a surprise to him, like what were they doing here. He stared at the pictures on the walls, looking at everything closely, like he didn't get out much, wandering down the hallway and back again, and you girls were looking at each other pointing at him shrugging your shoulders till finally Linda went up to him and introduced herself.

"Used to work with her at the Paper," he said. "Used to drive her home from the Paper." But that was all. He lingered a long time there. Kept going up to the coffin, then walking away. Was like he was waiting for something.

Of course Harold would come. He was a printer; they're all a little strange. Never married, lived with a crippled brother and his mother. I used to give him a few dollars a week for gas money for the ride. Wasn't far out of his way, he lived out on the North Side, but he always waited for me if I was running a few minutes late, always had a kind word.

He always sat down there by the vending machines, at the little round table, with his Styrofoam cup of coffee. We used to sit and talk or have a sandwich there, with the vibrations and clank of the printing presses shaking underneath the floor, printing up the news we had arranged that day.

Stories from everywhere, rolling out right under us. Then at 2:30 a.m. in the dark quiet of town he would give me a ride home.

Wouldn't be another soul on the dark streets, just Harold and me in the warm car interior on those winter nights, his car headlights moving into the only light in the world. What a wife never shares with her husband. There is so much we never share, a million layers of our not knowing each other, layers of distance, silence. Here in the Midwest we don't think of being seen, we are in the inside. Inside the car moving in the darkness. I gave him the money so I wouldn't have to be beholden, though he would have done it for free. I was glad for the ride, many a winter night it would have been tough to get home otherwise.

You see if we kept talking now we would still never run out of material, there is always more to any life than meets the eye.

You came here feeling you had missed something in your living so far away always, but I guess that turns out not to be so.

We were always connected. You were in this town as it was in you, all along.

～

All of us carrying each other. Going down this road or that one. Like the other night at your sister's place in Big Sur, walking down to the beach in a summer evening, down through the canyon below the redwood slopes, following the stream that spills out onto the beach. They call it Sycamore Canyon and they probably still will when the sycamores die. And they will die. You can count on that. Even now the trees with their gray roots in the still stream of water left from this year's late rains have some disease it seems, holding up their bare branches to the sky. The place has changed too as you walk remembering your son as a toddler, you would bring him down here to that wooden fence to see the horses that live in the pasture along the bottom of the canyon. You pass a beautiful swath of wildflowers by the roadside leading to someone's gate, lavender and pinks, bachelor buttons and other purple flowers; rich and lush there, you think of Shakespeare, *I know a place where the wild thyme blows where oxlips and the nodding violet grows....* You wonder did they plant it, they must have, and what wildflower mix was that to come out so well? Questioning everything, you wonder if you should stop that and just enjoy the bloom, if you can just see the beauty of the thing spread out before you, not the question of how it got to be there.

A few yards down the road some high hedges begin, and a few wild rabbits, small and brown, were out feeding on the roadside grass. One rabbit by his hedge root watched you pass but did not run or hide, simply watched you pass, your footsteps soft on the road. Who's to say the rabbit didn't know you as I do, that we have a familiarity rarely mentioned. Your body passed hers in the evening, she saw you, she heard you on the road. That's a certainty. You saw her small round body, felt for her smallness, saw the color of her mottled fur matched the color of the hedge roots where she lived, and when she did dart back into the hedge you went with her, felt into the darkness of the earth where she burrowed, all of that you sensed. And felt that you were the rabbit, didn't you feel that for a moment, we do we feel it about every living thing we encounter, that we are them for a moment, and think another thing before we even know it.

Maybe that's what it is, that longing for home, isn't some place at all but some kind of withness we need. If that's a word, all those years proofreading you'd think I would know, but word or no word I know what it is.

How close we are to each other if we just let ourselves feel that.

Who am I to say such things, but a mother ten times over. Said so yourself nursing your baby boy, where do I end and where does he begin, felt the river of life welling up in your chest and flowing to him like he was the sea. This isn't all ho-cus pocus sentimental now, I know that there is a science here as well, a kind of genetics that no one's discovered yet.

And while you're going down that road, down to Pfeifer Beach, you're thinking about what your old friend Terry Hoyle told you about a few nights ago when you went up to the top of the ridge for his Fourth of July party, dozens of people with bottles milling around in the dark and Hoyle was sitting by his fireplace holding court, doesn't seem like a party story but he wanted to tell it—that day he was thinking about it—another Fourth of July weekend, twelve years ago.

Child, mother and grandmother, all three.

He lived down in the canyon then in a little wooden cabin.

He said, "Locals came knocking on the door, yelling 'hurry can you, hurry. We need a surfboard and a surfer, there's a little girl in the water.' We drove fast, as fast as we could and I paddled out into the water, looking, looking. I couldn't see anything, started paddling back, there was an old man on the shore seemed to be yelling something so I went to the place in the waves where for some reason I thought he meant, and it was strange; right there she was. I pulled her onto the board, she was still alive too, then."

He stopped there in his story, stopped in the time he watched the little girl die; watched her last shuddering move-ment, her eyes blink shut.

The tears rolled down his wrinkled face, he couldn't say more.

You reached out your hand and touched his knee.

Didn't you see her too, when your hand touched him. See her dark hair and her pink striped shirt swaying in the clear green water by the rock, didn't you see her little body slung across the surfboard?

~

He saw it and you saw him see her, and I am with you, and we are her.

~

When the waves shoved Hoyle and the girl up onto the sand; the little girl's brother is hysterical because their mother was gone now too. She had gone in to try to get the daughter and her mother, their grandmother, had done the same and all drowned. Didn't even find the women's bodies for several more days.

Who wouldn't go in, just by instinct? Not thinking.

~

The year following that terrible tragedy we were at that beach together. I was out visiting your sister. We stopped to read the memorial plaque that had been put on the cypress tree along the shady path from the parking lot to the beach. It told the names of the three people who had died. How terrible, you said, to have the whole morbid story posted there, as if the place were haunted. And I said, no it wasn't terrible, it was best that people knew if that could help someone else, because you can't change what happened. But since then they've taken the plaque down. Now you wouldn't know unless someone told you.

Maybe some futures can be changed by telling about the past, or maybe it doesn't matter. You'll have to decide that about you and me.

It's not like one thing ever makes up for the loss of another. Doesn't work that way. There is all of what we did, good bad or indifferent. It remains. What happened remains and continues with us all.


2007
*Blanchardville*


I thought it was a shame to drag people out into that terrible cold, but there wasn't much I could do about it. What was it about five degrees, with the wind blowing and snow on the ground? Wind chill about minus nine, made your eyes water with the sharpness of it. Not fit for man nor beast. Any other time I would have stayed home.

They had a white awning set up over the cut-out square of the frozen earth, and they lined that with plastic green Astroturf that stood out against the snow in a strange way. I don't know why they don't want anyone to see that it's dirt where you're going, but they don't.

Along one side of the grave they lined up four black chairs, so if anyone needed to sit down they could. Front row seats.

The footsteps were crunching on the frozen ground, a powdery rime of frost on every pair of shoes. People gathering around the awning. No one wanted to sit in those black plastic chairs because it seems like well you were sitting in the waiting room. Have a seat death will be right with you. Next please, right this way. I know it's not funny but there it was.

Of course my sister Bess sat down, her knee is so bad. Well, she didn't cry or say anything. She just sat there alone, next to my grave. With her black stretch pants tucked into the top of her snow boots and her regular blue wool coat and hat. The poor thing. All those years she lived in that big house with Mother and her children but then her children grow up and get married and they have to sell off the big house to the demolition crew. She went to live in that small brick apartment with two rooms downstairs and two upstairs and she sits there for another fifteen years with nothing to do but smoke and doze off smoking, burning holes in her couch; thinking no one is coming, those that you love are only leaving.

Bess just sat there didn't weep or look around, stared at the hole in the ground as if no one else were there. Her son stood behind her as if to catch her if she decided to jump. Everyone worried the cold's going to do her in too.

The cold was so fierce that the bones in your face ache when you stepped outside in the cemetery, your face feels like a skull already, you know it is the cold of death.

The casket there under the awning and all around it such

an abundance of flowers you can't hardly see, a gaudy riot of blooming against the white snow, the glossy green ferns, pink carnations, roses, so many red roses dark maroon almost burgundy, roses, daisies, lilies and hyacinths, and how brilliant their colors are echoing through the frozen winter shadows. Maybe the only advantage of the cold was that it certainly did keep the flowers fresh. Not a wilted carnation in the bunch.

Then the VFW men, the Veterans of Foreign Wars draped an American flag over the coffin because I had served; and the red white and blue flag there along with the flowers under the awning, well if not for the unbelievable density of that frigid cold, which you might as well say it, was as cold as death. But if not for that and the darkness coming and poor Bess it might have almost been festive. Well at least my family was together.

The volunteers from the VFW, men in their 70's and 80's, all wore their military uniforms, braids of thick gold on the green blazers, and red patches saying Normandy, and Iwo Jima, but they didn't even have overcoats think of that. I worried they were going to freeze to death right then, think of the irony there. But they were quick with the white butt ends of the rifles they carried and cocked and raised when they shouted hup hup ready aim fire, then they fired the twenty-one-gun salute.

You were happy that they fired the guns that everyone would hear, the bang of it up over the cemetery and the park nearby, the sound of death, of disaster and the honor the old soldiers paid in braving the cold. A squadron of unknown men gathering for me, that was nice. Oh I must have known a few of them.

After the guns went off Aunt Bess thought it was over and started to get up but the priest had yet to say the final blessing.

*God, Father into your hands I commend thy spirit. Remember now that you are dust and to dust you shall return.*

"The family invites everyone to their home for a reception at Kingfish Way. This concludes our service, please go in the knowledge that your loved one will be buried with the utmost care and consideration."

You didn't see what happened after that. Walking stiffly back to your car. You all had to get out of the cold before you froze, close the door, turn the heater on quick. The cars start up and begin to roll away slowly. Under the sound of your engine you can hear another sputtering then humming. The engine of the mud-caked yellow tractor roars to life in the twilight quiet. Its iron claw, huge and hungry, digs at the frozen soil, scoops its dark weight deep like an ancient hand, scatters the earth upon my grave.